DEATH AT THE WORKHOUSE

Penny Green Mystery Book 8

EMILY ORGAN

First published in 2019 by Emily Organ

This edition © Emily Organ 2020

emilyorgan.com

Edited by Joy Tibbs

Emily Organ has asserted her right under the Copyright, Designs and
Patents Act 1988 to be identified as the author of this work.

ISBN 978-1-9993433-5-4

DEATH AT THE WORKHOUSE

Emily Organ

Books in the Penny Green Series:

ALSO BY EMILY ORGAN

Penny Green Series:
Limelight
The Rookery
The Maid's Secret
The Inventor
Curse of the Poppy
The Bermondsey Poisoner
An Unwelcome Guest
Death at the Workhouse
The Gang of St Bride's

Churchill and Pemberley Series:
Tragedy at Piddleton Hotel
Murder in Cold Mud
Puzzle in Poppleford Wood
Christmas Calamity at the Vicarage (novella)

Runaway Girl Series:
Runaway Girl

Forgotten Child
Sins of the Father

CHAPTER 1

"**M**r Torrance has been making complaints," said my landlady, Mrs Garnett.

"Who's Mr Torrance?" I asked as I adjusted my hat in the hallway mirror.

"The man who rents the room beneath you."

"That's who he is, is it? I didn't know his name. He's the man with the large moustache, I assume?"

"Yes. He's a clerk at one of those law firms. He's been making complaints about the noise."

"What noise?"

"From your new typewriting machine."

I laughed. "It doesn't make such a terrible noise!"

"He says it's like the pounding of a dozen tiny hammers."

"He must have exceptionally good hearing."

I stepped away from the mirror, and as I did so Mrs Garnett brushed her feather duster over it.

"Apparently, he's a light sleeper," she replied. "And you do have a habit of working at that thing until late into the evening."

"It's quite often the only time I have." I had recently

acquired my first typewriter and had been busy working on the book I was writing about my father's life.

"I realise that, Miss Green, but it's still noisy."

"Do you also hear it?"

"Yes, I could hear it from his room. Unfortunately, your writing desk is situated just above Mr Torrance's bed, and the poor man has to rise at five each morning."

"What would you have me do, Mrs Garnett?"

"There must be some agreed hours of use, and it cannot be late in the evening."

"But I do my best writing late in the evening!"

"That may be so, but Mr Torrance needs his sleep."

"Might I try moving my writing desk?" It was a reluctant suggestion, seeing as my desk sat in front of the little window in my garret room, and from there I could enjoy an easterly view over the rooftops of London.

"You could try that, but I doubt it would solve the problem completely. Mr Torrance would still be able to hear your machine."

"Perhaps he could push some cotton into his ears when he wishes to sleep."

"We can hardly expect him to go to such absurd lengths, Miss Green."

"Why not? If he's a light sleeper, as he claims to be, the cotton will ensure that nothing wakes him up. And besides, we're situated right beside the railway lines of Moorgate Station! How is it that my typewriter keeps him awake when the trains fail to do so?"

"It's easy to become accustomed to the noise of the trains, but a typewriter is a different kettle of fish."

"Most likely because I've only recently acquired it. I'm sure he'll become accustomed to the typewriting noise in time."

"That's hardly fair, Miss Green. I think the best solution would be to agree upon a curfew."

"Ten o'clock?"

"*Nine* o'clock."

"But that barely gives me any time at all to do my work in the evenings!"

"Then may I suggest that you discuss this issue directly with Mr Torrance?"

I sighed. "Well, I don't have time to discuss the matter much further, as I must go to work now. When you see him today, Mrs Garnett, tell him that he has nothing to worry about this evening as I shall be spending the night at the workhouse."

"The workhouse? Goodness, there's no need for you to go to such extreme measures in response to his complaint! I'm sure we can reach some sort of compromise. And besides, I shouldn't think you'd be allowed to take your typewriter in there."

"You misunderstand me, Mrs Garnett. I'm staying at the workhouse tonight as I shall be writing a piece about it for the *Morning Express*."

Mrs Garnett sucked her lip disapprovingly. "I don't think I'll ever understand your profession, Miss Green."

CHAPTER 2

I stepped off the omnibus on Hoxton Street that evening wearing a thin dress, bonnet and shawl I had bought from a second-hand clothes shop. A bitter January wind whisked along the street, and I shivered as I waited for my sister beneath a gas lamp outside the Britannia Theatre. A noisy crowd was gathering around me for the evening's pantomime performance.

"Hello, Penelope. Isn't it cold?" Eliza joined me beneath the gas lamp, rubbing her hands together. She wore a similar outfit but had managed to find a pair of fingerless woollen gloves to team it with.

"I wish I had some gloves," I said. "My hands are almost numb."

"I suppose this is only the beginning of the night's discomfort," she replied. "If you wish to write about a pauper's lot you must first experience it."

"Thank you for joining me, Ellie," I said gratefully. "I shouldn't have liked to do this on my own."

"I must say that I feel rather intrigued and nervous at the same time. I've heard so many stories about the workhouse."

"None of them good, I imagine."

"No, none. But I think it's important to see these things for oneself." She glanced around cautiously. "I can't say that I've ever visited East London before. It has a certain odour to it, doesn't it? Quite a different world from Bayswater. What are all these people here for? Oh, I see." She looked up at the billboard. "*Harlequin BonBon and the Golden Serpent*. I'd much rather be going in there than to the workhouse. Wouldn't you, Penelope?"

"Yes, but we must get on with it."

"What time do they open the doors to the casual wards?"

"Six o'clock."

It was a short walk up Hoxton Street to Shoreditch Work-house. The entrance sat between the Unicorn public house and an attractive red-and-cream building, upon which I could just discern the lettering 'Offices for the Relief of the Poor' in the lamplight. The little street that led to the workhouse entrance was named 'The Land of Promise', and within its confines a group of dishevelled people waited to be admitted to the foreboding building which lay beyond the walls.

The workhouse's casual wards provided food and a bed for the night for those who were too poor to pay the sixpence for a night at one of the city's squalid lodging houses. Having read several accounts of the men's casual wards in various publications, I was keen to discover for myself what the women's wards would be like. I hoped that by writing about the unfortunate conditions I was anticipating, more might be done to alleviate the suffering of London's destitute. I was expecting it to be a difficult experience, so I had been both surprised and grateful when Eliza had agreed to join me.

Although the gloom made it difficult to discern the faces of the others around us, I became aware of a stooped elderly lady whose chest rattled when she coughed. A younger woman was accompanied by two children who seemed unusually still and quiet for their age, while two old men were busy reminiscing about Bartholomew Fair, which had ceased running many years before.

We were startled by the slam of a door at the side of the Unicorn pub, and turned to see three loud young men sauntering toward us.

"Gotta match, old pal?" one of them asked a slumped figure.

The match was produced, and the smell of tobacco smoke soon drifted around our heads.

"Annuver night at Buckin'am Palace!" announced one of the young men. "We all lookin' forward to annuver night at Buckin'am Palace?"

One of the elderly men tutted at him.

"Bill, you ain't never stayed in this one afore."

"No, I ain't."

"What's the worse one as you've stayed in, Bill?"

"Poplar."

"That's a rotten one, ain't it? Tottenham's rotten an' all. This one ain't so bad."

"'Cause it's Buckin'am Palace!"

The men sniggered, and then one of them accidentally knocked me with his elbow.

"Beg yer pardon, m'lady."

"It's quite all right."

My polite reply seemed to amuse him, and he grinned at me. In the gloom I could see that he looked to be about twenty years of age, although his features were prematurely lined. He was dark-eyed and would have been quite handsome had his face not been so careworn.

As the workhouse bell chimed six, we heard the turn of a

key in the door at the top of the steps. The door swung open and the warden peered out at us.

"Any married couples here?" asked the beetle-browed man with thick, dark whiskers.

A middle-aged couple stepped forward.

"Have you stayed here before?" asked the warden.

"Yeah," said the husband.

"Come back to sponge off the rates then, have you?"

They nodded but said nothing.

Women and children were admitted next, and I felt distinctly nervous when our turn to be admitted came. *Would the warden realise that Eliza and I weren't genuinely destitute?*

As we stepped up to the desk in the dimly lit hallway, I felt keenly aware of how well-nourished we must have appeared.

The warden surveyed us through narrowed eyes. "Sisters?" he asked.

Eliza and I nodded.

He dipped his pen into the inkpot. "Have you stayed here before?"

"No," I said.

"'Tis a shame you've found yourself in a position in which you have no choice but to stay here tonight. Don't be coming back here again, will you? What are the circumstances that have brought you here?"

"My husband deserted us," said Eliza. "My sister and I have lost our means of income as well as our home."

"Can't you find any work?"

"We've been charring, and most days we can earn something, can't we, Penelope?"

I nodded.

"But we've been unable to find any money for our lodgings today."

The warden sighed and shook his head. "What a sorry

state when two gentlewomen find themselves down on their luck. Where did you stay last night?"

"At a lodging house in Drury Lane," I said.

He asked us for our names and ages, writing them down in the admission book.

"Who is your closest relative?" he asked.

"I suppose that would be our mother," said Eliza.

"What's her name and address?"

Eliza gave him the details and he jotted them down.

"Now, go through that door and it'll take you to the women's bathroom. The portress will meet you there."

As we walked on, I heard the warden call the next person forward.

"Where did you stay last night?" he asked.

"St Pancras."

"Staying at the ratepayer's expense again, eh? Can't you afford lodgings?"

"I'm a watercress hawker, but it ain't the season for it."

"May I suggest that you find something else to hawk? You can't keep staying at workhouses at the ratepayer's expense, you know. I don't want to see you down here again."

"The bathroom?" Eliza whispered to me. "Do we have to wash?"

"Yes, I think so."

"I fear that doing so will make us dirtier than we were when we came in!"

The stern-faced portress was a stocky woman of about fifty wearing a pale blue dress and a white apron. She showed us into a cold, whitewashed room with two dirty bathtubs in it.

"Have you any tobacco?" she asked.

We shook our heads.

"Tobacco is not allowed here. You'll be in trouble if we find any on you later. Take off your clothes and tie them in a bundle. You're some of the first here this evening, so you'll get the clean water."

Eliza and I removed our old garments and shivered, partly from the cold and partly from the lack of dignity. The order to have a bath seemed to be intended to demean poor people rather than to ensure their cleanliness. I peered into the bathtub and saw about six inches of grimy water inside.

"Wash your hair, too," ordered the portress as we stepped into the water, which still had some warmth to it.

I saw Eliza open her mouth to argue, but she evidently thought better of it. We reluctantly began to unpin our hair. We both had long, thick, fair hair and I knew that it would take a long time to dry in this cold place.

We were given threadbare towels to dry ourselves with, and I could see that they were quite unclean. Then the portress gave us rough blue flannel nightgowns to put on. These were clearly unlaundered and had an unpleasant musty odour to them, as well as stains around the neck. We were given three thin blankets each, and I tried to remain calm when I spotted a large louse crawling across one of them.

We left through a door which led into a room filled with long wooden tables. Around a dozen women wearing the same blue nightgowns were seated at these tables eating from enamel bowls.

Eliza and I collected our ration of thin gruel and dry bread from two pinch-faced women wearing the workhouse uniform, which comprised a thick, grey, collared dress with a matching apron. These women were from the main workhouse which admitted the destitute to live on a more permanent basis. In the main workhouse they were called inmates, as if poverty were a crime.

"I'm trying very hard not to cry," said Eliza as we sat down to eat. "This is a dreadful place. I wish we could leave it immediately."

"So do I."

"And that's just it. We *can*, Penelope," she whispered. "If we wished to, we could walk out the door this very minute and return to our comfortable homes. These other people, they..." She stopped to wipe her eyes with her hand.

"They have no choice, do they?" I whispered, a lump rising into my throat. "This is why I need to write about this, Ellie. All the people residing in their comfortable homes need to know that some people are forced to live like this."

"And it's so filthy!" Eliza gave a shudder. "Look at those bugs down there."

I reluctantly turned my head to look at the base of the wall, where beetles of some variety were scuttling past. "I won't be getting any sleep tonight."

"Me neither," replied Eliza. "How do you suppose anyone manages it?"

"I imagine they must drink a lot of gin and fall asleep from its numbing effects."

"It explains why so many paupers take to drink," said Eliza sadly. "That must be the only way to cope with it all."

The gruel was a watery mix of oatmeal and water with a slightly sour taste to it, and I could only manage a few mouthfuls. The bread was so dry that it was a job to eat any of it at all. The meal left me feeling rather thirsty.

"I thought we might get some tea," said Eliza. "Do you think they'll give us a cup?"

"There only appears to be water," I said, pointing toward a pail which stood beside the table where the gruel was being served from. A tin cup had been chained to the pail, and the women and girls gathered were dipping the cup directly into the pail and drinking from it.

"The warden who admitted us was rather ill-mannered,

wasn't he?" commented Eliza. "I can't believe he's allowed to speak to people in that way."

"Everything has been organised to dissuade people from staying here," I replied. "They don't want anyone to rely on poor relief."

"So what are they supposed to do instead? Everyone would surely prefer to work if they could find employment, but it's not readily available, is it? We both heard what the watercress seller said."

"I suppose the argument is that if they make it too comfortable here people would become dependent upon it."

"While I can understand that, it's such a miserable, demoralising place that it doesn't help people at all. I agree that no one should rely on charity, and many of the tenants I help look after manage to work hard and pay their rent. But I know that if they are unable to keep up with their payments they often end up in places like this."

A woman at a nearby table was trying to persuade her children to eat their gruel, but they were protesting loudly with wails and crumpled faces. It simply wasn't right that such young children didn't have a proper meal to eat, and my heart ached whenever I glanced over at them. The sight was also difficult for Eliza, who kept wiping tears away from her eyes with her fingers.

A drunk elderly lady joined us at our table, she ate her gruel and bread heartily. I had no doubt that it was a diet to which she had become accustomed.

"Ain't yer gonner eat yer skilly?" she asked, pointing at the gruel left over in my bowl.

"You may have it if you like," I replied.

She grabbed the bowl and helped herself. "What about yer toke?"

"Toke?"

"Bread. Ain't yer gonner eat it?"

I shook my head.

"Good, I'll 'ave that an' all." She took it from me and kept it in her hand, as if she intended to save it for later.

She proceeded to tell us about the pains she had in her back and legs, and Eliza and I listened patiently. Her lined skin was darkened by years of dirt, and when she grinned I saw that she had only three teeth. Her hair was dry, and I wondered how she had managed to escape washing it.

"Don't suppose you've got any bacca on yer, 'ave yer?"

"No," I replied. "We aren't allowed to bring any in."

"There's ways an' means of gettin' it in. Ways an' means," she said before getting up from the table and wandering off.

CHAPTER 3

Our sleeping quarters consisted of a stone shed with no heating of any kind, the air in which had a stale, pungent odour. The women there were beginning to make themselves comfortable, if that were possible, on straw-filled mattresses which lay directly atop the squalid floor. The whitewashed stone walls were furred with filth.

Once again I felt glad of Eliza's company, though many of the other women were on their own. They appeared to be well practised at wrapping themselves in the dirty blankets and lying down on the thin mattresses.

The portress had told us to place one rug on the mattress and two on top of us. There was no pillow. As soon as I laid myself down in this way, I realised my surroundings were too cold for my wet hair to dry at all, and the nightgown was not only itchy because of its rough fabric but also from the vermin crawling among the rugs.

I thought of James.

"I can't say that I envy you, Penny," he had said when I told him of my plan. "Have you ever been inside a workhouse before?"

I'd replied that I hadn't. "But I want to find out what it would be like," I had said. I now felt that I had already seen enough.

"Oh, this is miserable," whispered Eliza. We had placed our mattresses close together for warmth. "I don't think I can bear a single night of this, and to think that some people have to do it every night. And those children! They'll catch their death in here, it's so cold."

The pail of water and its chained cup were placed at the centre of the room. More and more women were shown in, each berated by the portress for their lateness, or for walking too slowly or being overly noisy. Many of the latecomers were clearly the worse for drink. They stumbled over the other sleepers, laughing and singing tuneless ditties as they went.

"I wonder how Francis is recovering," said Eliza with a sigh.

The new year had brought bad news from Colombia, where our friend Francis Edwards was searching for our father, the plant-hunter Frederick Brinsley Green.

"I hope he is much better now," I replied. "The fever sounded serious."

We had received a telegram from Francis at the end of November to say that he had heard tell of a European orchid grower in Cali, Western Colombia, and that he intended to visit him. A letter promising more detail had never arrived, but then we received a short letter from Francis' translator and travelling companion, Anselmo. Sent at the beginning of December, it had taken a month to reach us in London.

Borrero Ayerbe, United States of Colombia, 5th December 1884

To Miss Green and Mrs Billington-Grieg,

It is my regret to inform you that my good friend Mr Francis Edwards has been taken ill with fever and is resting at the house of a

*helpful gentleman, Mr Valencia, whose wife has been most attentive
to him. He asked me to write this letter to you, and to convey his hope
that he will soon recover so that we may continue our journey to Cali.*

I am reliably at your service,

Mr. A. Corrales

The news had filled me and Eliza with great concern for Francis, and having had no further updates from Anselmo we had no idea whether our friend was recovering. I had looked up Borrero Ayerbe on a map and discovered that it was a village about twenty miles north-west of Cali. I could not imagine a competent physician being easily found in such a place, and with no further detail concerning Francis' fever, Eliza and I had no idea whether it was a life-endangering affliction or one from which he could easily recover.

It was frustrating that there was nothing we could do to help Francis. All we could do at the present time was pray for his recovery.

The gas jet in the workhouse ward was turned off at eleven o'clock, and it was eerily quiet until a child began sobbing because she was afraid of the dark. Her mother did her best to comfort the little girl, and then a drunk lady began singing what she described as a "soothing ditty" to lull her to sleep. Instead, it provoked laughter among the huddled forms, though fortunately the child stopped crying before long. I began to wish I had eaten more of the gruel because hunger – along with the cold, fleas and lice – kept me awake.

The clocks chimed each hour, and I drifted in and out of a light sleep until my head ached. I was disturbed by people stumbling over me on their way to the water pail or to the lavatory. The sound of coughing was almost incessant; the cold winter appeared to have afflicted many with consumption. There were also occasional moans and groans as people complained about their illnesses or aches and pains. Eliza and I whispered to each other occasionally as we counted down the hours.

The chime of the factory bells at six o'clock was a welcome sound. Some women stayed put when the workhouse bell sounded soon afterwards, while others emerged from their beds of straw.

The portress marched in and ordered us to pile our mattresses over on one side of the room and to heap all the rugs together. We then filed into the changing room, where we collected our bundles of clothes and dressed. It was a relief to be rid of the uncomfortable nightgowns, and I couldn't wait to leave the unpleasant place behind.

My hair was damp and tangled, and I longed for a brush to pull through it. I tried to pin it out of the way as best I could for the time being. I noticed that a number of the women had their hair cut quite short, which no doubt made it easier to look after as they moved between workhouses and lodging houses.

There was more gruel and dry bread to endure for breakfast, and even though Eliza and I knew we would be able to find ourselves a good meal as soon as we left the place, we had to keep up the pretence that we needed the food. As I watched the others eat, I felt a shameful guilt that I would be returning to my comfortable life that same day while they faced yet another day of hardship. I couldn't imagine what it was like to struggle every day, being unable to eat properly and feeling demeaned and looked down upon by those in authority.

I couldn't eat all of my bread, so I pushed it up my sleeve

to give to someone who might be more in need of it than me. Eliza did the same.

After breakfast, a tall woman in a dark dress with a white collar swept into the room accompanied by several inmates carrying barrels filled with rope. The woman's steely gaze and smart dress suggested to me that she was a senior staff member at the workhouse; the matron, perhaps. The barrels of rope represented the work we had to complete in return for our board on the casual ward. Each of us had to pick three pounds of oakum before we could leave. We sat down at the tables as each of us was handed our ration of cut rope.

Eliza and I had never done such a thing as oakum picking before. We surreptitiously watched the women, who were much more adept at it, and saw that there was little more to it than separating the strands of rope until they were picked apart into fine little threads.

"What do they do with this?" Eliza wondered out loud.

"It goes down the shipyard," replied a sunken-cheeked woman. "And they puts it in the gaps in the ships' planks. Makes 'em watertight."

It seemed a useful purpose, and I supposed the workhouse made some income selling the oakum to the shipyard. However, what began as a seemingly simple task soon became onerous when I realised how much it hurt my fingers. Many of the women had hands as tough as old leather, and they worked quickly and effectively. For me and Eliza it was much slower going, and it wasn't long before the tips of our fingers began to bleed.

"There's tar on this piece of rope," commented Eliza. "It's almost impossible to pull apart."

I helped her with some of it, but my fingers felt raw and the coarse fibres had worked their way beneath my fingernails.

A few of the women rested a while. They seemed to be in

no hurry to get their work done and leave. The old lady we had spoken to the previous evening had found some tobacco and was smoking it in a clay pipe. I feared she would find herself in trouble if caught, but perhaps she didn't care. One lady in possession of a needle was called upon to make repairs to well-worn skirts and bodices with the strands of oakum.

Just when it seemed as though our work would never come to an end, Eliza and I finally finished picking our quota. A nod from the lady in the dark dress confirmed that our work was deemed adequate and that we could be on our way.

The bell chimed eleven as Eliza and I stepped through the workhouse door back into The Land of Promise. The street seemed aptly named for those leaving the workhouse, but only providing they were never forced to return.

An elderly lady rested against the wall. She was wrapped in layers of old clothes and wore a shawl over her head and shoulders.

"You've a long wait before they admit people for this evening," I said to her. "Would you like us to help you find somewhere warmer?"

"I ain't allowed in," she replied.

"They won't admit you to the workhouse?" I asked incredulously. "Did you spend the night out here?"

"Yeah." She shrugged.

"But that's awful!"

She shrugged again. "If yer seek refuge more 'n three times a month yer get sent to the work'ouse fer good."

"Staying in the workhouse is surely better than living on the streets," I said.

"Sactly. So I keeps tryin', and 'opefully soon they'll let me in."

Her face brightened enormously when Eliza and I gave her our bread.

"Thankee!"

"Why would they not let her in?" I asked Eliza as we walked away. "It makes no sense."

I glanced back at the lady as she contentedly ate the dry bread. She appeared to harbour no anger or sadness about her predicament, and I could only assume that those feelings had long since passed. She had somehow accepted her position in life and felt able to find contentment in the smallest of things, such as a morsel or two of bread.

"There is a great deal to write about," I said as we paused outside the Unicorn public house. "I think it will need to be serialised! Thank you for accompanying me, Eliza. I couldn't have endured that without you."

"I can't say that I enjoyed the experience, but it has certainly opened my eyes and made me feel determined to do something about it."

"Such as what?"

"I don't quite know." Her eyes grew damp. "There must be something that can be done to improve their lot in life. Nobody would wish to find themselves in this situation, would they?"

"I wonder what the rest of the workhouse is like."

"I wouldn't have thought it was much better."

The pale, haggard faces of two young men caught my eye as they stepped through the workhouse gates. Although I was now accustomed to seeing anguished faces at the workhouse, it appeared as though something particularly dreadful had occurred. I watched as they walked up to the door of the Unicorn, at which point the taller of the two paused and lowered his face into his grimy hands.

"Is something wrong?" I asked.

The other man looked back toward the workhouse gates, his eyes red. "'E's died."

"Someone's died?"

"Yeah, Bill."

I thought immediately of the three young men who had waited outside the workhouse with us the previous evening. I looked at the two men and realised neither was the one who had grinned at me.

"Bill?" I said, associating his face with the name. "What happened to him?"

"'E got sick an' they took 'im to the infirmary. We went lookin' for 'im just now, an' Old Sawbones told us 'e's dead."

"But what was the cause?" asked Eliza.

"'E 'ad a problem with his 'eart."

"There weren't nuffink wrong with 'is 'eart," said the taller man.

"There was, 'cause 'e died of it. 'E was arright when we was makin' our beds, then all of a sudden 'e starts gaspin' and 'oldin' his throat and neck, like." The shorter chap demonstrated a man struggling to breathe. "The master come then, got the doctor and they took 'im away. That was the last we saw of 'im."

"That's awful," said Eliza.

"I only knowed 'im a short while," added the taller man, burying his hands in his pockets. He stared at the ground. "Never would've thought it of 'im. Can't believe 'e's gone."

"I'm so sorry to hear it," I said, appalled that such a young man should have died so suddenly.

"We needs a drink," said the shorter man as he pushed open the door to the pub. "Bill would've wanted us to 'ave a drink."

The two men stepped inside and the door slammed shut behind them.

CHAPTER 4

"I wish I could ask the doctor exactly what has happened," I said.

"Go and tell him you're a news reporter," replied Eliza. "He might be willing to speak to you."

"Dressed in these rags? He'd struggle to believe me, I imagine. And besides, I don't suppose it's really any of my business. People must die at the workhouse on a regular basis, and it sounds as though Bill had a problem with his heart. It just seems so terribly sad."

"It does."

A hansom cab pulled into The Land of Promise, and two respectable-looking ladies laden with books stepped out.

"Books?" commented Eliza as they made their way toward the workhouse entrance.

"I beg your pardon?" asked one of the ladies, pausing to look at us. She was a dark-haired lady of about thirty, and wore a lilac woollen dress with a high lace collar.

"I do apologise," replied my sister, "but you strike me as rather unusual visitors to the workhouse."

"We're quite usual visitors, in fact," replied the woman.

"We come here twice a week to read to the patients in the infirmary."

"Oh, I see! What a wonderful idea!" enthused Eliza.

I noticed the lady and her companion looking Eliza up and down, as if confused that her manner and speech did not match with her appearance.

"Perhaps we should explain who we are and what we're doing here," I suggested. "I'm Miss Penelope Green, and I'm a reporter for the *Morning Express* newspaper. This is my sister, Mrs Eliza Billington-Grieg. The pair of us spent the night on the casual ward as I'm writing a report on it for the newspaper."

The dark-haired lady's face broke out into a smile. "Well, you are brave ladies indeed! And I can see that you came dressed for the part. I'm Miss Lucy Russell and this is Mrs Jane Menzies."

Her companion gave us a friendly nod.

"We've been working for some time to help the inmates in the workhouse," she continued. "How did you sleep? Or perhaps I should ask whether you managed any sleep at all!"

I gave a laugh. "Eliza and I achieved very little sleep," I replied. "In fact, I don't believe anyone should have to endure such conditions. Not even criminals."

Her smile faded. "I agree. The conditions are particularly bad for the *tramps*, as the visitors to the casual wards are called. It's because the authorities want to dissuade them from staying and to encourage them to find alternative solutions to their poverty."

"And what might those alternatives be?" asked Eliza. "How are mothers caring for young children supposed to find opportunities? I couldn't bear to see those little children suffering so, and as for the poor old lady who is too old and infirm to work, she spent the night lying beside the workhouse steps. They wouldn't even let her in!"

Miss Russell nodded sadly. "Conditions need to improve. They have improved in recent years, believe it or not, and the inmates in the main workhouse are now afforded a little more comfort than they used to be. But there is a great deal more that needs to be done. We're fortunate that the board of guardians for the Shoreditch Union is quite receptive to our help and suggestions."

"Well, I've a good mind to tell them what I think of their casual wards!" Eliza said indignantly. "The nightgowns and rugs could at least be washed! And the warden is so very discourteous."

"Oh dear. We've heard complaints about him before. Is he still speaking to people in a rude manner?"

"Yes. He seems to be the sort of man who enjoys doing so."

"When your article is published, Miss Green, may I suggest that you bring it to the attention of the board of guardians?" asked Miss Russell. "They'll be interested to read it, as they're not always aware of the finer points. The master and matron, Mr and Mrs Hale, are ultimately responsible for the day-to-day running of the workhouse, and they are the ones who must be held to account. The chairman of the board is Mr Buller, and you might be interested to hear that there is also a lady, Mrs Hodges, on the board. We think it's wonderful progress, because she can help to improve the care of women in the workhouse and the attached infirmary."

"That is certainly very interesting indeed," said Eliza.

"When will your report be published?" asked Miss Russell.

"Hopefully next week," I replied.

"I shall keep a look out for it. The *Morning Express*, did you say?"

"Yes."

"It's certainly a valuable thing to do. There have been accounts published regarding the men's wards before, but not the women's. I think that the more the public learns about what happens behind these walls the better the conditions will be for those poor souls who are confined within them. If either of you would like to assist us in our work we are often in need of more readers."

"Thank you, Miss Russell," I said. "We may just take you up on your offer."

CHAPTER 5

"You look rather tired, Miss Green," commented my colleague, Edgar Fish, when I arrived at the *Morning Express* offices that afternoon. He was a young man with heavy features and small, glinting eyes.

After leaving the workhouse, Eliza and I had visited the public baths, changed into decent clothes and consumed a large luncheon.

"I didn't sleep very well on the casual ward," I replied. "I don't know how anyone manages to sleep in a place like that."

"No doubt you've resolved never to find yourself in the sort of situation that could lead you to the workhouse," he said.

"Absolutely. I don't know what I'd do if I were ever to become that destitute. I don't even like to think about it. I realise now just how lucky we are."

"I spent the night in the casual ward at the St Giles Workhouse," replied Edgar. "Do you remember that time when I was undercover in St Giles? I've never forgotten it; in fact, I don't think I've ever truly recovered from it."

"And I don't think you've ever stopped talking about it," added our corpulent, curly-haired colleague Frederick Potter.

"That's easy for you to say, Potter," said Edgar. "What has been your most challenging experience to date as a parliamentary reporter? A particularly dull bill reading, perhaps? Or having to endure yet another debate on agriculture?"

"It is extremely difficult to get through some of those."

"And I suppose you manage to endure them by taking a little nap," Edgar continued.

"Not on those uncomfortable benches the reporters have to sit on."

"Ah yes, the uncomfortable benches! A terrible state of affairs, wouldn't you say, Miss Green?"

"I've managed to fall asleep on them once or twice, actually," added Frederick.

"After some particularly strenuous drinking at one of the bars, no doubt."

"Yes indeed. The drinking can be very strenuous, in fact. As is all the lunching."

"Doesn't your heart bleed for him, Miss Green?" asked Edgar with a laugh.

With the image of the children struggling to eat their gruel lingering in my mind I found it difficult to share the joke.

"Are you all right, Miss Green?" asked Edgar, noticing my dour expression.

"I'm fine. Just a little tired."

"How was it then, Miss Green?" asked our editor, Mr Sherman, as he entered the newsroom and left the door to slam closed behind him.

"Quite awful."

"Good. I'm looking forward to reading about it, in that case." His dark, oiled hair was parted to one side and he wore a blue waistcoat.

"A man died," I added. "I saw him yesterday evening, and he seemed fine then. There were three young men all together, and they stayed on the men's casual ward. Apparently, he was taken ill and admitted to the infirmary, and then he died quite suddenly. His friends told me there was a problem with his heart, but I found the whole episode rather odd and unsettling."

I could feel tears pricking the backs of my eyes as I spoke.

Mr Sherman gave a deep sigh. "That is sad news indeed. Unfortunately, the lives these paupers lead mean that many are in poor health."

"It's probably rather common for paupers to keel over without warning," added Edgar, "especially in the winter. Many of them have consumption, and they spend so much of their time worse for drink."

"But it's not fair," I said. "If they had proper homes and sufficient food and warmth it simply wouldn't happen. And besides, this man supposedly had something wrong with his heart."

"Well, that could be something one is born with and could die from no matter what one's living conditions are," replied Edgar. "The chap was simply unlucky."

"I'm afraid to say there isn't a great deal you can do about it, Miss Green," added Mr Sherman. "You cannot allow your emotions to get in the way of your reporting."

"Impossible for a lady!" Frederick piped up. "Perhaps a chap should have done the reporting instead."

"The purpose of asking Miss Green to do it was to obtain a report of the *women's* casual wards," replied Mr Sherman. "There have been plenty of reports from the men's wards; we're all tired of reading them. Now, on a lighter note, Miss Green, do you recall my suggestion of a weekly ladies' column?"

"I can't say that I do, sir."

"I'm entirely sure that I mentioned it to you. Anyway, I noticed there is a trend for ladies' columns in our rival publications, so I thought perhaps you could get onto it and write one."

"And what should I include in it?"

"Anything that you ladies might be interested in. The latest fashions, perhaps? Menu suggestions? Tips and advice for running a household?"

"Three subjects I know very little about, sir."

"You're a writer, Miss Green. Surely you've learned how to make these things up by now."

"I could do, but presumably there needs to be a measure of actionable advice in the column."

"A little, yes, but I wouldn't dwell overmuch on the matter, Miss Green. The ladies' column is merely intended to add a little frivolity to the publication, and to ensure that our lady readers feel catered for. Fish, where have you got to with your article on Lord Wolseley's mission to relieve Major General Gordon in Khartoum?"

"It's almost done, sir."

"One day I'll ask you that question and you'll tell me your article is complete. I'm truly looking forward to that day."

"Me too, sir."

"Well, get on with it then!"

I sat down at my desk with a pencil and paper and began to write down everything I could recall from my miserable stay at Shoreditch Workhouse. My fingers still felt sore from the oakum picking, and I felt extremely fortunate as I considered it unlikely that I should ever have to do such a thing again.

CHAPTER 6

A young police constable stood outside Lord Courtauld's townhouse in Carlos Place, Mayfair. It was a grand six-storey townhouse with an elegant curved facade of red-and-cream brick.

I joined two other reporters who were busy questioning the constable. A housekeeper with a stern face opened the front door to glare at us, then closed it again. Moments later she peered through one of the wide bay windows and scowled at us.

"A large number of valuables have been taken," said the constable, "and a maid has gone missing."

"What's the maid's name?" asked one of the reporters.

"Maisie Hopkins."

"How long has she worked in this household?"

"About three years."

"And what is her age?" asked the other reporter.

"She's twenty years old."

"So the maid has run off with the valuables?"

"It certainly looks that way."

"What sort of valuables are missing?" I asked.

"Quite a number of items, including silver marrow spoons, a butter dish and butter knife, wine glasses, and a purse containing gold rings and coins. An inspector from the Yard has been called in at the personal request of Lord Courtauld."

"Do you have any idea where the maid is now?" I probed.

"None."

"When did she run away?" asked the first reporter.

"Some time during the night."

"Can you be any more specific?"

"We know that she retired at eleven o'clock last night and was nowhere to be found by six o'clock this morning."

The front door opened again, and I felt a grin spread across my face as James stepped out, bowler hat in hand.

"Penny!" There was a sparkle in his blue eyes. "I should have guessed you'd be here before long."

The constable and reporters stared at us both, surprised by the young inspector's familiar tone. James walked down the steps to join me.

"So Lord Courtauld chose you above the inspectors at C Division," I commented with a smile.

"Not me personally, but he requested the services of the Yard. The maid has stolen rather a lot of valuables, and it seems she has been doing so over the period of a good few months."

"And no one noticed it earlier?"

"It seems not. There are a great many valuables in that home, so it was only when she ran away that suspicions were aroused." He put on his hat. "I'm going to make some enquiries at the nearest pawnbroker's shop. Do you have time to join me?"

"I'd love to."

We exchanged a smile, and as we crossed the road together I could feel the gaze of the constable and reporters still lingering upon us.

. . .

"You survived the workhouse, then," said James.

"It was rather grim."

I told him about my stay there as we turned to walk between two smart shops and joined a path that took us through the gardens of the vestry hall.

"The workhouse is a horrible place," said James once he had heard my account. "I pray that none of my acquaintances will ever find themselves there."

"No one should," I replied. "Perhaps it wouldn't be so awful if these people could somehow find a way out of their grinding poverty, but very few ever do. It's all most of them have ever known."

"The answer to London's poverty lies beyond our capabilities, Penny."

'But that doesn't mean we should just accept it!"

"No, we shouldn't, and we must do whatever we can. For my part, I would afford the same level of respect to a tramp from the workhouse as I would to Lord Courtauld. I like to think that I treat people the same way no matter their class, but it's possible that my conduct occasionally falls short. For your part, you're writing about people in poverty and educating the middle and upper classes about the realities the poor have to face. That's about all you can do."

"I wish that I could do more."

"What you're doing is enough."

A lone blackbird sang sweetly from a bare-branched tree. The sky was a dark grey, and lights glimmered in the windows of the buildings overlooking the gardens.

"You'll be pleased to hear that I've paid Charlotte the sum of four hundred pounds," said James.

"I'm not pleased to hear that at all!"

"Neither was I pleased to pay it. But the breach of

promise hearing ruled that I must pay her six hundred pounds, so we should both be pleased that there is only two hundred pounds outstanding."

"What a lot of money," I said angrily, "and she doesn't even need it! I don't think for a single moment that she would attempt to donate a portion of it to the poor who wait outside the workhouse every evening. We met an elderly lady who spent the entire night out in the cold. The workhouse wouldn't even admit her!"

"We can't expect Charlotte to share your views on philanthropy, Penny."

"Do you think she might donate any of the money to people in need?"

"I have never known her to do such a thing in the past."

"Exactly!"

"But she may do so in the future."

"It's unlikely."

"What I began this conversation with the intention of saying, Penny, was that once the final two hundred pounds is paid we shall be free of any association with my former fiancée."

"Good."

"Which means that I can give other matters some consideration."

I stopped. "You mean marriage?"

James laughed. "What else could I mean? Not a week goes by without you dropping a thinly disguised hint that it is your wish to tie the knot."

"But is it *your* wish, James?" My heart began to pound excitedly.

He stepped toward me and took my gloved hand in his. "Of course it's my wish."

I smiled. "Good."

He leaned in to kiss me, but the sound of a cough nearby

made him draw back. The person from whom the cough had originated – a smartly dressed man with a walking cane – glowered at us as he passed by.

"That's a shame," muttered James. "I thought we were alone."

"We're not," I replied, glancing at a couple who had just entered the gardens. "And we should really have a chaperone with us," I added with a grin.

We continued on our way.

"Is your sister available to act as a chaperone this weekend?" he asked.

"Yes, I should think so."

"This weather rather limits what we can do," he said, glancing up at the leaden sky.

"Let's go to Madame Tussauds!"

"Really?"

"Yes! I read that there's a new portrait model of the Queen."

"Then it will be even busier than usual."

"And Elizabeth Gibbons has been added to the Chamber of Horrors."

"The lady who shot her husband and claimed it was a suicide? That is exceptionally quick. Her trial was only last month!"

"They're extremely clever at Madame Tussauds."

"So that's where we're going this weekend, is it?"

"Of course!"

We found a pawnbroker's shop on South Street, which was marked with the sign of three golden spheres. Gathered inside the wood-panelled establishment were several sorrowful-looking people, while three smartly dressed men briskly saw to their needs from behind the polished counter.

Beyond it, glass-fronted cases filled with silver, jewellery and other valuable paraphernalia stretched right up to the ceiling.

One of the men appeared to notice in an instant that a detective had entered the shop. He gave James a nod, as if to beckon him over. He was a slightly built man with a greying moustache and keen grey eyes.

"How can I be of help, Inspector?" His face remained impassive, as if wary of giving anything away.

James introduced himself, then asked, "Are you the proprietor?"

The man gave a nod. "Mr Gregson."

"You've heard about the thefts at Lord Courtauld's home, I assume?"

"There's been a theft there?"

"Yes, and a maid named Maisie Hopkins has gone missing. Do you know her?"

Mr Gregson shook his head. "I can't say that I do."

"But you've heard of Lord Courtauld?"

"Oh yes."

"Has a young woman recently visited your shop to pawn anything?"

"Yes, quite a few of them have."

"A young woman whom you suspect might be a maid? She may have had some silver spoons to sell or a butter dish. Or perhaps a purse containing coins and jewellery."

"Yes indeed. We get all sorts in here."

"Do you think Maisie Hopkins may have tried to pawn something here?"

"She might have. I can't rule it out."

"Has a young woman with brown hair and brown eyes visited your shop this morning with something valuable on her person?"

"Not this morning, no."

"Do you recognise the young woman from my description?"

"It's not much of a description, if you don't mind me saying so."

"She would have been wearing the clothing of a maid."

He shrugged. "I can't recall having seen her."

"But you think she might have visited your shop to pawn something in the past?"

"It's possible."

"Can you be any more certain than that?"

"I can't say that I remember."

"If I ask my officers to carry out a search of your premises, do you think they might find anything from the Courtauld household here?"

Mr Gregson's expression hardened. "You'll have to get a warrant if you want to do that, Inspector."

"I will, but that won't be much trouble. The magistrates at Marylebone Police Court are always quick and obliging with such requests."

The pawnbroker scratched his chin. "Brown hair, you say?"

"And brown eyes. A young woman of about twenty years of age."

"I think she has been in here, now you mention it."

"Recently?"

"Yes."

"How recently?"

"I'd say about two days ago."

"I presume you keep a record of all your transactions."

"Of course."

"Perhaps you could check them for us and find out what she pawned on that occasion."

"I'll have a look. Excuse me for a moment." He disappeared through a door between the glass cases.

"These men rarely question the provenance of the items they buy," muttered James. "In some cases they're complicit with the thieves themselves." I watched one of the pawnbrokers as he counted out a few coins for a woman who had just handed over a bundled-up package. I wondered what was inside, and how long it had taken the poor woman to make the difficult decision to part with it.

"I suppose many of these customers live in hope that they'll be able to buy back their belongings," I whispered to James. "But in reality I don't suppose many of them do."

"They'd have to buy them back with interest even if they did," he replied. "It's a rather desperate situation to be in."

Mr Gregson returned. "I think she was here two days ago," he said, "though she used a different name."

"How do you know that it was her?" asked James.

"She pawned quite a valuable salt cellar, and that's why I recall her. She was young and dark-haired."

"Did she not strike you as suspicious at the time?"

Mr Gregson glanced around the shop, then lowered his face. "A good number of our customers appear suspicious, Inspector, but we're too busy to question the origin of every item they bring in."

James sighed. "What name did she give you?"

"Betsy Combe."

"And has she visited you on any other occasion?"

"Her face did not appear unfamiliar when she visited with the salt cellar."

"I shall take that as a *yes*, then. We believe this maid has been stealing from Lord Courtauld for some time. I'd like to examine your records, if you please, and make a note of everything she has pawned here."

"Of course, though there's still a possibility that she's not the maid you're looking for."

"I'd like to have a look all the same."

"Of course."

"I should get back to work," I said to James. "See you at Madame Tussauds!"

James rolled his eyes, then smiled. "See you on Saturday, Penny."

CHAPTER 7

"Your workhouse article has been well received, Miss Green," said Mr Sherman later that week. "We've had a good number of letters about it, many of them expressing concern about the conditions which paupers are forced to endure. We'll publish a selection of them."

"I'm pleased to hear that there has been some response," I said. "Debate is all well and good, but something needs to change."

"It will in due course. This is just the beginning, Miss Green. A little patience is required."

With this in mind, I returned to The Land of Promise the following day in the hopes that I might encounter Miss Russell and Mrs Menzies again. If I could read to the inmates I would be able to access parts of the workhouse I had not yet seen.

I assumed that Miss Russell and her companion would arrive at eleven o'clock, as they had on the morning Eliza and I had first met them. I waited beside the workhouse entrance in the cold drizzle and was pleased to find myself in luck when a hansom cab drew up and the two ladies stepped out.

It took Miss Russell a moment to recognise who I was in my respectable attire.

"Miss Green! If only I'd told you my address you could have called on me," she said with a smile. "I do apologise that you've been waiting in the rain for us." She gave me her carte de visite.

"It's no trouble at all," I replied, handing her my card in return.

"I read the remarkable article you wrote about your stay here," she continued. "It quite saddened me. I understand that those on the board of guardians were extremely interested to read it, and intend to discuss it at their next meeting."

"They do? That's wonderful news! I hope they might be encouraged to make some changes."

"We shall see. It usually takes a long time for change to happen, as you are no doubt well aware."

"Then we need to keep reminding them, don't we? Would you like some help this morning with reading to the inmates?"

"Do you plan to write an article about it?"

"Not at this time, no. At the moment I'm simply interested in visiting other parts of the workhouse to increase my own understanding."

"I see. I'm afraid it will only be the infirmary today. Is that good enough?"

"Of course. I've never been inside a workhouse infirmary before."

"Well, do come and join us in that case."

"Would you mind not mentioning to the inmates or staff members that I'm a news reporter? People are often suspicious with regard to reporters and their intentions."

Miss Russell gave this some thought, and I wondered whether my choice of profession made her a little uneasy.

"Shall I just introduce you as an acquaintance of mine?" she suggested.

"That would be most helpful. Thank you."

We were met by the matron, Mrs Hale; the tall, steely-eyed woman who had issued me with my quota of oakum to pick. I felt an uncomfortable pang in my stomach as I feared she might recognise me from the casual ward, but she gave no such indication. Instead, she chatted quite politely as she led us along the covered walkway which ran between two high walls. Rain drummed onto the iron and glass roof above our heads.

Mrs Hale opened a door, and the walkway turned into a whitewashed corridor which led through a building that smelled of stale sweat and soap. Inmates in their grey uniforms glanced at us with interest as we passed them, books in hand. We soon left this building and entered another covered walkway. I observed through the rain spattered glass roof that ahead of us was a gloomy brown building. It was four storeys high with tall, narrow windows.

The gloomy building was the infirmary, and once we were inside it I felt pleasantly surprised by its cleanliness. The walls had been freshly whitewashed, and there was a vague scent of carbolic soap.

Mrs Hale left us by the door to an office marked 'Medical Officer'. We were greeted by a smiling nurse, Miss Turner; a lady of about forty wearing a crisp white apron and a tall cotton cap.

"Good morning, Miss Russell, Mrs Menzies." These words were spoken by a man who had just stepped out of the office. He wore spectacles along with a dark jacket and waistcoat, and he had thick, fair whiskers. "And another volunteer, I see?"

Miss Russell introduced me to the medical officer, whose name was Dr Kemp. "Thank you for joining us," he said to me. "I'm extremely grateful to Miss Russell and her friends for doing such a wonderful job of keeping our patients occupied. When they're being read to they forget all about their illnesses and pains, and they give us a bit of peace for a while. It can be rather a struggle, as our wards are always full."

"I expect you're glad of the extra help," I said.

"Oh, we are. The priests from St Monica's in Hoxton Square are also regular visitors. We are fortunate that so many people are willing to give up their time to assist us."

I remembered how dismal the casual ward had been and noted that the infirmary seemed to be a different place altogether.

Dr Kemp explained that it was divided into two wings: one for the women and the other for the men.

"How many wards are there?" I asked as we walked into the women's wing.

"For the women we have the general ward, the lying-in ward, the nursery ward and the lunatic ward. For the men we have two wards: one for general patients and the other for lunatics. We also have a children's ward and a small ward for fever and other infectious cases. We try to send fever patients to the fever hospital as quickly as possible, as we don't want them infecting everyone else."

"The winter must be a particularly busy time for you."

"It certainly is, and we admit paupers from outside as well as from within the workhouse. There's a great deal of influenza about, and a number of patients have bronchitis, phthisis, pleurisy and other conditions that afflict the lungs. These people usually have to endure cold, damp living conditions, which exacerbate their illnesses. We have no space for people to convalesce here, so we send patients to the convalescent hospital as soon as we're able to."

We entered the general ward for women, where the beds were placed so close together that there was barely any space between them. I was relieved to see that the blankets looked a good deal cleaner than the ones in the casual wards. Each bed contained a patient. Some were sleeping, while others coughed and grumbled.

"I shall take my leave of you here," said Dr Kemp. "It's a pleasure to meet you, Miss Green, and I do hope that you'll consider becoming a regular visitor to our wards."

"Thank you, I should like to," I replied.

As I watched him walk away, I felt a slight pang of guilt that I hadn't informed him of the fact that I was a news reporter.

"This is Mrs King," said Miss Turner as we approached one of the beds. "How are you feeling today, Mrs King?"

"No better." She gave a hacking cough. Her cheeks were sunken and her skin was so delicate it was almost transparent.

"Hello again, Mrs King," said Mrs Menzies, stepping forward. "Would you like to hear a bit of *Treasure Island* or *Great Expectations*?"

The old lady smiled. "*Treasure Island*! You've read me that one afore, and I enjoys it."

"Would you like Miss Green to read it to you this time?"

"Yeah, I'll 'ave the new 'un read it." She turned her head and gave me a toothless smile.

Mrs Menzies handed me the book, so I opened it and began to read.

"What's 'is name?" Mrs King asked before I had reached the bottom of the first page.

"I don't know. He's described here as the 'brown old seaman'. I expect we shall find out fairly soon."

"I knows 'is name, I jus' can't remember it."

As I continued to read, Mrs King tutted. "'E drinks a lotta rum, that one."

"I suppose most seamen do."

"Yeah, they does. I wouldn't want the likes o' them staying in *my* inn."

"Me neither."

"They should of kicked 'im out!"

"I think they must have been too frightened."

"He don't frighten me. I'd of kicked 'im out."

I soon realised that reading to Mrs King consisted of reciting a few sentences and then being interrupted to discuss them. Before long, her conversation became more general.

"I ain't never sailed in a ship. Don't spect I ever will now."

"You might be surprised. There's plenty of life left in you yet!" I said with a smile.

The old lady gave a loud laugh. "No there ain't, and you knows it! You're pulling me leg, you are. I'm dyin'! I won't see out the week."

"That may still give you enough time to sail on a ship!"

She laughed again. "It won't, and you knows it!" The laugh became a cough, which alarmed me as I saw that she was struggling to breath.

"Are you all right, Mrs King?"

"No, I ain't. I'm dyin', I tell yer. But I'm one o' the lucky ones, as the Lord's given me four score years. Can't do no better 'an that."

She yawned, and I continued to read. It wasn't long before the interruptions stopped and I noticed that she was sound asleep. I closed the book and observed her for a moment. Her gnarled hands were folded neatly on the blanket.

Miss Russell approached and smiled as she looked down at the sleeping Mrs King.

"I must have bored her," I commented.

"I think you made her feel at ease. Thank you. Shall we visit the children now?"

· · ·

Our appearance on the children's ward created some lively interest, and when Miss Russell paused beside the bed of a little boy there was no stopping a number of others climbing out of their beds and clambering onto his.

"Be careful with Tom, he's quite sick," said Miss Russell.

The nurse brought some blankets over to cover the children's shoulders as Mrs Menzies read from *Gulliver's Travels*. The children sat and listened, wide-eyed.

"It's the ladies what do the readin'!" announced an old man as we entered the men's ward. "Come and read ter me. I need ter 'ear a good story."

"Miss Green, perhaps you could read to Mr Dyers over there," suggested Miss Russell, pointing toward a young man who was lying in bed staring up at the ceiling.

I walked over and introduced myself. His skin had a yellowish tinge and he moved his thin, chapped lips as if to say something, but he seemed to lack the strength. I decided to read *David Copperfield* to him, and before long I found myself quite enjoying the story.

"Thank you for your help, Miss Green," said Miss Russell as we left the workhouse.

"It was no trouble at all," I said. "I enjoyed it, in fact. Having experienced the casual wards, I had assumed the rest of the workhouse would be just as awful, but the infirmary seems very well managed."

"It is; they do a marvellous job. Dr Kemp is excellent, though the board of guardians has no idea how fortunate they are to have him. He has implemented a number of changes since he took charge as medical officer, and it really shows in how well the infirmary is run. His job isn't easy."

"Do you visit the other inmates at the workhouse?"

"Occasionally. We always go when there's a treat put on for them. That's when there's musical entertainment or a play, along with a good meal. Much of the time the fit and able ones must work, of course."

"Picking oakum?" I asked.

"Yes. The women and children do that, as well as working in the kitchen, the bakehouse or the laundry. There are many other chores too, such as portering and carpet beating. And there's stone breaking, of course, which the men do. Would you like to join us again sometime?"

"Absolutely!"

CHAPTER 8

"Where have you been, Miss Green?" asked my editor, Mr Sherman.

"I've been visiting Shoreditch Workhouse."

"Again? But why? Your article about the women's casual ward has already been published."

"I was interested to see what the rest of it was like."

"And what was it like?"

"I visited the infirmary and acquainted myself with Miss Russell and Mrs Menzies, who visit regularly to read to the patients there."

"That's nice of them," Edgar interjected. "Did you read to the patients yourself?"

"I did, and I think they appreciated it."

Mr Sherman sighed. "Miss Green, while I appreciate that your work this morning was that of a philanthropic gentle-woman, may I remind you that I employ you as a news reporter?"

"Yes, and I hadn't forgotten it, Mr Sherman."

"I was beginning to wonder if you had. Reading to sick people down at the workhouse is not part of your job."

"But I could write an interesting account of the work-house infirmary, sir."

"Is it as miserable as the casual wards?"

"No."

"Then we don't need an account of it for the time being. The birthday party of Lady Agnes Courtauld, daughter of Lord Courtauld, will be held at the Metropolitan Hotel this afternoon. Could you please head down there and make a note of the attendees and the menu, and perhaps describe some of the gowns the ladies are wearing? I'd like you to include the piece in Saturday's ladies' column."

Reporting on a birthday party was the very last thing I wished to do, but I knew that I had little choice in the matter. "Lord Courtauld is the man whose maid stole from him, isn't he?" I said. "He's having an eventful week!"

"He certainly is."

Young ladies in bright gowns and furs stepped down from a row of carriages outside the Metropolitan Hotel. They skipped hurriedly across the wet pavement and in through the hotel doors. I waited for a convenient gap between them and followed in their wake.

"May I help you, ma'am?" asked a uniformed man who had immediately spotted that I wasn't one of the guests.

I introduced myself and told him I was there to report on the event for the *Morning Express* newspaper.

"Is there someone I can speak to about the attendees and the menu?" I asked.

He told me Mrs Roberts was arranging the event and that he would find her for me. I waited in the foyer as the young ladies continued to arrive. I took out my notebook and pencil to make a note of any gowns that particularly caught my eye. One young lady wore a satin bustle dress, which shimmered in gold. Another wore turquoise with a bustle and train patterned with blue, green and gold, like the colours of a peacock's tail. I was struck by how tiny many of the women's waists were. Jewellery glittered at their ears, throats and wrists, and there was a lot of excitable chatter as they headed toward a room from which the music played by a quartet was drifting out. It all seemed rather extravagant for an afternoon tea party.

Mrs Roberts was a pleasant lady, and she was happy to share with me the names of the most distinguished guests.

"How nice to see the press take an interest in this happy event!" she commented. "All too often news reporters are only interested in reporting on misery and tragedy. I suppose it's what the readers want. But an event like this should be celebrated; that of a young woman coming of age! It's a happy event indeed, and I'm sure readers of the *Morning Express* will be delighted to read about it."

"I shall mention it in the new ladies' column, which will be published this Saturday."

"What a marvellous idea! So many ladies read the newspaper now, don't they? And there are so many pages filled with men's business, such as politics, money and the law. That's not interesting to us at all, is it? I think it's a wonderful idea that the ladies will have a section of the newspaper all to themselves!"

"I should like to include the menu, if I may."

"I can fetch a menu card for you to take away, if you like."

"That would be very kind of you."

"Would you like to stay for the speeches? They're to take place in an hour."

I felt my heart sink at the thought of waiting around for them. "I suppose my editor would like me to. Is there somewhere I can wait until then?"

"Of course. I'll show you into the lounge and ask someone to bring you some tea."

"Thank you."

I spent the next hour in the lounge with my notebook and a pot of tea listening to the happy laughter and chatter coming from the room further down the corridor. I thought of Mrs King, and how unlikely it was that she had ever attended a party like this. In fact, many of the patients from the infirmary would have had little or no idea of what a society birthday celebration might entail. They would never wear the bright, expensive gowns or the family jewels kept under lock and key in the grand townhouses of Mayfair. I reflected on the fact that these differences existed for no other reason than the virtue of one's birth.

CHAPTER 9

"Just as I thought," said James once we had paid our entrance fee to Madame Tussauds. "It's rather busy."

"That's the problem one faces on a cold, wet Saturday," said Eliza. "Everyone wants to do something indoors."

"Don't you want to see the latest portrait models?" I asked them.

"Yes, if we get a chance to see them through this crowd," replied James.

"We just need to push our way through," I said.

We entered a large, high-ceilinged room filled with people, all of whom were bustling around the costumed wax figures displayed on ornate plinths.

"There's Ellen Terry as Ophelia," said Eliza, pointing at a model of the actress in a flowing cream gown clutching a bunch of flowers. "What a lovely dress."

"Hamlet was one of Father's favourite plays," I said as we pushed ourselves nearer. "Do you remember?"

"Of course I remember," she replied. "I thought Miss Terry would be taller, somehow."

"They're all smaller than what you'd think, ain't they?" a lady in a large blue hat chipped in.

"No they ain't," said her male companion with a grin. "They're all tall; look at 'em. Head and shoulders above ev'ryone else."

"That's 'cause they're on them pedestals, Charlie!" The lady shook her head in bemusement. "Can't take 'im anywhere!"

"Who's that bedraggled-looking fellow?" asked James, pointing toward a thick-whiskered man wearing dishevelled clothing.

"Captain Dudley o' the Mignonette," replied the lady in the hat. "You know all about *'im*, don't yer?"

"I do indeed," replied James.

"Cannibals, the lot of 'em," she continued. "Ate a cabin boy while driftin' away at sea."

"That cabin boy were dyin' anyway," interrupted her companion. "He never would of made it."

"That ain't no excuse."

"They thought they was protected by the custom o' the sea."

"Turned out they weren't, though, din't it? And quite right too, I reckon."

"What would you rather 'ave?" asked her companion. "One dead man and three alive, or four dead men?"

We slipped away to look at the model of General Gordon as the lady in the hat paused to consider this.

"I wonder if he can hold out until Lord Wolseley reaches Khartoum," commented James.

"He seems fairly confident that he will," I replied.

"Speaking of people in foreign climes, has there been any word on Francis Edwards' condition?"

"No," replied Eliza sadly. "Nothing at all! I'm quite desperate for news, and it's so terribly frustrating when letters take a month to reach us. I can only hope that we shall receive good news from Anselmo very soon."

"Poor Francis," said James. "He had covered such a lot of ground, and news of the European orchid grower sounded so promising. Let's hope that he is well recovered and meeting with the European as we speak."

"I should like to think so," I said. "And how nice of you to be so charitable about Francis, James."

He shifted from one foot to the other. "I like the fellow; he's a decent chap. And if he hadn't wished to marry you I'd like him even more!"

"That was long ago now."

"Not terribly long ago."

"Long enough to be forgotten about. It was before your proposed wedding day."

"There's no need to remind me of that!"

"Let's stop the bickering, shall we?" interrupted Eliza. "The past is in the past, and all that matters now is what the pair of you wish to do about your future. I'm quite sure that you have no wish for me to keep chaperoning you every weekend."

James and I exchanged a glance, and he smiled.

"Well?" asked my sister. "Is there anything you'd like to share with me?"

"We haven't set out any plans in detail yet," I ventured. I could feel a warmth rising in my face. "And we thought, perhaps, that we should wait until James has paid Charlotte the outstanding damages before anything else is decided."

"And then?" A smile began to spread across Eliza's face.

"And then we may be in a position to discuss marriage a little further," said James.

"*In a position to discuss it?* I hope you're not dragging your heels, James! Either you wish to marry one another or you don't."

"We do," said James.

"Then that's wonderful news!" Eliza clapped her hands together with glee. "How exciting!"

I glanced around us, slightly embarrassed by the fuss she was making. "We've only just begun to discuss it, Ellie. Please don't become too exuberant."

Her face fell. "How else do you expect me to be, Penelope? Here I am petitioning for divorce, and then I hear that my sister is to be married! The sister I thought would never marry! It's the most wonderful news I've heard in years!"

"I'm pleased that you're so happy about it."

"Happier than you, it seems!"

"I *am* happy. We both are." I turned to James and smiled. "We're just not ready to make a big announcement yet."

Eliza tutted. "Thirty-five years old and not yet ready to make an announcement! I suppose you're about to ask me not to mention it to Mother?"

"Yes."

"I should like to visit Mrs Green to formally request her daughter's hand," said James.

"Of course, replied Eliza. "Mother would like that very much. You must do it soon, though, as I shall grow terribly impatient having to keep this news quiet!"

"Once I've paid Charlotte the outstanding balance we shall get everything moving," said James.

"I've a good mind to pay it myself just to hurry things along!" said Eliza with a laugh. "Now, let's find this new portrait model of the Queen. I don't suppose we should leave here without seeing her."

There was quite a crowd around the Queen, who stood before the throne in a dark gown and a long white veil of lace.

"You might be interested to know that I returned to the workhouse this week," I said to Eliza.

"Don't tell me you stayed there again!"

I explained how I had helped Miss Russell with the task of reading to the patients.

"That sounds like an extremely helpful thing to do, Penelope. Well done! I wonder if the West London Women's Society might consider doing something similar at Paddington Workhouse, and perhaps Kensington, too."

"I'm sure they'd be delighted to hear from you."

"I might just write them a letter about it."

"I have to return to Shoreditch Workhouse again on Monday," I said. "The board of guardians has asked to meet me to discuss the article I wrote about our stay there."

"Oh goodness! Are they likely to scold you?"

"They shouldn't do, as I merely reported on my findings. The article didn't contain any untruths; nor was it sensationalised in any way."

"You're right, it wasn't. Oh good luck, Penelope, I hope they're kind to you. I still think about that poor man Bill who died there."

"So do I."

"Now where? Have we seen most of the exhibition?"

"There's the Chamber of Horrors to see yet."

"Oh no, count me out of that. I've no wish to see a host of dreadful criminals. I shall wait outside."

"I'm rather looking forward to it," said James. "There might be a few familiar faces in there."

CHAPTER 10

The following Monday I found myself waiting in a wood-panelled corridor, listening to the murmur of voices beyond a door marked 'Boardroom'. Despite straining to make out individual words, I felt disappointed that I was unable to hear what the members of the Shoreditch Union board of guardians were discussing.

I stepped back when I heard footsteps approaching from the other side of the door. The handle turned, and a bald man with a thick grey moustache pushed his head out. It was the clerk, Mr Lennox.

"The board is ready for you, Miss Green."

He swung the door open so that I could enter the room. I was greeted by a wall of a dozen faces all silently watching me from around a long, polished table. The chair nearest the door was empty. Everyone stood to their feet, and the bushy-whiskered man at the head of the table greeted me, gesturing for me to sit. There were two women in the group, one of whom I recognised as the matron, Mrs Hale. I guessed that the other woman was the poor law guardian Mrs Hodges, whom Miss Russell had mentioned to me.

There was a scraping of chair legs on floorboards as everyone took their seats again. The bushy-whiskered man at the head of the table was Mr Buller, the chairman, and he cleared his throat as he leafed through the papers piled in front of him.

"Thank you for joining us, Miss Green," he said. "We have all read, with great interest, the report you wrote regarding your stay on the women's casual ward here at Shoreditch Workhouse."

"That's encouraging to hear, sir." My voice sounded timorous in the large room, and the palms of my hands felt damp beneath my gloves. "May I ask what you thought of it?"

"Oh, you'll hear what we all thought of it in due course, Miss Green, there's no doubt about that. You're not the first to have undertaken this sort of reporting, you know. We've suffered a few individuals over the years who have stayed with us at the ratepayer's expense."

"My newspaper will recompense you for my stay," I said.

He gave an impatient nod, as if to indicate that he didn't like to be interrupted. "You're the first woman who has done it here, although I can't say that you'll find much difference between the women's casual ward and the men's. The work is different, but that's all there is to it."

"Can I ask whether my report was as you might have expected?"

He scowled, as if irritated by me speaking. "We're not managing a hotel, Miss Green, and we have no wish to encourage people to stay here. Quite the opposite, in fact. So in answer to your question, your report is broadly in line with what we expected. We don't expect people to come here and enjoy themselves. There is no joy in poverty."

"I realise that, but I believe the conditions could be a little more comfortable than they are."

"They don't need to be, Miss Green. We already have

more people wishing to spend the night here than we can accommodate. If we make the conditions *more comfortable*, as you suggest, we will simply have longer queues outside the workhouse door each evening. Word would spread, and then the paupers would abandon the other workhouses and make demands upon us instead. Can you imagine the difficulties that would cause us?"

The other board members nodded with agreement upon hearing this. I felt outnumbered but decided it was best to soldier on.

"If all the workhouses improved their conditions," I ventured, "you wouldn't be placed at a disadvantage."

My comment was met with light laughter.

"Each poor union must manage itself," replied Mr Buller. "I have no authority to tell other unions how they should run their workhouses! As the situation stands, the workhouses are very much alike at present. The pauper knows what to expect from each one."

"Which isn't much."

"Exactly, and nor can it be! We cannot encourage dependency, Miss Green."

"I witnessed young children who were cold and hungry. Such innocents have no say over their circumstances."

"They don't, but that's the role of the parents! Would you allow your children to wear rags and go hungry?"

"Of course not."

"And neither would any other respectable parent. Paupers must take responsibility for their children, and often a few nights on the casual ward helps them learn their lesson. At least the children have a roof over their heads and a bed for the night. There are many poor urchins who live on the streets and have no parents at all! There is provision for them, of course, in the form of orphanages and poor schools. We send countless children to these establishments once it becomes clear that their parents are either absent or unable to feed, clothe and send them to school."

A walrus-faced board member named Mr Webster addressed me next. "We would like you to write another article for your newspaper, Miss Green, about the excellent work we and other poor law unions are doing in providing for the poor. We do our very best to ensure that paupers are kept away from the workhouse, you know. Each week we have significant numbers applying to us for poor relief and medical relief, and we are extremely generous with what we grant them. A great many people remain in their homes and receive what is termed 'outdoor poor relief' from us. Our intention is to assist them for a short while until they are able to find work."

"What about those who are too infirm to work?"

"There is usually something they can do. A man who has lost a leg in a factory accident could take on some sewing instead and work alongside his wife, for example. We do whatever we can to encourage people to find work, and the children are also encouraged to do so once they have left school. And what we are experiencing here is a problem that will improve. Compulsory schooling has only been enforced for fifteen years, and we are beginning to see a generation of children who are far better educated than their forebears. Just twenty years ago young children were a common sight within our factories. That's changed now, and instead we ensure that they attend school up until the age of ten."

"If the families can afford schooling, that is."

"And if they can't, the children are sent to a poor school or a ragged school."

"Separated from their families?"

"Sometimes that is unavoidable, Miss Green. I cannot help but think that you are determined to dwell on the more negative side of this issue. We asked you here in order to provide you with details of all the good we're doing. Perhaps, Mrs Hodges, you could explain to Miss Green the excellent work we have been undertaking with the young women in the workhouse."

"Of course, Mr Webster," said Mrs Hodges, a grey-haired woman with pointed features. "We have been working extremely hard to ensure that girls over the age of twelve and unmarried women are trained in all matters pertaining to housekeeping. We also teach them good manners and show them how to look after their personal appearance. In doing so, we are training these women to find viable employment as maids. There is great demand for maids in London, as you know, and servants' wages have been increasing of late. Households can employ the girls we train at a slightly lower rate given that they have come directly from the workhouse. But many of the girls we train are just as proficient as those with several years of experience.

"I, myself, have been working with Lady Courtauld, who had been struggling to find good maids for her household. She has since enlisted the help of numerous friends, and we have supplied a good many maids to them all across London. This means that we no longer need to spend ratepayers' money on these girls, and that they have an opportunity to earn their own wages."

"*Lower* wages," I commented, noticing her lips scrunch thin as I did so.

"Initially, perhaps. After all, these girls have come straight out of the workhouse. But once they have held a position for a few years they are usually able to command a higher wage. We are preparing them for an independence that will last them until they marry. And of course a maid is a much better marriage prospect than a pauper from the workhouse; I'm sure you'd agree with that! The sad fact of the matter is that if we do nothing with these girls they may turn to drink... or worse."

"Worse?"

"I'm talking about *prostitution*." She whispered this last word. "It isn't nice to consider, but we cannot house young women in the workhouse forever, and if they have no skills for work, they usually fall by the wayside."

"And then use the workhouse infirmary for their lying-in!" added Mr Webster.

"Yes, indeed. It's sorrowful. Weak little babies are then born of these mothers, and sadly few survive. Who must care for them when this happens? The poor law unions, of course."

"I think your scheme to help young women find work is quite commendable," I said. "Are they encouraged to seek any work other than service?"

My question was met with general laughter.

"They don't have the propensity, Miss Green," said Mrs Hodges. "I realise that you speak as a lady who has a profession, and of course a fair number of women have a profession these days. But that is not something a girl from the workhouse would ever be capable of. It's hard enough teaching some of them to carry out the duties of a mere scullery maid!"

"Lord and Lady Courtauld were the victims of a theft last week," I said, "and the suspect is believed to have been their maid, Maisie Hopkins. Was she recruited from the workhouse?"

"I believe she was," replied Mrs Hodges tartly, "but the vast majority of workhouse girls make for good servants. There is clearly a bit of bad blood in Miss Hopkins."

"So what do you think to all that, Miss Green?" asked Mr Buller. "Perhaps your readers would like to hear about the good work we're doing with the girls and young women."

"What about the young men?" I asked.

"Apprenticeships," he replied. "They don't initially receive a wage, but if they show promise these opportunities may lead to employment. We work so hard to get these people off our hands, and when they complain that the gruel is tasteless and the bread is stale we explain to them that there is always an alternative. Perhaps you'd like a tour of the workhouse, Miss Green? I think it is important for you to see that the casual wards are only a small part of it."

"Thank you, I should like that."

I was accompanied on my tour by Mrs Hodges, along with the master, Mr Hale, and the matron, Mrs Hale. The latter observed me quizzically in the corridor outside the boardroom.

"You're an acquaintance of Miss Russell's aren't you, Miss Green?" she asked.

"I am indeed."

"And you were here just last week visiting patients in the infirmary, were you not?"

"Is that so?" asked Mrs Hodges.

"I don't recall you mentioning that you were a news reporter on that occasion," said Mrs Hale.

"Oh really?" I replied with wide-eyed innocence. "Well, the intention of my visit was to assist Miss Russell and Mrs Menzies rather than to carry out any reporting."

"And during your previous visit you stayed on the casual ward," continued Mrs Hale. "Your face is certainly quite familiar to me now. Were you not accompanied by another woman during your stay here?"

"Yes, my sister. I didn't feel brave enough to stay here alone."

Mrs Hale gave a dry laugh, and by the haughty look she gave me I deduced that she didn't care for me much.

Mr Hale was tall, like his wife, and walked with a stoop. He had a brooding presence, and I sensed that he hadn't warmed to me either. He led us on a brisk tour of the women's wing, where the elderly sat sewing in the day room, and the women and girls in their grey workhouse uniforms swept and dusted the dormitories. Inmates were peeling potatoes in the kitchen and kneading dough in the bakehouse. I could hear lively conversation just before we entered the laundry, but when we stepped inside the voices fell silent. Some of the women were slaving away at steam-filled tubs, wringers and mangles. Others were pressing linen with irons at long tables.

"Why are the blankets and nightgowns from the casual wards not washed with the other laundry?" I asked Mrs Hodges.

"They are," she replied.

"They can't be," I said. "They're filthy!"

"There isn't always time to wash them," said Mrs Hale, "but they are always stoved."

"I didn't see any being stoved."

She glared at me as though I were an insolent child.

A series of featureless yards sat between the workhouse buildings and perimeter walls. These were exercise yards segregating the men and women, boys and girls. Another yard had been set aside for stone-breaking, where the sound of hammers against rock was almost deafening. A long shed ran along one side of the yard, the wall of which featured an iron grill.

"The men have to break the stone small enough to fit through the holes in the grill," explained Mr Hale. "They must break half a yard a day, or more if they are being disciplined."

Some of the men were clearly well practised at the work,

while others appeared to be struggling. Their arms and shoulders seemed too weak to wield the heavy hammers.

"And what of those who are too infirm to break the stone?" I asked.

"We give them women's work," replied Mr Hale with a mocking smile. "They pick oakum, beat carpets, bake bread and that sort of thing."

"Inmates over the age of seventy are permitted to spend their time in the day rooms," said Mrs Hodges, seemingly keen to demonstrate that the workhouse offered some degree of compassion.

After leaving the stone-breaking yard we encountered one of the priests Dr Kemp had mentioned. Introduced to me as Father Keane, he was about thirty with a clean-shaven, youthful face. Mrs Hodges was keen to explain the good work he and St Monica's carried out on behalf of the workhouse. The tour concluded with a visit to the two classrooms, where girls were taught as well as boys. Even the children fell silent when we entered the room.

"We look forward to reading your next article on the subject of Shoreditch Workhouse," said Mrs Hodges as I took my leave. "I think it's quite important that your readers understand the full picture, don't you?"

"I must say that I was impressed by the infirmary when I visited last week," I said. "Dr Kemp appears to be doing a good job."

"Well there you are, you see. Are you planning to publish something about it?"

"The decision lies with my editor," I replied, "but I shall certainly mention it to him."

CHAPTER II

"**M**iss Green, this is Mr Torrance," said Mrs Garnett when I arrived home that evening.

I had climbed the stairs to my room only to find my landlady and the tenant with the large moustache blocking my way. He wore a smoking jacket over his shirt and waistcoat.

"It's a pleasure to meet you, Mr Torrance," I lied.

He gave me an officious nod.

"We thought it was about time that a typewriting curfew was agreed upon," said Mrs Garnett.

"Now? I'm only just returning from the office."

"It's a good a time as any, isn't it? Mr Torrance will retire for the evening shortly."

"And therein lies the problem," he interjected through his moustache. "It appears that Miss Green keeps the hours of a night owl."

"How about nine o'clock?" I suggested.

Mr Torrance shook his head. "Too late, I'm afraid."

I turned to my landlady for support. "I think nine o'clock is quite reasonable. Don't you agree, Mrs Garnett?"

"Well, if Mr Torrance says that it's too late, then I'm afraid it's too late."

"Can't you move your bed, Mr Torrance?" I asked gruffly.

He scowled. "The only other location would be next to my window, where there's a terrible draught."

"You could fold up a few sheets of newspaper and push them into the gaps," I replied.

"That would hardly be a long-term solution, Miss Green."

"May I ask what time you propose?"

"An eight o'clock curfew."

"Do you retire at eight o'clock every evening, Mr Torrance?"

"I do indeed. And I rise at five. You are quite welcome to begin your work at five o'clock. I don't mind hearing the typewriter while I'm breakfasting."

I forced a smile. "How very accommodating."

⚜

"An article about the good work of the Shoreditch Union sounds like a defence of their position," said Mr Sherman. "There's no doubt that the public has a low opinion of workhouses and their conditions, and reformers strongly believe that changes need to be made. To state that the workhouse is an effective solution for managing those in poverty is to suggest that the system should continue as it is. Nothing could excuse the misery of those casual wards, and publishing an article on the supposed good work of the union merely lets the board of guardians off the hook."

"They were quite keen for such an article to be printed."

"I'm sure they were! They have a reputation to uphold, after all. But the fact of the matter is that many of these boards have been poorly run over the years. And has the workhouse system achieved any perceivable change? There are still queues of people at their doors despite the miserable conditions. And for every person queueing at the workhouse door there are many who daren't go anywhere near it. Only last week we reported on the story of a man who froze to death in the doorway of the Alhambra Theatre, and all because he couldn't face returning to the workhouse. A freezing cold doorway – and likely death – was preferable to him!

"They may be doing good works in training young women to become maids and suchlike, and I've no doubt that some of those guardians are well-meaning. However, to report on the supposed good work they're doing is simply to deflect from the problem at hand. The problem is that these are hellish places, filled with misery. Prison inmates receive better treatment!"

"The guardians have a tough job, Mr Sherman," said Edgar.

"Of course they do."

"There is only so much money in the ratepayers' pot."

"So there is. And perhaps there should be more."

"I think you'd have a difficult task persuading hard-working, everyday Londoners to pay higher rates so the work-shy can eat better, sir," said Edgar.

"Very few people in the workhouse are work-shy," I said. "Some are unable to work because of old age or illness, while others have suffered an accident or misfortune. And there are many children there."

"It's different for the children, of course, but many of the adults are simply drunks," Edgar replied. "Surely you've seen all the inmates from the Strand Workhouse for yourself on liberty day, Miss Green. What do you suppose they do with their free time? They spend it at the public house, that's what! Don't ask me where they find the money to spend on drink, but find it they do."

"They beg," Frederick chipped in.

"Ah yes, many of them do that. And even worse, they make their children beg! Sometimes they wrap them in dirty bandages and sit them in the street, instructing them to pretend to be poor, crippled orphans! They're showered with coins in no time, and then mater and pater spend it all on gin."

"A few of them may do that," I said, "but not many. The majority have found themselves in difficult circumstances for one genuine reason or another. Those people would give anything to have regular work and a proper home."

"I consider them the minority," said Edgar. "If a man puts his mind to it he can always find work."

"Not if he is too elderly or infirm," I said.

"What we're really talking about here are the deserving and undeserving poor," said Edgar. "No one has any problem with the deserving poor, and we're all agreed that they deserve help. But when it comes to the undeserving—"

"I think this debate could rage on all day," interrupted Mr Sherman. "In the meantime, Miss Green, we won't be publishing anything that serves to defend how the board of guardians manages relief for the poor. I don't bear a personal grudge against its members; I suspect all poor law unions are run in the same manner up and down the country."

"And it's the only system that works," added Frederick.

"In what way does it work?" I asked. "Poverty still exists."

"Of course it does, and it always will. There will always be the haves and the have-nots, and then a whole horde of people in the middle like us."

"So you see no need at all for reform, Frederick?" I asked.

He shrugged his shoulders. "None. It is what it is. If you can't fend for yourself, you end up in the workhouse. If it wasn't for the threat of the workhouse, we'd have a good many more people claiming poverty."

"Interesting point, Potter," said Edgar. "If the workhouse was a pleasant place one wouldn't be able to threaten people with it, would one?"

"Not at all. It would be the same as saying to someone, 'Find work or you'll end up at Claridge's.'"

Both men gave a hearty laugh.

Mr Sherman sighed. "Get back to your work please, everyone."

There was a knock at the newsroom door, which Mr Sherman flung open to find James standing on the other side.

"Inspector Blakely!" he said. "And what can we do for you?"

"I have news for Miss Green," he replied, removing his bowler hat and giving me a gentle smile.

"Is it relevant to her work?"

"Yes, of course. I wouldn't wish to disturb her otherwise."

"Good," replied Sherman. "Then what is it?"

"I was called out to a murder this morning."

"Oh no!" I said. "What happened?"

"It was the result of an argument between two men, but I thought you might be interested to know about it, Penny, because of the location."

"Where did it occur?"

"At Shoreditch Workhouse."

CHAPTER 12

J ames instantly had the attention of everyone in the
newsroom.

"A fight, you say?" said Mr Sherman. "Were there
weapons involved?"

"No conventional weapons, no. A shovel was involved but
the cause of death was strangulation."

"Have you made an arrest?"

"Not exactly. The culprit died from his wounds."

"Goodness. Does that make it a double murder?"

"Well, no. It means that the victim put up a good enough
fight to cause fatal injuries to the other."

"How do you know that he was the victim?" asked Edgar.
"Perhaps he had attempted to murder the other chap first?"

"The other chap, or the culprit as we might refer to him,
was a known troublemaker."

"And both men are dead?" I asked.

"Unfortunately, yes. You may be interested in attending
the inquest, Penny. It's to be held this evening at the Green
Man public house on Hoxton Street, just opposite the workhouse entrance."

"Thank you, James. I'll be there."

An inquisitive crowd had gathered in Hoxton Street by the time I arrived at the Green Man that evening. The inquest was held in an upstairs room where the jurors were seated around a table. There was limited room around the table for everyone else to stand, so I joined the other reporters in the corner of the room and readied myself with my notebook.

A police inspector with grey whiskers and gold-rimmed spectacles entered the room, accompanied by James and a young constable. James and I caught each other's eye and exchanged a smile.

The coroner, Mr Welby, entered the room with his two assistants and everyone fell silent.

We waited while the jury was led out to the workhouse's dead house to view the bodies of the two men who had died. Then they returned to the room and official proceedings began.

"This morning at half-past seven o'clock, Mr Lawrence Patten, aged twenty-four and an inmate at Shoreditch Workhouse, was found dead in the stone-breaking yard," the coroner began. "Beside him lay the body of Mr Thomas Walker, aged thirty-one, who was also an inmate of the workhouse. As the deaths of these two men were the result of a singular incident, I shall consider both in the same inquest. I would like to call Mr George Simms as a witness, please."

A young, nervous-looking man in a rough suit rose to his feet and removed his flat cap.

"Mr Simms, may I confirm that you are an inmate at Shoreditch Workhouse?"

"Yessir."

I could see his hands trembling as he held his cap tightly.

"Can you describe what you discovered in the stone-breaking yard this morning?"

"Yessir. I was walkin' to the coal store an' I saw the pair of 'em laid out."

"And at what time was this?"

"First light; abaht 'alf past seven, sir."

"And what was your immediate thought when you saw Mr Patten and Mr Walker lying on the ground?"

"Surprise. Din't know what to fink!"

"Was it obvious to you that they were both dead?"

"Yessir. They both looked dead a'right."

"And what did you do then?"

"I called for the master!"

The coroner also called for the master of the workhouse.

"What was your first thought, Mr Hale, when you saw the bodies of these two men?"

"That they'd come to blows."

"You didn't suspect a third party?"

"No, Your Honour. I'd had words with Walker in the past about fighting."

"They had fought each other before?"

"Not each other. But Walker was handy with his fists, if you know what I mean."

"When were the two men last seen alive?"

"Patten was put to work at eight o'clock yesterday evening by the labour master, Mr Cricks. The work was given as punishment for the use of foul language, and he was told to shovel pieces of stone from one heap to another for the duration of three hours."

"So Mr Patten was last seen by Mr Cricks at eight o'clock yesterday evening in the stone-breaking yard."

"That's correct."

The coroner furrowed his brow. "If Mr Patten was put to work at eight o'clock for three hours then surely the labour master would have checked that his work was complete at eleven o'clock that evening? Once the three hours had passed?"

Mr Hale shifted from one foot to another. "Well he should have done."

"And he didn't?"

"No, I don't believe he did."

"Do you have any idea why not?"

The Master cleared his throat. "I believe he finished his duty early that evening."

"So where was he?"

"He was off-duty, Your Honour."

"Where does he spend his time when he's off-duty?"

"On this particular occasion he was in The Unicorn public house."

The coroner pursed his lips. "I see. Is that what he told you?"

"I know it for sure, Your Honour, I saw him there myself."

The coroner raised an eyebrow and gave a sigh.

"Mr Patten was the sort to be trusted to work for three hours, Your Honour," continued the Master.

"Had Mr Cricks returned to the stone-breaking yard, then the sorrowful scene would have been discovered much sooner," commented the coroner. "Perhaps it could even have been avoided?"

"I'm not sure, Your Honour."

"And Mr Walker?" asked the coroner. "When was he last seen?"

"He was last seen by fellow inmates in the men's day room, and then he crossed the yard to fetch some coal from the coal store."

"What time was that?"

"About a quarter after eight, I believe."

The police constable who had been summoned by the

master then gave his deposition. He described the scene, with Mr Patten lying on his back and Mr Walker lying close by on his left side. Found beside them were a shovel, two extinguished lanterns and an empty pail, which Mr Walker had been seen carrying when he left for the coal store.

The constable's deposition was followed by that of the police surgeon, who had examined the bodies at the scene and carried out the autopsies. He confirmed that Mr Patten had died of strangulation, while Mr Walker had died of severe injuries to his head.

"Which man do you suspect died first?" asked the coroner.

"I think it must have been Mr Patten, who had been subjected to a sustained strangulation. I'm quite sure Mr Walker would have ensured that he carried out the act until Mr Patten was completely dead."

"And you state that Mr Walker sustained injuries himself during the altercation."

"Yes. His death was caused by a head injury that didn't cause immediate death but was quite swift."

"So you believe that Mr Walker carried out a murderous act upon Mr Patten before succumbing to his own injuries?"

"Yes, I believe that to be the case."

"And what do you suspect was used as a weapon?"

"A shovel was found next to Mr Patten's body, and the injuries to Mr Walker were consistent with being hit by a shovel."

The police surgeon went on to give details of the injuries suffered by both men.

"And what is the estimated time of death?"

"Both men were quite cold when I examined them, and there was a hard frost last night, which was evident on their clothing. There's no doubt that they had lain there all night. Cold conditions delay the onset of rigor mortis, so that cannot be relied upon to calculate a time of death in this case. As the settling of frost made it quite evident that the bodies had lain in the yard for some time, I estimate that both deaths occurred no later than midnight, though there is every chance that they occurred much sooner; perhaps shortly after the two men were last seen."

The bald, grey-whiskered clerk, Mr Lennox, was called.

"What do you know of Mr Patten?" asked the coroner.

"Only what we have in the admissions book," Mr Lennox replied.

"Which is what?"

"His name and last known address, which was a lodging house in Southwark. He was admitted to the workhouse three weeks ago, and had visited as a casual pauper before then."

"Have you located any family members or friends?"

"None. His entry in the admissions book confirms that he had no known friends or family."

"Do you know anything else about the man?"

"He gave his occupation as a labourer."

"And what of Mr Walker?"

"He was admitted to the workhouse seven weeks ago."

"And this man has family?"

"Yes. He has a sister, Your Honour."

The judge called the sister, Mrs Holmes, who wore a scruffy bonnet and shawl.

"Mr Walker was your brother, I believe."

"Yeah, 'e were."

"When did you last see him?"

"Afore 'e went inter the work'ouse."

"And how was he occupied before being admitted to the workhouse?"

"'E were a costermonger."

"And why did he cease that line of work?"

"Couldn't make it pay. 'E was buyin' apples for more 'an 'e could sell 'em for. 'E said they 'ad summink against 'im down the market and only sold 'im rotten apples. And 'e couldn't sell rotten apples ter no one! 'E 'ad 'is troubles, but 'e weren't no murderer! 'E never 'armed no one, Lord's truth!"

"How did he end up at the workhouse?"

"'E kept gettin' harrested because o' the drink, an' then 'e got put in the work'ouse. But 'e never laid a finger on no one!"

"He was sent to the workhouse for being drunk?" asked the coroner.

"Yeah."

The bespectacled, grey-whiskered inspector was summoned to explain this. He stated his name as Inspector Ferguson of Commercial Street police station, H Division.

"Is it true that Mr Walker was admitted to the workhouse for being drunk?" the coroner asked him.

"He was admitted to the workhouse infirmary a number of times because he was *unwell*, Your Honour."

"Unwell from drink?"

"As I'm not a medical man, sir, I'm unable to elaborate further, but the police doctor had certified that he was ill and sent him to the workhouse infirmary."

The coroner frowned. "Is the medical officer for the infirmary present?"

Dr Kemp stood up and introduced himself.

"Do you recall treating Mr Walker?" the coroner asked him.

"Many times, Your Honour," replied the doctor with a sigh.

"And what was the nature of his illness?"

"On each occasion he was under the influence of strong liquor, and in some instances he had sustained a wound that required dressing. He was swiftly discharged again each time, but after countless readmissions I recommended that he be admitted to the workhouse."

"And was he treated in the infirmary after his admission?"

"No. My action had the desired result of keeping him away."

This reply was met with light laughter.

"Are paupers the worse for drink frequently admitted to the workhouse infirmary, Dr Kemp?" asked the coroner.

"Yes, and the matter has been a bone of contention between myself and the officers at Commercial Street station for a while. Time and again I have been awoken in the early hours of the morning to admit persons with certificates stating that they are ill when they are merely drunk. Police doctors receive a fee for certifying such cases, while I receive no fee at all."

"Is what the doctor says correct, Inspector Ferguson?" asked the coroner.

"As I explained, Your Honour, I'm not a medical man and am merely guided by the advice of our own doctors."

The coroner shook his head and looked down at his papers. "There is a risk that we may preoccupy ourselves with matters irrelevant to this inquest. Inspector Ferguson, have you learnt anything of Mr Patten to supplement what the workhouse clerk, Mr Lennox, has already told us?"

"I spoke to a number of the inmates, who told me that he claimed to have been born near Birmingham. The owner of the lodging house in Southwark, which was his last known address, confirmed that he was a regular visitor there and a considerate one. He had never known him to be in any sort of trouble. Mr Patten mentioned that he had also stayed in the Paddington and Millwall workhouses, when I examined their admissions books I found no further details about him. It appears that he conducted himself well and was not given to drink. He was a well-liked man who found the odd bit of work down at the docks, but not a great deal."

"So although the man was a pauper he was of good character?"

"He was indeed, Your Honour."

"With the exception of his using foul language in the workhouse, which led to his punishment of breaking stone, that is. Can you tell us anything more of Mr Walker, Inspector Ferguson?"

"He was very much given to drink, Your Honour. Although all efforts were made to keep substances away from him at the workhouse, he did manage to get his hands on the stuff from time to time."

"And he had been arrested by the constables at your station several times."

"Yes, Your Honour."

"On how many occasions?"

"On six occasions."

"For drunkenness in each case?"

"Yes, Your Honour. He may also have been arrested by constables at other stations, but I haven't had time to make enquiries with them yet."

The coroner conferred with his assistants, then addressed the jury. "You have heard all that you need to hear about these two unfortunate souls. Mr Patten was a man of generally good character, who had been tasked with breaking stone at the workhouse yesterday evening. Shortly after he began his work, Mr Walker, a known drunkard, entered the yard to fetch coal from the coal store. He made his presence known to Mr Patten for reasons we have been unable to establish. It is clear, however, that a disagreement ensued, and this altercation escalated into a physical conflict with fatal consequences for both men. Please take your time as you consider your verdict."

CHAPTER 13

"Have you ever come across a case before in which two men have fought to the death?" I asked James as we walked down Hoxton Street after the inquest.

Gas lamps on the path ahead of us illuminated a crowd of people leaving the Britannia Theatre after the pantomime performance.

"Only once," said James. "I remember two chaps fatally injuring each other in a fight outside a public house in Marylebone."

"Do you consider it a rare occurrence?"

"I should say so, yes."

"There's something rather odd about the case of Mr Patten and Mr Walker, don't you think?"

"Insofar as that it's unusual, yes."

"Too unusual, I'd say."

"The facts of the case have been considered by Inspector Ferguson and Mr Welby."

"And they have concluded that each man killed the other."

"That's also what the jury surmised."

"But no one seems willing to consider that a third person might have been involved."

"There is no evidence to suggest such a thing."

"But that doesn't mean the possibility can immediately be ruled out! You know that, James."

He laughed. "Oh, Penny. Why must you question everything?"

"Because I feel that we shouldn't necessarily accept all that we are told. There was one dissenting voice at that inquest, and it came from Mr Walker's sister. She strongly believed that he would never murder someone, and she knew him better than anyone else in the room. The two men were found dead in the yard, and the assumption was that one had murdered the other. But who made that assumption?"

"Everyone. And the fact that they died in quite different ways supports it. If a third man had been involved, surely he would have used the same method for both? After all, he would have been outnumbered, and he'd have had to quickly dispatch both of them before they could do him any harm. Strangulation can take a few minutes, so how could he have done it without Walker trying to stop him?"

"Perhaps he killed Walker first."

"In which case, why didn't he also kill Patten with the shovel? Why go to the trouble of strangling him?"

I couldn't think of an immediate reply to this.

"And a supposed third man might well have been injured in the attack," continued James. "The other two would surely have fought back, in which case we'd be looking for another inmate with injuries."

"Has Inspector Ferguson searched for another inmate with injuries?"

"I doubt it, as no one has seriously considered that a third person might have been involved."

I sighed. "I think the coroner should have called for an adjournment so that further investigations could take place."

"But he judged the case as it appeared. Two men fell into a disagreement, which resulted in fatal consequences. Let's consider for a moment that a third man murdered them both. What might his motive have been?"

"Perhaps the three of them argued. Perhaps it was a revenge attack for something one or both of them had said or done. Perhaps one man was murdered because he witnessed the attack on the other. The motive doesn't have to be obvious or even rational; you've said that yourself before now, James. But the intent was there. Someone wanted those men dead."

"You're not content with the explanation that Mr Walker simply succumbed to his injuries?"

"He died from a fatal head injury, which Mr Patten supposedly inflicted upon him. Could he have throttled Mr Patten while nursing that dreadful injury? Surely such a blow to his head would have incapacitated him."

"It's likely that it would have done so, but not a certainty."

"Nothing about this case is a certainty, but I think my theory holds just as much weight as the current theory that the two men killed each other."

"Then where is the third man now?"

"He's lying low somewhere, pleased that he has managed to get away with it."

"And presumably injured. I suppose we could present this theory to Inspector Ferguson; not that he'll be happy to hear it, given that he considers the case to be closed now."

"The case is not closed if there's a murderer lurking within the walls of that workhouse."

"How many inmates does it have in total? About five hundred?"

"There are various assumptions we can make to decrease

the number of suspects," I said. "We can count the children out, and perhaps also the women. A lady hanging about in the men's yard would have been easy to spot."

"Unless she had disguised herself."

"That isn't impossible, is it? But to begin with we might assume a simpler explanation: that another man carried out the attack. After all, it would have had to be a strong woman to overpower two men. So if the women and children are ruled out, that would probably leave about two hundred men."

"At the maximum, I'd say."

"It can't have been a patient in the infirmary as he would have been too weak or infirm to commit the violence. And it can't have been an elderly man, so perhaps that reduces the suspect list to between one hundred and one hundred and fifty."

"That's still rather a lot of possible culprits, Penny!"

"But then we need to consider who would have been in the vicinity at the time. Some men may have been in the dormitories while others were in the day room. How many were in close proximity to the stone-breaking yard at the time the attack was carried out?"

"We would need to question everyone and establish their alibis. Can you imagine asking Inspector Ferguson to do that on a case that is already solved?"

"But it's *not* solved."

"He thinks it is. And what if the findings of the inquest were correct? The police could spend all their time inter-viewing countless inmates only to realise that the details were exactly as described!"

"So what do you suggest, James? Should we accept the findings of the inquest and assume that no one else was involved?"

"That's what everyone else intends to do."

"And what if there is still a murderer at large?"

"If there's a murderer at large he'll strike again, Penny."

"And you think it acceptable that he be allowed to prowl around the workhouse in search of his next victim?"

"No, not at all. But I must also consider the amount of police time required to investigate this properly. Although I think there is a possibility that a third person may have been involved, it is still only a theory. We have no evidence. We cannot possibly persuade the police to go around interviewing hundreds of inmates when the coroner's inquest has already presented its findings."

"A little too hastily, I'd say."

"Yes, perhaps you're right. But do you understand what I'm trying to say, Penny? Our hands are tied."

"Yes, until the next person dies."

CHAPTER 14

S *ilk and satin dresses with velvet designs continue their trend in evening wear. Velvet stripes, spots, leaves and flowers are proving particularly popular this season, while velvet bodices and lace skirts trimmed with velvet are more in vogue than ever. Tulles and gauzes are lightly draped and decorated with appliquéd flowers.*

Pale china pink is teamed with myrtle green or bronze, though Louis green, a bright shade of emerald, is also making an appearance. Black lace remains popular for evening wear, especially when worn with a contrasting colour.

In Paris, emu feathers are replacing ostrich feathers in hats. These can be curled into little rings or arranged as a long plume.

"This piece of writing seems rather lacklustre for you, Miss Green," my editor commented as he read it through.

"I can't say that I enjoy writing about fashion, sir," I said. "I find it rather tedious."

"A good reporter can turn her hand to anything, Miss Green."

"I realise that, but it's difficult when the topic holds no interest at all."

"It doesn't matter what interests you, Miss Green. It's what interests our readers that sells copies, and any ladies' column would be incomplete without a few notes on the subject of fashion."

"Ladies are interested in other things too, Mr Sherman."

"Of course they are, but the purpose of the ladies' column is to include topics that are not currently featured elsewhere in the newspaper. Ladies can read all about parliament and the money markets if they so wish and then turn to enjoy these lighter topics. I think you'll find that a few gentlemen may also have a surreptitious read of the ladies' column."

Edgar gave a loud laugh. "You wouldn't find *me* reading it, sir!"

"Why not? It might enlighten you on a matter or two."

"Trivial matters, perhaps."

"Are you saying that ladies' interests are trivial?" I asked Edgar.

"Quite a lot of them are, yes. Many of them are to do with running the home, in which case decor and menus are important. And appearance is also important to a lady, isn't it? She must run a respectable home and look respectable at the same time."

"These issues are not necessarily trivial," said Mr Sherman. "They constitute essential reading for the day-to-day life of a lady."

"I suppose so," replied Edgar.

"And the husband wishes to return to a well-managed home in the evenings, doesn't he?" continued the editor. "So perhaps it's not quite so trivial for him after all."

"Well, yes. I agree wholeheartedly with that," said Edgar. "The focus of my home is the cats more than anything else. Georgina spends all her time grooming them, tying little bows around their necks and shopping for the finest cuts of meat to feed them with."

"Perhaps I could write about cats for the ladies' column," I suggested with a smile.

"Georgina would certainly enjoy that," said Edgar. "In fact, she would probably be willing to become a guest writer for the column. If there's anything she doesn't know about cats it's not worth knowing at all. In fact, she would do well to spend a little more time focusing on other household matters. She's so busy fussing over the cats that she doesn't always pay attention to what's going on below stairs."

"And what *is* going on below stairs?" enquired Mr Sherman.

"The servants please themselves, that's what! The cook concocts whatever she pleases. She's served us game three times within the past week, despite me telling Georgina that I dislike game. I've told her she needs to agree the menu with the housekeeper every Sunday evening, but it never happens."

"Miss Green, I think some tips for managing one's housekeeper should be included in next week's column," said Mr Sherman.

"I wouldn't have the first idea about that," I replied. "I could just about manage a few words on fashion, but housekeeping is something I know nothing about. Perhaps you could write some housekeeping tips yourself, sir. You have a housekeeper, don't you?"

"Yes, but only for a small household. It's just me, the housekeeper and a maid."

"I don't run a household at all, sir."

"That's an interesting point, Miss Green. I'm asking you to write the ladies' column, yet you're not exactly representative of the average lady, are you?"

I laughed. "No, I'm not."

"I'll happily jot down the housekeeper tips for you, Miss Green. Would that help?"

"It would indeed, sir. Thank you."

"So while I tackle the trivial matters, how would you like to write about something a little more intellectual for the ladies' column, Miss Green?"

"I should like that very much. What is it?"

"My brother informs me that one of London's most eminent physicians, Dr Charles Macpherson of St Bartholomew's Hospital, is to speak on anatomy at the School of Medicine for Women this evening. The invitation to attend is extended to all members of the fairer sex; not only to those who are studying medicine. His attendance at the school demonstrates the increasing significance of women's medicine. I should think that a summary of his lecture would be of interest to our learned lady readers."

"A medical lecture!" Edgar laughed. "I bet you wish you hadn't complained about fashion now, don't you, Miss Green? I expect you'd far rather write about hats than body parts!"

❧

Dr Macpherson proved to be an engaging speaker that evening. He was able to maintain my interest in a subject to which I had previously given little thought. He was a short, affable man with an intelligent, hawk-like face and a quick wit. I glanced around the auditorium as he spoke, impressed by the number of interested female faces I could see.

CHAPTER 15

The following Tuesday I met Miss Russell and Mrs Menzies at the Shoreditch Workhouse infirmary and read to the patients once again. I had been worried that the frail Mrs King would no longer be there, so it was with some relief that I was able to read her a little more of *Treasure Island*.

"Stop interruptin'!" she scolded.

"What do you mean, Mrs King?"

"Miss Turner over there. She's openin' an' closin' that door, and I can't 'ear the words."

I looked across the room and saw the nurse locking a door in the corner of the room.

"What's in there, anyway?" demanded Mrs King.

"Never you mind," replied the nurse with a smile. "I'll return to it once Miss Green has finished reading."

"In and out of it all day, she is," muttered Mrs King. "Gives me an 'eadache."

"How was your meeting with the board of guardians?" asked

Miss Russell as we walked over to the children's ward. "I heard they spoke to you about your article."

"They're keen for me to write a second piece about all the good work they're doing here, such as the scheme to help young women find work as maids."

"And will you?"

"The decision rests with my editor," I replied, keen to make it clear that the matter was out of my hands. "He is reluctant to publish an article which praises the board of guardians when the conditions here are still so bad."

"I can understand why he would feel like that, but change cannot come about if we ignore the efforts being made to improve the situation."

"Are they genuine efforts?" I asked. "Or are they just small gestures the board of guardians hopes will atone for the misery people suffer here? I dislike the general insistence that conditions have to remain bad – especially on the casual wards – to deter people from seeking refuge here."

"It's a dilemma. I can understand why the conditions cannot be too appealing."

"But surely a bit of warmth, a comfortable bed and good food are required. I struggle to believe that fulfilling these basic human needs would result in people coming here in their droves."

"There's a great deal of debate to be had on the subject, and that's why I think it a shame that your editor refuses to publish a second article. Perhaps the piece could be more of a discursive essay mentioning the positive work that has been carried out but also reminding people of the wider problems."

I nodded. This seemed to me to be a good approach.

"After all, the problem stretches way beyond the walls of this workhouse," continued Miss Russell. "There is so much poverty on London's streets, and the population of the city's slums is so great that the workhouses are unable to accommodate everyone who needs assistance. Just think of the thousands who must part with a sixpence to spend the night at one of those dreadful lodging houses.

"I think there is very little that a board of guardians can do all by itself. There needs to be an orchestrated approach from all the unions that administer poor relief, and the unscrupulous landlords of slum properties need to mend their ways too. The solution lies with the government, so we can only do what we are able to and report back on what's happening. Articles such as yours could help with that, Miss Green.

"A good number of organisations are doing their best to improve the daily lives of the poor. There are countless charitable causes providing food, companionship and occasional shelter. If we can simply do a little to help someone in need feel better, our day's work will be well spent.

"I suppose that's all we can do, isn't it? And we must keep reminding the government that changes need to be made. I read recently that the British Empire covers a fifth of the globe and encompasses more than three hundred million inhabitants, yet we're unable to feed and clothe those living right on our doorstep. It doesn't seem right, does it?"

We encountered Dr Kemp as we were walking from the children's ward to the men's ward and I told him that I had found his deposition at the inquest of Mr Patten and Mr Walker most interesting.

"In what sense?" he asked.

"It was the fact that the police officers at Commercial Street station refer drunkards to you, claiming they're ill, that intrigued me."

"I think it's the fault of the police doctors rather than

the constables themselves," he replied. "The doctors are paid for each patient they certify, so it's an easy income for them."

"But the police are duty-bound to put a stop it!"

"They are, but who are they to doubt a medical man's word? Doing so could result in a genuinely ill drunkard being refused treatment at the infirmary."

"So what can be done about it?"

"I wish I knew, Miss Green. I don't have an easy answer; all I know is that the services of this infirmary are always under a great strain."

"I think you have an unenviable job, Dr Kemp," I said. "On the subject of the inquest, do you think the events of that evening occurred as the inquest described?"

"Yes, I should think so."

"You don't think that it could have played out rather differently?"

"In what way?"

"Perhaps a third person could have been involved."

"Someone who got away, you mean?"

"Yes."

He pondered this for a moment. "I suppose there's a possibility. But the culprit would have had to overpower two men, and I don't think that sounds likely. Sadly, we'll never truly know what occurred in that yard, but many queer things have happened here over the years. It seems to be the way of the workhouse, I'm afraid."

I could recall what the stone-breaking yard looked like from my tour of the workhouse, but in the light of the recent tragedy that had taken place there I wished to see it again to satisfy my curiosity. We finished reading to the patients and I parted company with Miss Russell before we walked to the entrance, informing her that I needed to visit the clerk, Mr Lennox.

I made my way along the covered walkway toward the building that housed the dormitories and day rooms. The stone-breaking yard could be accessed from the men's wing of the building. I paused in the corridor and waited until there was no one about before slipping in through the doorway of the men's day room.

A few elderly inmates gave me a cursory glance as I walked through the room, but I simply smiled and hoped to remain unchallenged until I reached the door at the far end. Beyond it I could hear the sound of hammer against stone. I opened the door a little way and peered out into the yard, where a great number of men were wielding their hammers against the blocks of stone and shovelling piles of it through the iron grill. Small flakes of ice floated down from the thick clouds overhead as the men laboured, their uniforms as grey as the sky.

I stood at the door for a while and surveyed the yard. There were three other doors that opened out onto it. One had a sign beside it that read 'Coals', and I surmised that this had been the original destination for Mr Simms, the man who had discovered the bodies of Mr Patten and Mr Walker. With the yard now busy, it was difficult to identify where the bodies of the two men had lain.

The second door was closed, but the third had been propped open with a barrel. Nearby, a large young man with close-set features stooped down to pick something up from the ground. A sign on the wall behind him read 'Store'. As he wasn't breaking stone, I wondered whether he regularly worked in the storeroom instead. There was no sign of the labour master in the yard; a fact that some of the inmates were taking advantage of as they sat on the ground and exchanged lively banter.

I decided to talk to the man standing beside the store. I sidled out of the doorway and walked around the perimeter of the yard, hoping to remain unnoticed. A few men glanced over and leered at me, but my presence did not appear to surprise them too greatly.

As the young man lingering beside the store saw me approaching, he stood to his feet, put something in his pocket and ducked through the doorway. I reached the entrance and peered inside the gloomy room, which was filled with shelves. Each was piled high with bundled items tied up with string. The small windowsill was covered with odds and ends, such as little bottles, broken clay pipes and discarded snuff boxes.

"Hello?" I ventured.

The young man was watching me from the far corner of the storeroom. I noticed that he was cross-eyed.

"I'm a missionary," I said, feeling ashamed at my brazen lie. "Do you work here all the time?"

He nodded.

"I heard about the sad deaths of Mr Patten and Mr Walker," I said. "Did you see anything yourself that night?"

He gave a slight nod.

"What did you see?" I asked.

"I heard," he replied.

"What did you hear?"

"Shoutin'."

"A lot of shouting?"

"Just some."

"And did you hear anyone say anything in particular?"

He shook his head.

"Do you know who was shouting?"

He shrugged his shoulders.

"Did you hear anything else?"

He shook his head.

"What time were you here in the store until?"

"Ten o'clock."

"I presume you crossed the yard when you left?"

He nodded.

"Did you see anything unusual in the yard?"

"No, it were too dark."

"Has a police officer spoken to you about this?"

He shook his head, then turned away from me and began to examine one of the bundles on the nearest shelf. I took this as a sign that he was reluctant to talk any more. It was apparent that he struggled with conversation, and I guessed that he was perhaps a man of limited intelligence. However, there was a possibility that he could turn out to be an important witness to the events of that evening.

Aware that I was somewhere I wasn't supposed to be, I decided it was time to leave. I walked back toward the men's day room and briskly sauntered through it again before stepping out into the main corridor.

"Miss Green?"

I felt a plummeting sensation in my chest as I turned to see who had become aware of my presence.

"Oh, hello, Mr Hale," I replied cheerfully.

He stood over me, his shoulders hunched. I felt as though I were about to be admonished by a schoolmaster.

"May I ask what you're doing here?"

"I've been assisting Miss Russell and Mrs Menzies with reading to the patients in the infirmary."

"We are a long way from the infirmary, Miss Green, and I have just observed you stepping out of the men's day room. Women are not permitted to enter."

"I do apologise, Mr Hale."

"What were you doing in there?"

"I became a little lost, I'm afraid."

"The men's day room is clearly marked as such on the

door. And even if you hadn't taken the time to read the sign, it would have been quite obvious once you stepped inside the room that it was occupied entirely by men."

I felt a warmth in my face as I struggled to concoct a sensible reply to this. Rather than continue to lie, I decided it would be best to tell Mr Hale at least part of the truth.

"I took a wrong turn when I left the infirmary, Mr Hale, and as I did so I realised that I was walking in the direction of the stone-breaking yard where the tragic deaths of—"

"I see." He grinned insincerely. "And because you are a news reporter you were keen to see where the two men lost their lives, were you?"

"I can't say that I was keen to see it, Mr Hale, but—"

"But you are a news reporter, and this is the sort of thing news reporters do. I might have guessed that the supposed assistance you have been giving Miss Russell was little more than a ruse to gain access to the murder scene."

"No! That really isn't true, Mr Hale. I volunteered to assist Miss Russell before the deaths occurred."

"Did you speak to any of the inmates?"

"No. Well, I did speak extremely briefly with the young man in the storeroom."

"Horace? Well, I'd be surprised if he spoke a single word to you. You managed to get all the way to the storeroom in the stone-breaking yard, you say?"

"It was just a brief visit."

"Please come with me, Miss Green, and I shall escort you from the premises. I am quite astonished that you were able to enter the men's wing of the workhouse without being challenged. Your conduct has been both reckless and improper."

He strode on ahead, so I followed him out of the block and along the covered walkway. We marched through the infirmary and down the walkway that led to the workhouse entrance.

"I had hoped you were here to inform me that you would be writing an article about the good work of the workhouse, as the board of guardians requested," said Mr Hale over his shoulder.

I had to quicken my step to keep up with his stooped form. "My editor has no plans for such an article to be written at the present time."

"I can't say that I'm surprised," he snapped. "Lurid details about the deaths of Mr Patten and Mr Walker are of far greater interest, I suppose. The press would far rather print sensationalist nonsense than good news these days. However, I think it only fair after your criticism of the casual wards here at the workhouse that such an article were required to provide an alternative viewpoint. Not everything about the workhouse is bad, Miss Green."

"I agree."

"Then perhaps you can convince your editor of that."

"He feels that if we were to publish an article praising the work of the workhouse, the criticisms we have made so far would be disregarded."

"The majority of your readers will already have disregarded your article, Miss Green."

I chose not to react to his provocation. "There is no doubt that improvement in the casual wards is needed," I said.

"So you're a workhouse inspector now, Miss Green. You do realise that an inspector visits us on a regular basis and is always content with the way we manage things here, do you not?"

"I'm sure you manage them as well as any other workhouse does, Mr Hale, but conditions need to improve at all the workhouses."

He gave a dry laugh. "It amuses me that do-gooders and members of the press think they're doing everyone a service by complaining about the conditions when they have hardly any knowledge of how poor relief works in this country. It's all very well for people such as yourself, Miss Green, to loudly complain about such matters before retiring to your agreeable homes for the evening. I'm sure you would view matters rather differently if you were a pauper yourself."

"The fact that someone is a pauper does not mean they would find the conditions acceptable," I retorted. "News reporters such as myself can speak up for people who are unable to make their voices heard. If a pauper complains about the conditions at a workhouse, he or she is rebuked. When a newspaper does it on the pauper's behalf the people responsible are forced to listen."

We paused in the entrance hallway. Mr Hale towered over me, and I resisted the urge to take a step back.

"We are not the reason these people are poverty-stricken, Miss Green. We are part of the system that provides relief to them. We *help* them. Is it so impossible for your newspaper to acknowledge that? Now, I don't know why you have singled out Shoreditch Workhouse as a target for your ire, but if you're unhappy with the system your time would be better spent down at Westminster haranguing the people who put these systems in place. If I find you hanging around this workhouse again I shall involve the police and make an official complaint to the *Morning Express* newspaper. Good day to you!"

CHAPTER 16

"Horace, the man who works in the storeroom, told me he heard shouting in the stone-breaking yard the night the two men died," I told James. "And he says he was in the storeroom until ten o'clock that evening, so he must have seen or heard something else. I think he may be an important witness, and I'm quite surprised that Inspector Ferguson and his men have neglected to speak to him."

I was standing beside James' desk in his dingy office at Scotland Yard. A cloud of tobacco smoke drifted over us from a police officer who was smoking a pipe nearby.

"What have you been doing, Penny?" replied James. "You can't just wander around a workhouse trying to find out if someone else murdered those two men!"

"No one else intends to, do they?"

"But this is just an idea of yours. It's a whim—"

"It's not a whim! I know the inquest is closed, but its findings may well have been wrong."

"Or they may have been right."

"But there is definitely some uncertainty!"

"In your mind, perhaps."

"Is there no uncertainty in yours?"

"A little, I suppose."

"Can you be sure that the events decided upon at the inquest describe exactly what happened?"

"No, I cannot be sure of that."

"So there is some doubt over whether the right verdict was returned."

"Only a tiny bit."

"Then we need to do something about it, James, and Horace can help us."

James shook his head. "How do you know you didn't plant an idea in his head? Witnesses must be questioned in the proper manner. It's imperative that the person asking the questions doesn't make any suggestions as to what the witness may or may not have seen."

"I know how to speak to potential witnesses!" I snapped. "I merely asked him whether he saw anything in the yard that night, and he replied that he had *heard* something. He heard shouting, and that was all he told me. I don't know what time he heard the shouting or how long it lasted for, but I think that would probably best be discussed with a police officer or yourself, James."

He gave a low sigh. "It would be useful to make further enquiries, I suppose. That way we could establish for certain whether he was there or not when the two men lost their lives. But I'll have to speak to Inspector Ferguson about this, and he won't be happy."

"Then perhaps he should have done his job properly in the first place!"

"Perhaps he already has. He will not appreciate the Yard suggesting that he reopens the case."

"Fine, then don't speak to him!"

"Don't be like that, Penny."

"You seem quite determined to disagree with everything I've suggested regarding this case!"

"I don't disagree with you, and there is a possibility that the deaths haven't been investigated thoroughly enough. However, you seem so convinced that I feel the need to encourage you to consider all possibilities. The words of this Horace fellow have played into your hands, and now you are convinced that your theory is correct. But we must keep our minds open to other—"

"Just as Inspector Ferguson has? And the coroner?"

"Please don't convince yourself of this one theory, Penny. Perhaps events unfolded in a way that we haven't even considered yet."

"Perhaps they did. In which case Inspector Ferguson needs to start all over again."

"We can't order him to do so, can we? But I can certainly have a conversation with him about it and see what he thinks."

"Could you not speak to Horace yourself?"

"I probably could if Inspector Ferguson has no wish to do so, but I must be careful not to tread on his toes."

"So you'll speak to him?"

"Yes, I'll speak to him."

"Should I come with you?"

"Perhaps not. Ferguson is unlikely to be impressed by my suggestion that he hasn't investigated the case properly, and he'll be even less impressed by the presence of a news reporter. I don't know how you managed to walk around the workhouse and speak to a potential witness without being spotted."

"I was spotted. Mr Hale found me there."

James groaned and placed his head in his hands. "I can't imagine that he was particularly happy with you."

"You're right, he wasn't. Apparently, if I set foot in the

workhouse again he'll report me to the police. That's not such a serious problem because you *are* the police, aren't you?" I smiled.

He lifted his head and gave me a stern glance. "The closeness between us doesn't give you the right to ride roughshod over protocol, Penny." I felt the smile leave my face. "Don't ever assume that you can do whatever you like and rely on my position to get you out of hot water."

"I would never think that, James!"

"Good." He began to tidy the papers on his desk into a neat pile.

"But I'm sure that Horace could provide a crucial clue as to what happened that night."

"Maybe he will, maybe he won't." James rose to his feet and retrieved his overcoat from the coat stand. "Just be careful how you go about this one, Penny. Be very careful indeed."

CHAPTER 17

"Unfortunately, my solicitor thinks that I need to change my petition for divorce," said Eliza as she made herself comfortable in the chair beside my writing desk that evening.

Tiger, my cat, observed her from beneath my bed.

"He thinks that a simple cause of cruelty wouldn't be enough."

"But he assisted a criminal!" I said. "And he expected you to live on earnings obtained from a criminal source. If that's not cruelty, what is?"

"Physical cruelty."

"Oh, I see. And was he never physically cruel?"

"No, though I wish that he had been now so the divorce could be over and done with."

"Don't say that, Ellie! You cannot mean such a thing. It would have been dreadful if he'd been physically cruel to you."

"And yet his criminal behaviour seemingly isn't cruel enough. My solicitor has explained the problem I face, Penelope: the simple fact that it is easier for a man to divorce his wife than it is for a wife to divorce her husband."

"I have heard as much before, but I still think you're perfectly entitled to a divorce, Ellie."

"*You* might think that, but a judge may not. George could petition to divorce me for just a single act of adultery on my part, yet I cannot divorce him for adultery."

"But he hasn't committed adultery, has he?"

"Not to my knowledge, no. But even if he had it would need to be combined with another offence, such as bigamy or desertion."

"Or cruelty."

"Indeed, or cruelty. But as I say, that usually pertains to acts of physical cruelty, which George has never committed."

"So what does your solicitor suggest?"

"He thinks I would have a far better chance if I were to petition for adultery and cruelty, at the very least."

"But how can you petition for adultery?"

"I would need to prove somehow that he had committed it at some stage during our thirteen-year marriage."

"Oh goodness, Ellie. How would you even begin to prove that?"

"By finding a woman with whom he has committed adultery."

"But are there any?"

"I don't know."

"And even if you found one, would she admit to it?"

"I should think it unlikely. There would no benefit for her in doing so, especially if she happened to be married herself. So it seems that my hopes of obtaining a divorce from George are rather remote."

"Is there any chance that George might petition for a divorce from you?"

"Not at the moment. He's still holding out hope for a

reconciliation. Only last week he sent me a great long letter professing his deep regret and undying love for me. It only served to make me like him even less. There's something rather unattractive about desperation, isn't there?"

"Yes, there is. Well, I can think of one other possible solution, Ellie."

"What is it?"

"That you find yourself a chap to commit adultery with yourself."

"Penelope! What a suggestion!"

"Just one act of adultery and George could petition for divorce from you."

"I suppose he could. But would he?"

"I'd like to think so! Why would he wish to remain married to you if you'd done such a thing?"

"Oh, I don't know, Penelope. It's too scandalous to even consider! I have my reputation to think of, and besides, I never encounter any eligible men to be adulterous with. The thought that I would even consider such a thing is dreadful enough! Where do you get these ideas from?"

"I was trying to think of a viable solution."

"Well, it's an interesting idea, but I cannot possibly consider it."

"So instead you will attempt to find a woman with whom your husband may or may not have committed adultery?"

"I could begin with looking through his old letters and diaries, couldn't I? He left them all at the house. Perhaps there's a love note amongst them. That would be very convenient, as it would count as evidence that could be used in the courtroom."

"But consider how you would feel if you discovered such a note, Ellie. Don't forget that you loved the man once, and I've no doubt that you still harbour some affection for him now."

"I suppose it would be rather upsetting, but I want to be able to divorce him, and at this present moment my hands feel quite tied."

We were interrupted by a knock at the door. I answered to find Mr Torrance standing there in his smoking jacket.

"Oh, good evening, Miss Green." He forced a smile from beneath his thick moustache that I didn't reciprocate. "I'm here to inform you that it is past the curfew time."

"Yes, I'm aware of that," I replied. "I haven't worked at my typewriter at all this evening, and nor will I now that the hour of eight o'clock has passed."

"Ah, but there is still noise."

"What sort of noise?"

"Loud chatter."

"I'm merely having a conversation with my sister," I said. "I wasn't aware that it was loud in any way."

"Oh, but it is quite loud."

"My sister has visited me here more times than I care to remember. You have never complained before, Mr Torrance."

"That was before the curfew was agreed."

"I thought the curfew merely referred to my typewriter."

"No, it refers to all noise, Miss Green."

"That wasn't my understanding of it at all."

He gave a hollow laugh. "We can hardly agree on a curfew for typewriting noise and yet allow all other noise to continue late into the night!"

"The only noise here is the conversation taking place between myself and my sister, and neither of us have raised our voices once. I don't know how you would be able to hear our conversation unless you were standing on a stool immediately beneath my floorboards and listening in with the aid of an ear trumpet."

"There's no need to be facetious, Miss Green."

"I'm not being facetious. I'm merely highlighting the

ridiculousness of the situation. I'm entitled to converse quietly with any visitors to my room."

"I think Mrs Garnett needs to introduce a few rules about visitors to tenants' rooms."

"She already has rules in place, and rest assured, Mr Torrance, that I am not breaking any of them."

His moustache gave a twitch as he handed me a tatty envelope. "I accidentally picked this up amongst my pile of post the other morning."

My heart skipped a beat when I saw the Colombian postmark.

"Thank you, Mr Torrance!" My words were more gracious than I had intended, as I was so pleased to finally receive word regarding Francis.

"I shall be speaking with Mrs Garnett about this infringement of the curfew."

"You do that, Mr Torrance. Goodnight."

I shut the door on him and walked over to the desk to show Eliza the letter. My fingers fumbled as I ripped the envelope open.

"Oh, Penelope! Is he still alive? I don't think I can bring myself to hear the news! Is it good or bad?"

I opened out the letter. "Good, I think. I feel sure that this is Francis' hand." I checked the signature at the bottom of the letter. "Yes, this is from Francis! He has survived his fever!"

"Oh, thank goodness!"

I read the letter aloud to my sister. "'My dearest Penny and Eliza. A little misfortune has befallen me, and for these past three weeks I have suffered with a most terrible tropical illness. I am grateful to Anselmo for writing to you and informing you of my predicament, though I hope his letter didn't give you too much cause for concern. I find that my health is recovered just enough to be able to write this letter and to reassure you that I am gradually recovering.

"'Alas, I remain bedridden, and although I am gaining strength with each day that passes I do not yet know when I will be able to resume my journey to Cali to visit the European orchid grower I mentioned in my previous letter. If my recuperation delays me for too long I may ask Anselmo to travel on ahead of me and bring whatever news he can of this elusive European.

"'If all goes to plan I shall be on my way again before long, and I hope to bring you more encouraging news very soon. With fondest regards from your faithful friend, Francis Edwards.'"

I glanced up at my sister, who was wiping the tears from her eyes. "Oh, poor Francis. He must have suffered terribly! And to think that he has been so poorly in a foreign country with little idea as to whether he would live or die! It's simply awful."

"But he's recovering now, Ellie, and I'm sure he'll be able to resume his travels very soon."

"When is the letter dated?"

"The twenty-fourth of December."

"Christmas Eve. Goodness, how miserable it must have been to spend Christmas Day in bed. Is there an address on the letter?"

"Yes. Mr Valencia's home in Borrero Ayerbe is given, but hopefully Francis has moved on from there by now. This letter was written a month ago. We can only hope that he has made it to Cali by now."

"And if he hasn't?"

"We shall just have to wait until we receive word from him, Ellie. That is really all we can do for the time being."

CHAPTER 18

I worked in the reading room at the British Library the following morning, researching the details I had not fully understood from Dr Macpherson's lecture at the School of Medicine for Women.

I heard the doughy-faced reading room clerk, Mr Retchford, scolding someone for talking above a whisper, and as I watched him bustle about imperiously I recalled the days when Francis Edwards had worked here. I had valued his help, and although it had only been four months since he had departed for Colombia it already felt like a long time ago. I prayed that he was fully recovered and closer to discovering my father's fate.

Not having found the information I needed, I left my desk and climbed the elaborate iron staircase up to the galleries that encircled the domed room. After a quick search I happened upon a book entitled *Gray's Anatomy,* which I decided to take back to my desk. When I returned I found another book lying there.

"Excuse me, does this book belong to you?" I whispered to the man sitting next to me.

He shook his head.

"Did you see who placed it here?" I asked.

"I'm afraid I didn't."

The desk on the other side was empty, so I asked the man sitting opposite whether he had seen anyone place the book there.

"No," came the reply.

"What's the problem here?" came a harsh whisper from behind me.

I turned to see Mr Retchford glaring at me.

"It's Miss Green, isn't it?" he whispered.

"Yes, that's me."

"You're disturbing the other readers."

"Someone left this book on my desk and I was trying to find out who its owner might be."

I set down *Gray's Anatomy* and picked up the other book. I was surprised to see that it was entitled *A Practical Guide to Journalism*.

Mr Retchford took the volume from me and examined it, his nose wrinkling as if there were a bad smell in the air.

"This doesn't belong in here," he announced. "It doesn't have a British Library bookplate inside it."

He handed it back to me and I leafed through the pages. Its condition was almost new, unlike many of the books in the library, which were well-thumbed.

"Someone must have placed it here by accident," I said. "I'm sure they'll come looking for it before long. Perhaps you could hold on to it in case the owner asks after it."

He sighed and took the book from me. "I'll put it on the lost property shelf."

"Thank you."

The clerk opened the book again as he began to walk away, then stopped and returned to my side.

"This book is *yours*," he said with a roll of his eyes.

"But it isn't. I have never owned that book."

Mr Retchford opened the book at the page he had just stumbled across and showed it to me.

"It has your name in it. You are Miss Penelope Green, are you not?"

I looked down at the title page, where my name had been written in black ink. My heart gave a heavy thud.

"Yes," I replied. "Someone must have left it on my desk as a gift."

"How very kind of them," he said, snapping the book shut and handing it back to me.

I glanced around the reading room as the clerk strode away, looking for anyone who might have been watching this scene unfold, but everything appeared as normal. Most people had their heads bent over their desks or were busy perusing the bookshelves. I felt slightly annoyed with the people sitting around me for failing to notice who had placed the book on my desk.

I sat down, and my hands trembled a little as I leafed through each page of the book. *Could there be a message for me hidden within its pages?*

But as I flicked through the pages I found nothing of the sort. The only handwriting in the book was my name on the title page. I examined the handwriting again. *Did it look familiar?*

I didn't recognise it as having been written by anyone I knew. Perhaps I was mistaken, but the title of the book seemed to be some sort of jibe, implying that I required further instruction in my chosen profession.

Was this really a malevolent gift, as I suspected? Or was it a genuine gift for which I had simply misread the intent? I conjectured that a genuine gift would have included the name of the person bestowing it. There was something rather sinister about the anonymity.

I pushed the book to one side and returned to my work, trying to appear as unaffected by the episode as possible. If my mysterious benefactor were still in the room and watching me, he or she would no doubt gain great satisfaction from any discomfort I displayed. I tried to steady my hand as I wrote, but it wasn't easy.

Someone was watching me. They had known which desk I was sitting at, and they had known when I was away from it.

But who could it be?

I tried to think of anyone I might have upset recently, but the only person who sprang to mind was Mr Hale from the workhouse. *Was it possible that he had placed the book on my desk?* It seemed extremely unlikely, as his work would surely have kept him too busy to do such a thing. *Perhaps it was one of my colleagues, Edgar or Frederick, playing a practical joke on me.*

I finished my research, then carefully packed my work and the guide to journalism into my carpet bag. I checked behind me when I left the reading room, but the only person who looked over in my direction was Mr Retchford.

I scurried down the steps of the British Museum and looked around as I went. I couldn't see anyone who appeared to be following me.

CHAPTER 19

"I apologise that I shall be unable to assist in reading to the infirmary patients for the foreseeable future," I said to Miss Russell as we stood beside the workhouse door in The Land of Promise.

"There is no need to explain any further, Miss Green," she replied. "I have already received a visit from Mr Hale."

"Oh, I see."

"He told me that he found you poking around in the men's wing."

"I must admit that I was. I have been reporting on the sad deaths of Mr Patten and Mr Walker."

"But you're not permitted to wander around the workhouse alone."

"No, I realise that now and have apologised to Mr Hale."

"He said that you didn't immediately explain to him that you were there in your role as a news reporter."

"Not immediately, no."

"Instead, you told him that you had been helping me and Mrs Menzies with reading to the patients in the infirmary."

"I did, yes."

"So he was rather cross with me that one of the people who came to assist me with reading decided to wander off to places she wasn't supposed to go."

"Oh dear. I'm sorry he was cross with you, Miss Russell. He strikes me as a singularly grumpy man."

"And he has every right to be if people are found wandering around the men's wing! You weren't supposed to be there!"

"No, it was rather unfortunate that he found me there."

"What exactly were you doing there, Miss Green? Trying to get information for your newspaper?"

"I apologise, Miss Russell. To be completely honest with you I was rather concerned by the verdict of the inquest into two deaths that occurred in the stone-breaking yard."

"Yes, I heard about that."

"It was assumed that one man murdered the other and then died from his injuries. That may have been the case, but I think other possibilities also need to be considered. Therefore, I took a detour to see the stone-breaking yard for myself and identify any possible witnesses. I found a man there who may have heard and seen something significant that night."

"Isn't that a job for the police?"

"Yes it is, and I have been able to convince a good friend of mine, who happens to be a Scotland Yard inspector, that further questions need to be asked of the inmates."

"I'm not sure I understand your role as a news reporter, Miss Green. I thought your responsibility was to report on events rather than to get involved in investigating them."

"You're not the first person to say that to me, Miss Russell. Although my job is to report on what is happening around me, I prefer to report the truth. The truth is not always what the authorities like us to write about. I want to make the public aware of what is *really* happening. We cannot simply accept everything the authorities and the courts tell us; we need to question things. And as a reporter I think I am well placed to do so."

"I think your cause is admirable, Miss Green, and I wish you luck in establishing the truth of the case. However, the fact of the matter remains that your motive in helping us read to the patients was not an altruistic one. You were doing so to gain access to places you would otherwise have been prohibited from."

"No, that wasn't my motive at all. I wanted to help!"

"You used it as a cover with Mr Hale. You didn't tell him you were a news reporter who was concerned about the verdict of an inquest; you told him you were a volunteer who had got herself lost. Now he's angry with me about it, and there is a risk that we shall be forbidden from doing the work we and the patients enjoy so much!"

There was a long pause. I didn't know what to say other than to apologise again.

"I really am sorry, Miss Russell. I was wrong to do what I did. I should have been honest with Mr Hale, as you say, and not brought you and your cause into it. I believe you are doing great work here, and I should be extremely upset if it were to stop as a result of my foolish actions. Please don't think that I only volunteered in order to further my own professional interests. It was with genuine enthusiasm that I asked to join you, and for no other reason. If you would like me to explain that to Mr Hale—"

"There's no need."

"Or perhaps I could write an article about the good work you're doing here. It's high time that people heard about it."

"There's no need for any sort of appeasement, thank you. Mrs Menzies and I shall go and read to the patients now. We only have two hours with them."

"Of course. I shan't hold you up any longer."

I watched Miss Russell and Mrs Menzies climb the workhouse steps with their books in their arms and felt devastated that I wouldn't be joining them. I had well and truly broken their trust.

I felt a lump in my throat as I thought of old Mrs King and her toothless smile, and the children listening, wide-eyed, to *Gulliver's Travels*. I had truly enjoyed my time reading to them. I'd had an opportunity to do something worthwhile, but sadly I had ruined it.

CHAPTER 20

"Maisie Hopkins has been a busy woman," said James as we met on Market Street in Mayfair. "We've found three shops where she pawned the belongings of Lord Courtauld, and have managed to recover around thirty items so far. The fate of others may have been less traceable. There's a known criminal who calls himself a blacksmith near Shepherd Market I need to have a conversation with."

"Any sign of Miss Hopkins herself?"

"None, I'm afraid. She knows this area well, however, so we're hopeful that she hasn't strayed far."

"I wonder where she's staying."

"All being well, it won't be too long before we find out."

We began to walk along narrow Market Street, where the awnings of the little shops met over our heads.

"Inspector Ferguson and I spoke with Horace yesterday," said James.

"How did you get on?"

"You didn't tell me he was simple-minded!"

"Is he?"

"Penny, you must have realised. You told me yourself that he didn't say a great deal."

"Not a great deal, but he communicated in the best way he knew how. He may not be particularly talkative but that doesn't mean he's an idiot. He clearly has enough intellect to work in the storeroom and to know that he heard something that night."

"Well, he didn't strike me as being particularly articulate, and you wouldn't like to hear what Inspector Ferguson made of the matter!"

"I certainly would. What *did* he make of it?"

"Well, the conversation in which I introduced the idea that the inquest might have been flawed did not go down well with him, as you can imagine. He considered the case to have been closed. After a great deal of persuasion he finally agreed that we could go to the workhouse and interview this witness you spoke to. That required us to obtain permission from the clerk and the master, and they were quite perturbed to hear that a third person might have been involved! They didn't want to consider the idea that there may be a murderer in their midst."

"Of course not, but it might still be true."

"Oh, Penny." James shook his head. "The situation worsened from there. Mr Lennox was particularly amused to hear that we wished to speak to Horace, and when I met the lad I could see why! He is not a reliable witness, I'm afraid."

"Why not?"

"Because of his limited intellect!"

"But that doesn't necessarily mean that he was mistaken."

"Perhaps it doesn't, but can you imagine him standing as a witness in a courtroom? Suppose we manage to find a culprit and put him on trial. What would the jury make of a boy who is unable to string two words together? Not to mention the fact that the lad would be terrified by such a prospect. He was quivering when Mr Lennox, Inspector Ferguson and I questioned him."

"I'm sure he was! Poor boy."

"Can't you see that he is of no help to us? Inspector Ferguson was appalled that I had taken up so much of his time by asking him to go and speak to the boy."

"But what did Horace tell you?"

"Very little."

"Did he mention that he was in the storeroom until ten o'clock and that he heard shouting in the yard?"

"He did, though not in so many words."

"Did you believe him?"

"Well yes, I did. Although he doesn't speak much, he seemed quite honest and earnest."

"Was he able to tell you at what time he heard the shouting?"

"There's a clock in the storeroom, and he thought that it was at about ten minutes past eight that he heard the shouting. That doesn't fit with what we already know about the crime, as Mr Walker didn't leave the day room until a quarter past eight."

"Ah, but it does fit, don't you see? It fits with the idea that a third person was involved. There must have been an altercation between the culprit and Mr Patten, and then Mr Walker arrived a short while later. Perhaps Mr Walker was killed because he was a witness to the murder."

James gave this some thought. "It's possible, I suppose."

"Of course it is!"

"But we cannot be sure that Horace is correct about the time. He says it was ten minutes past eight, but it could have been an hour earlier or later for all we know. He is not a very reliable witness."

"Did he look out into the yard when he heard the shouting?"

"He said that he did, but it was dark and he couldn't see anything."

"You'd have thought Mr Patten would have had a lantern with him. In fact, he did! Two lanterns were found beside the bodies of the men, weren't they? How had Patten's lantern been extinguished by the time Horace looked out?"

"That's an interesting thought."

"The culprit must have extinguished it so that no one was able to witness the murder."

"Then why was Walker killed if it was too dark for him to have witnessed the murder?"

"Because he walked into the yard with his lantern!"

"Of course. So he might have seen something.

"Maybe there are other witnesses," I suggested.

"Inspector Ferguson told me he had issued an appeal for witnesses when he first investigated the case. There was no word from anyone then, not even Horace."

"Perhaps some people felt nervous about talking to the police. Besides, some may have seen or heard something they didn't consider to be suspicious but might actually serve as a clue."

"They may well have done, but finding them and extracting the relevant information is often like squeezing blood out of a stone!"

"So what can we do next?"

"If we want to prove that a third person was involved we need to uncover some sort of evidence that he was in the yard with those two men. Reliable witnesses would help, but it's unlikely that there are any to be found."

"Then what can we do?"

"I don't know. Inspector Ferguson isn't interested, that's for sure. As soon as he started speaking to Horace the inspector felt convinced that he was wasting his time. He accepts the findings of the inquest and has other cases to be focusing his attention on."

"So he doesn't care."

"I'm sure he does, Penny, but he and his men are busy. And this case is rather obscure. In fact, there may not be a case here at all."

"Then we must simply wait for the murderer to strike again."

"If there is one."

"I suppose there's a small chance that there isn't."

"And there is only so much we can do. I wish we had the time and capacity to question every inmate who passed through or happened to be near the stone-breaking yard that evening, but we don't. Nor will we be granted the men to work on it given that the inquest found there was no case to answer."

"And how will you feel if the murderer strikes again?"

"Upset and angry, as I'm sure you would be. But that may never happen, Penny."

We passed through the market stalls in Shepherd Market and found the blacksmith's forge in a narrow street behind the King's Arms tavern. James knocked at a paint-splintered door, which was swung open by a man dressed in a leather apron and a dirty, collarless shirt with rolled-up sleeves. His bare forearms rippled with muscle, and the beads of perspiration running down his face left trails in the grime.

"I ain't done nuffink, Hinspector," he said with a lop-sided smile.

Even though James wore plain clothes, it amused me that men with any hint of criminality about them were always able to identify him as a police officer.

"What, nothing at all, Mr Brooks?" asked James.

"Nuffink. Who's this?" he asked, looking me up and down with a glint in his eye.

"This is Miss Green of the *Morning Express* newspaper. She is reporting on the disappearance of the maid Maisie Hopkins, who ran off with some of the Courtauld family's treasure. Have you heard about her?"

"Yeah, I fink I 'eard summink about it."

"And I'm Inspector Blakely of Scotland Yard. We've come to talk to you about Maisie."

"Well, I ain't gonna be of no 'elp to neither of yer."

"May we please come in?"

"Course!" He flung the door wide in an exaggerated gesture of welcome. "Come in and yer'll see that I ain't got nuffink to 'ide these days. I ain't hashamed to say that it ain't always been the case. But I've learnt me lessons and mended me ways."

"That's good to hear," replied James, surveying the room as we stepped inside.

Smoke from the blazing fire curled around the heavy oak beams in the ceiling. Greasy sackcloth hung across the windows, and the worktables were laden with hammers, tongs and pliers of all shapes and sizes. Two large anvils sat in front of the fire. My eyes began to water from the smoke, and I wondered how anyone could work comfortably in this environment.

"Well, 'ere you are. This is me 'umble hestablisment, Hinspector."

"Have you ever received a visit from Miss Hopkins?" James asked.

"Can't say as I 'ave. Who might she be?"

"The maid I was just telling you about."

"Oh, 'er. Nope."

"Are you quite sure about that?"

"What's she look like?"

"About twenty years old with dark hair and dark eyes."

Mr Brooks grinned. "I'd of knowed abaht it if she'd of paid me a visit!"

"Has she been here, Mr Brooks?"

"Can't say as I remember."

"Because one of your neighbours said that she called at this place about three days ago."

The blacksmith's brow instantly furrowed. "Who's goin' abaht sayin' stuff?"

"A witness."

"They tryin' ter get me inter trouble again? Just when I've gone an' got meself on the straight and narrah?"

"No one's trying to get you into trouble, Mr Brooks. I'm merely following up on what someone told me."

"I wish I knew who's said it. Bet it were that nosey beggar Iron'ead over the road."

"It doesn't matter who said it," replied James. "I simply wish to know when Maisie Hopkins visited you."

"I don't remember 'er ever comin' in 'ere."

James leafed through his notebook and held it aloft so that he could read it by the light of the fire.

"You spent two years in Newgate for melting down stolen silver, am I right?"

"Yeah. Like I told yer, I ain't hashamed ter say it."

"Good. Because it would be a terrible shame if you had returned to your old ways, wouldn't it?"

"Terrible, it'd be."

"We have a witness who saw a young woman call at this address late on Tuesday evening. The witness was unsure as to the sort of business a young woman might be wanting at a blacksmiths at that hour of the evening, which is why it stuck in this individual's mind."

"That was my gal!" said Mr Brooks proudly, hitching up his trousers.

"I see. And what is her name?"

"Maggie."

"Maggie who?"

"Maggie Smith."

"And where does she reside?"

"Dunno 'er address. Somewhere over St James's way, I reckon."

"Where did you meet her?"

"Why you askin' me all these questions, Hinspector?"

"I'm simply trying to establish whether Maggie is a real person or not."

"Course she's real!"

"Where did you meet her?"

"Down the King's Arms."

"So they would know her at the King's Arms, then?"

"I dunno."

"Mr Brooks, you realise this moment is the perfect opportunity for you to tell us anything you know about Maisie Hopkins, don't you? If we later discover that you melted down any stolen goods for her the punishment will be far more severe than if you were simply to admit it now, especially if your past conviction is taken into consideration. You could be looking at an extremely long stretch in prison."

He swallowed nervously. "I ain't done nuffink."

"The sooner you recall what you may or may not have done the better the outcome will be for you," said James. "In the meantime, we have a lot of people out looking for Miss Hopkins, and we're confident that we shall find her before long. When you do remember something, perhaps you could call in to Vine Street station at your earliest opportunity."

CHAPTER 21

"I'd say that Mr Brooks knows more about Maisie Hopkins than he's letting on, wouldn't you, Penny?"

James and I left Shepherd Market and walked toward Piccadilly.

"He did look rather guilty," I replied.

"I feel certain that he had an arrangement with her to melt down some of the pieces, and he probably kept his share, too. It's the sort of thing he's done before. I'll ask Kit the shoeshine boy to watch his premises for a few days to see whether Miss Hopkins returns. We could also obtain a warrant to search his premises if needs be."

We turned into the wide thoroughfare of Piccadilly. A row of bare-branched trees lined the perimeter of Green Park on the opposite side.

"I've upset Miss Russell," I said. "She's the lady who reads to the patients in the Shoreditch Workhouse infirmary. Mr Hale spoke to her after he happened upon me in the men's wing."

"I'm not surprised she was upset."

"Oh, don't make me feel even worse about it, James!"

"You do tend to take liberties, Penny. I'm used to it, but many people wouldn't understand it at all. You used Miss Russell as an excuse to get into the workhouse, and no doubt she thinks you were acting dishonestly."

"I wish I could make it up to her. I enjoyed helping with the reading! I can't deny that it gave me the opportunity to wander off and find out more about the tragic deaths that took place there, but it certainly wasn't my intention to upset Miss Russell. I'm worried she might never forgive me."

"She might not."

"Oh, James. You're no comfort at all!"

"Do you want me to speak to you in platitudes, Penny? To tell you not to worry about it; that she will surely forgive you in time?"

"Not exactly. You cannot be sure that she will, after all."

"There you go, then. Perhaps she will, perhaps she won't. But I suppose if you didn't do these things you would never get anywhere. I know that your intentions are good, and that you have strong feelings about any form of injustice, but the pursuit of truth can lead us down a lonely path at times."

"It does."

"And you know that I will always support you, don't you? I may argue the point with you on a regular basis, but I only do so because I want you to feel quite sure that you're doing the right thing."

"Do you think I'm doing the right thing in this case?"

"That's for you to decide."

"Oh, James!"

He smiled. "Yes, I do."

James hailed a hansom cab, and as we travelled toward Whitehall I showed him the book that had been left on my desk in the reading room.

"What a strange business," he said, leafing through it. "And are you quite sure there isn't anything else written in here? No message of any kind? Nothing written in invisible ink?"

"How would I know it was there if it was written in invisible ink?"

"You'd simply heat it by the fire."

"But I'd need to do so with every single page. It would take days!"

"Perhaps there was a message hidden in the book that has slipped out. Or could there be false pages concealing a folded message?"

"All the pages look normal to me."

"They do indeed. How mysterious."

"The title of the book must provide a clue," I said. "*A Practical Guide to Journalism.* Someone surely meant something malicious by it."

"Are they suggesting that your knowledge of journalism is deficient?"

"Yes, it's exactly that. But what worries me most is that someone must have been watching me in the reading room when he or she left this book on my desk. And I really couldn't tell you who it was. I've been able to spot the person on occasions when I was followed before, but not this time. It's made me feel rather vulnerable."

James rested his hand on mine. "I'm quite sure the individual doesn't mean you any harm, Penny. The perpetrator simply wished to make you feel perturbed."

"In that case he is succeeding!"

"He probably thinks he's being very clever indeed, but it's cowardly behaviour. The locks on your door and window at Mrs Garnett's are working properly now, aren't they?"

"Yes."

"In that case, keep to busy places and don't go out on your own after dark."

"It's dark by five o'clock in the evening at this time of year. I'll still be working in the office at that time!"

"Then hail a cab to take you straight to your door."

"What a lot of unnecessary expense."

"I would happily pay it."

"No James, there's no need. I want you to use all your money to pay off that awful Miss Jenkins."

"You will be careful, won't you?"

"Of course I will, though you said yourself that this person probably only wished to make me feel perturbed."

"I'm sure of it." He gave my hand a reassuring squeeze. "I never thought I'd say this, Penny, but I sometimes wish that you had a different profession."

CHAPTER 22

"Why did you think that I might have left this book on your desk in the reading room, Miss Green?" asked Edgar, leafing through *A Practical Guide to Journalism*.

"I knew it was unlikely," I replied, "but I thought I would check that it wasn't some sort of joke on your part."

"It might be a joke," said Edgar, "but I'm not responsible for it. What about you, Potter?"

"I haven't been inside the reading room for about a fortnight."

"I'd wager that it was Tom Clifford from *The Holborn Gazette*," said Edgar. "Did you see him in there, Miss Green?"

"I didn't. I saw no obvious culprit there at all."

"It's a very strange thing to do, but quite useful as well. I must confess that I have a copy of this book at home and haven't yet read it. It contains some helpful tips, doesn't it?"

"And so it should," said Frederick. "Otherwise it wouldn't be true to its title."

"Do either of you recognise the handwriting on the title page?" I asked.

They both examined it.

"I can't say that it's familiar to me," replied Edgar.

"Nor me," added Frederick.

I sighed as Edgar handed the book back to me.

"You seem to have yourself a secret admirer, Miss Green," he said.

"I don't think *admirer* is quite the right word," I retorted. "I believe the person who left this on my desk wished to intimidate me."

"But whoever it was gave you a gift!"

"An *anonymous* gift," I replied. "There's something slightly malevolent about it, if you ask me."

A slam of the newsroom door announced the arrival of Mr Sherman who held a copy of *The Holborn Gazette* in his hand.

"It seems Shoreditch Workhouse can do no wrong according to Tom Clifford," he said, dropping the newspaper in front of me and poking his finger at an article entitled 'Philanthropy in the Workhouse'.

I quickly read through it and saw that Tom Clifford had written the article that the board of guardians had hoped I would write. It described the honourable work of Lady Courtauld and the manner in which she had helped many workhouse girls gain employment as maids within London's wealthiest households. It also described improvements that had been made to the workhouse conditions in recent years and mentioned the work of Miss Russell and Mrs Menzies. The article concluded as follows:

Other publications describe the workhouse as if nothing has changed since the days of Oliver Twist; sensationalist accounts that belong within the pages of a Penny Dreadful. However, our hardworking Poor Law Guardians have ensured, in these modern times, that the workhouse, although still a last resort for paupers, gives every consideration to the well-being of its inmates.

I felt my jaw clench once I had finished reading.

"Thank you, Mr Sherman. I'm sure the Shoreditch board members are overjoyed with this piece."

"Oh, they will be. I have come to expect as much from the editor, Mr Cropper, who will publish anything he can find in a bid to sabotage our work. I hope I live to see the day when he comes up with some original ideas of his own! May I speak with you in private for a moment, Miss Green?"

I felt an uncomfortable twinge in my stomach as I followed Mr Sherman into his office. He usually only asked his staff to join him there when he had something important to say.

He took a seat behind the desk in his office, which had greasy, yellowing walls and a strong odour of pipe smoke. Piles of books and papers were stacked on the desk, and a fire burned brightly in the small grate.

As I took a seat opposite him he rested his hands on his desk, his fingers linked together.

"I was visited yesterday by Inspector Ferguson of H Division."

I felt my heart sink. "Were you, sir?"

"Yes. He was rather concerned by what he described as the *hold* you have over a certain Inspector Blakely of the Yard."

I couldn't help but laugh. "I can assure you, sir, that I have no hold whatsoever over Inspector Blakely!"

"You may not consider that you do, Miss Green; however, that is not how Inspector Ferguson perceives the situation. He told me that you have not only convinced Inspector

Blakely that the verdict of the inquest into the deaths at Shoreditch Workhouse was flawed, but that you had also found someone who claims to have seen the murderer. Only this witness turned out to be an idiot boy."

"He's not an idiot, sir. And he didn't actually see the murderer. I merely suggested that he might turn out to be a useful witness."

"Inspector Ferguson said he had spoken to the chap and that he was an imbecile of some sort."

"He could perhaps be described as simple-minded, but I think he knows what he heard."

"May I ask why you feel that you can overrule the findings of an inquest?"

"I don't believe all the possibilities were considered at the inquest."

"So you know better than the coroner, do you?"

"No sir, I don't. I feel that the coroner and the jury were led by the work of Inspector Ferguson, and I don't believe he considered all potential scenarios."

Mr Sherman sighed. "This is not the first time I have needed to remind you that you are a news reporter, Miss Green, and not a detective."

"I realise that, sir, but—"

"Can you imagine how embarrassing it is for me to hear this from a police inspector, and to have to defend your actions? I shouldn't have to do it, Miss Green. And while I'm fully aware of your relationship with Inspector Blakely, I'm extremely concerned that you have been persuading the man to act against his better judgement."

"I haven't, sir, really I haven't. He isn't as convinced of my theory as I am, but he did feel that it warranted further investigation."

"Do you think he would have considered it if you hadn't mentioned it to him?"

"I'd like to think so, sir. I'd like to think that police offi-cers consider all of the possibilities when investigating a suspicious death, but unfortunately that isn't always the case. I realise I'm only a news reporter, but I do believe that part of my responsibility is to ensure that the truth is uncovered."

"And what makes you suspect that the verdict is incorrect?"

"It's entirely feasible that a third person may have been involved in the incident, sir."

"And have you discovered any evidence of that?"

"Horace says that he heard shouting—"

Mr Sherman lifted his hand to stop me in my tracks. "We have already discussed him. Do you have any other evidence?"

"Not yet, sir, but if the police continue their—"

"They have plenty of other business to attend to, Miss Green. Inspector Ferguson is already angry that he was persuaded to go back to the workhouse as it is. The coroner has done his job, and there is no case to answer. No shred of evidence has been found to support your theory. It's possible to theorise on what might have been an alternative series of events, but that doesn't mean you should be using your newly found influence to direct the work of the police. I have no idea what the commissioner of the Yard will make of this."

"Do you intend to tell him, sir?" I was aware that the commissioner was Mr Sherman's cousin.

"There's no need for me to do so. Inspector Ferguson will be making his feelings known himself." He sat back in his chair and sighed. "I've known you for a number of years now, Miss Green, and I know that you approach your work with dedication and an enthusiasm that is unrivalled by your colleagues. I also realise that in the reporting of stories it is likely that one or two questions will arise in a reporter's mind about a particular situation. I have no wish to dissuade you from doing the excellent work you do, Miss Green, but I do think you have overstepped the mark by encouraging your friend to re-examine a case just because you don't feel particularly content with the outcome of an inquest."

"Inspector Blakely would do no such thing if he didn't believe there was cause to do so, sir."

Mr Sherman shook his head. "It's not for me to speculate on how a man is able to be convinced of something by a lady, but if I were his superior I would hope that my trusted detective inspector happened to be using his own judgement when carrying out his work rather than being influenced by anyone else. The long and short of it is that Inspector Ferguson felt his time had been wasted. May I also remind you, Miss Green, that you also have other reporting to be getting on with. Your work on this should have stopped as soon as you reported on the verdict of the inquest. Have I made myself clear?"

I nodded.

"I don't want to hear anything more about the sad deaths of Mr Patten and Mr Walker at the workhouse. The matter is concluded. Is that understood?"

I nodded again.

"You have this week's ladies' column to finish. Miss Welton has typewritten my tips for managing a housekeeper, so please have a read of that."

"I will sir."

"You can assess how feminine my tone is and tweak it accordingly." He gave me a dismissive wave to let me know that the conversation was at an end.

❦

I worked on the book I was writing about my father that evening, pressing the keys of my typewriter slowly and carefully so that Mr Torrance wouldn't hear me in the room below. This meant that my progress was slow, and that the letters weren't imprinted as clearly on the paper as I would have liked, but this was preferable to not being able to work on the book at all.

Was it possible that my father was the European orchid grower in Cali? Although I liked to think so, I didn't relish the thought that he had built a new life for himself without ever contacting his family. *What sort of man was he if he had been content to allow his wife and daughters to fear the worst?*

My hope was that the orchid grower was not my father but knew something of his whereabouts. It was likely that Francis had met with him by now and had news one way or the other. *Would he travel to the telegraph office to let us know if he had important news? Did the fact that we hadn't yet received a telegram mean that the orchid grower had been of no help?*

My mind whirled with possibilities. Tiger jumped up onto my desk and pushed her head into my face, as if to suggest that this endless speculation was doing me no good at all.

I stroked her and thought about the workhouse. *Was it possible that I was thinking too much about the deaths of Mr Patten and Mr Walker? Having imagined there was a third man involved, perhaps I had convinced myself of something that had never happened.* In my quest to pursue the truth, it was possible that I was misleading myself. Knowing when to continue my work and when to stop often proved difficult for me. However, the decision in the case of the workhouse had been made for me. The message from James and Mr Sherman was clear: I had overstepped the mark.

I resumed my quiet typewriting as soon as Tiger jumped down from my desk. I had no choice but to forget about the workhouse and the poor unfortunates who dwelt within it. Their situations were replicated countless times across

London and the rest of the country, and I had to accept that there was little more I could do. But while I was determined to push all thoughts of Shoreditch Workhouse away, little did I know that events would soon turn my mind back to it.

CHAPTER 23

"Interesting news from Commercial Street police station," whispered James, who had surprised me with a visit to the reading room. "A complaint has been received from the family of a man who died at Shoreditch Workhouse."

"What sort of complaint?"

"Stop that!" came a hiss from behind us.

I didn't need to turn around to confirm that the sound had come from Mr Retchford. I quickly pushed my papers into my carpet bag and rose to my feet.

"No talking in the reading room!" scolded the clerk.

I forced a smile at him. "We are just leaving," I hissed.

A freezing fog hung over the courtyard of the British Museum.

"Rather inclement, isn't it?" commented James. "Shall we seek refuge in the Museum Tavern?"

The smoky warmth of the tavern caused my spectacles to

mist up. James and I sat at our usual table with a tankard of porter and a glass of sherry, respectively.

"I thought I was doing rather a good job of forgetting about Shoreditch Workhouse," I said. "What's happened now?"

"The family of a man who died there say that the workhouse failed to notify them of his death."

"Oh dear, how awful. How did they find out that he had died?"

"They hadn't heard any information about him for some time. They knew that he had stayed in lodging houses and in the casual wards of workhouses, so they made enquiries. After a while they discovered that he had died at Shoreditch Workhouse."

"And the workhouse hadn't told them?"

"No. But in their defence, workhouse staff can only inform the family if the deceased has left details of family members or close friends."

"That's right. They can only use what has been written down in the admissions book."

"It's possible that he gave no details, or that he gave incorrect details."

"In which case, how can the workhouse be at fault?"

"Indeed. But it seems that there has been some careless record-keeping somewhere. The family asked to see a record of the man's burial, which the workhouse had recorded properly. However, when they visited the cemetery there was no record of him being buried there."

"So either the workhouse or the cemetery made a mistake in their records."

"It would seem so."

"You might expect one mistake to occur from time to time," I said, "but two mistakes have been made here. The family weren't notified and there is also a contradiction in the burial records. Perhaps this is a regular occurrence when it comes to the poor because the authorities don't really care about them."

"That may well be the case," said James. "And it just so happens that this man's family is particularly vigilant and keen to raise the issue with the police. I can't say that it's our job to get too closely involved; it's something for the district's poor law inspector to look into. In fact, I can't see that any crime has been committed, but I thought you would be interested to hear this latest piece of news."

"I certainly need to report on it." I took a sip of sherry and sighed. "People shouldn't be treated in such a way," I said. "It's just not right. The family reported the incident to Commercial Street station, you say?"

"Yes."

"Do you think Inspector Ferguson would be happy to speak to me about it?"

"I doubt it." James grinned.

"I haven't been making many friends recently, have I?"

"Would you really wish to be friends with Inspector Ferguson?"

"No, I can't say that I would."

We both laughed.

"We should plan our next excursion," said James. "Madame Tussauds was rather too busy for my liking."

"You enjoyed the Chamber of Horrors, though."

"Yes, that was my favourite part. I felt quite at home there! How would you like to go to a music recital next time?"

"I would like that very much, James. In fact, I don't mind where we go. I enjoy any time we spend together when we don't have to talk about criminals and suspicious deaths."

"As do I, although you always seem to end up talking about them anyway." There was a twinkle of mischief in his blue eyes.

"I do not!"

"It's all reporters seem to want to talk about," he continued.

I gave his shin a nudge with my foot beneath the table.

"Now, now. There's no need for violence," he added.

"We'll have to work very hard on not discussing cases in the evenings," I said. "It's important that we have other interests in common."

"Easy for me, Penny, but a little more difficult for you I think."

"If you're not careful I shall kick your shins again!"

"Is that a way to treat your..."

"My *what?*"

"Oh, I don't know," he laughed. "I was about to say the word *husband*, but we're not at that stage yet, are we?"

"I wish you would hurry up and pay Charlotte her remaining two hundred pounds."

"Just a few more months' salary and then it'll all be settled."

I sighed. "I'm tempted to borrow the money and pay her myself."

"It's supposed to come from me."

"Then I shall give it to you to pay her with."

"Please don't borrow any money, Penny. There really is no need."

"Perhaps my mother will lend it to us. We could visit her and explain that we intend to marry, and that we could do it even sooner if she would be prepared to lend us two hundred pounds."

"We can't do that! What about my pride?"

"What about it?"

"Your mother needs to know that I can provide for you. If we're asking to borrow money from the very outset of our marriage she'll assume that I am an unreliable spendthrift."

"There's no need to worry about my mother's opinion of you. She already thinks far worse of me!"

"I'm sure that's not true."

"I'm a working woman and a spinster. She gave up on all her aspirations for me many years ago."

"But she must still be fond of you."

"I don't doubt that she is, but I can't bear to see her expression of disapproval."

"What does that look like?"

"She sucks her cheeks in like this."

I pulled a face and James laughed.

"That's quite an extreme expression of disapproval."

"You wait until you meet her. It's even worse in person."

❧

"What do you want, Miss Green?" asked Inspector Ferguson impatiently as he walked away from me down the station corridor with a pile of papers in one hand.

"Just one minute of your time, sir. I'd like to learn more about the family that wasn't notified that a relative had died in the workhouse."

He stopped and turned to face me. "That's not really a matter for the police."

"Perhaps it isn't, sir, but it's certainly a matter for a news reporter."

He sighed and shook his head. "You've already wasted my time with the case of Mr Patten and Mr Walker. What do I need to do to ensure that you will leave me alone?"

"Just give me the name and address of the family, Inspector, and then I shall look into their claims myself."

"Don't be bothering the board of guardians at the workhouse again, Miss Green."

"I won't."

"Sergeant Wilkins at the desk will give you the family's details."

"Thank you, sir. I appreciate your help."

"I'm not helping you, Miss Green. I'm trying to get rid of you."

I gave him a broad smile. "Well thank you all the same."

The address the desk sergeant gave me was in Bethnal Green. The Connolly family lived in the upper rooms of a bow-fronted cottage that overlooked Regent's Canal. It was bordered on one side by the Imperial Gas Works and on the other by railway lines.

Children in thin, ragged clothes paused from their games to watch me call at the door. Once I had introduced myself to the occupants, I was surrounded by a small group of women, all telling me who they were in relation to the deceased – sisters, aunts and even his mother – but I struggled to establish who was who among the clamour.

"What was his name?" I called out.

"Joe Connolly. Joseph or Joe. Some called 'im Joey."

They told me he had been just twenty-four years old at the time of his death.

"When did you last see him?"

This question invited a whole host of responses, but I managed to deduce that it had been about two months previously. They had heard he had entered a workhouse but that was the last anyone had seen of him.

"It weren't like 'im not ter visit 'is ma," said a grey-haired woman wearing several headscarves. "They get liberty days in the work'ouse, and the fust fing 'e would of done was visit 'is ma."

"Then you are his mother?"

"Yeah." She gave me a look that suggested I should have already known this.

"When did you visit the workhouse?"

"This side o' Christmas."

"And you asked to see Joseph?"

"They told me 'e was dead!"

Her face crumpled and another woman embraced her tightly.

"Not only was 'e dead," added the other woman, "but they'd already buried 'im!"

"Buried 'im and no one 'ad told us!" cried another.

"Whom did you speak to at the workhouse?"

"Dunno. Mr..."

"Lennox?" I suggested.

"Yeah, 'im. Mis'rable cove."

"He's the clerk," I said.

"You knows 'im, does yer?"

"I've met him a few times."

"Ask 'im what's 'appenin', then! Ask 'im what's 'appened to our Joe! Ask 'im 'ow comes 'e's dead and buried with none of 'is fambly knowin' abaht it!"

"Did Mr Lennox tell you the date that Joseph died?"

"It were afore Christmas! Twenny-third o' December. And ter fink that when it were Christmas none of us even knew 'e was dead!"

Fresh tears began to flow, and I felt a flush of anger at the injustice this family had suffered. They had been unable to say goodbye to their brother and son.

"Where did the workhouse say he had been buried?"

"Tower 'Amlets. So we went there!"

"And?"

"Weren't no sign of 'im. Some warden took us to the newest bit, where they're buryin' folks, and there weren't no sign of 'im! Warden said 'e'd 'eard no mention of our Joe!"

"Then Joseph is definitely not buried at Tower Hamlets cemetery?"

"'E ain't there! But where is 'e? Are yer gonna 'elp us?"

"I'll certainly try. And I'd like to write about this for the *Morning Express* newspaper if that's all right with you."

"The noospaper?" one of the sisters asked, her face lighting up.

"Yeah, write abaht it in yer noospaper so all the folks who reads it 'ear abaht Joe!" said the lady in the headscarves. "We need ter find 'im!"

"I'll do what I can to help, and if I manage to find out where he's buried I shall let you know immediately."

"Thankee, m'lady!" she said.

"Miss Green will do just fine."

"You's a kind lady, Miss Green. Gawd bless yer!"

CHAPTER 24

I travelled by omnibus to the City of London and Tower Hamlets Cemetery in Mile End, keen to ensure that the Connolly family hadn't been mistaken. I felt sure that they hadn't been.

A cold wind whipped across the cemetery as I made my enquiries with the warden at the lodge beside the cemetery gates.

"I remember 'em," he replied once I had asked him about the Connolly family. "They came 'ere lookin' for a chap the workhouse 'ad buried. But he ain't 'ere."

"Joseph Connolly?" I asked. "He may also have been known as Joe."

"Yeah, they told me all that. I looked and there ain't nuffink 'ere."

"And every name is written in your burial register even if they receive a common burial, is it?"

"Yeah, ev'ry single one of 'em. We bury a lot o' paupers 'ere, as yer might expect, but there ain't no Joseph Connolly among 'em."

"Does Shoreditch Workhouse bury many of its inmates here?"

"Yeah, an' Whitechapel an' all." He gestured toward the nearby walls of Whitechapel Workhouse.

"Could he have been buried in another cemetery?"

"'E must of been!" The warden laughed. "'Cause he ain't 'ere, that's fer sure!"

"But does Shoreditch Workhouse use any other cemetery for pauper burials?"

"Not as I knows of; you'd 'ave to ask 'em yerself. Second thoughts, ask Barnes."

"Who's Barnes?"

"'E's the undertaker or funeral director, whatever 'e calls 'imself. The one what's got the contract wiv Shoreditch. Come ter fink of it, 'e's got contracts wiv most o' the work'ouses."

"I see. He derives a good business from them, does he?"

The warden laughed again. "I'll say!"

W. Barnes and Son's was a smart establishment compared with its neighbours on Bethnal Green Road. Situated between a pie shop and a grocer's store, the funeral director's facade was constructed from sharply cut stone and polished black marble.

As soon as I stepped inside, a quietly spoken man in a smart black suit was by my side. A softness in his expression suggested that he was prepared to support me in my grief.

"May I help you, ma'am?"

"I'd like to speak to Mr Barnes, please."

This wasn't the reaction he had been expecting. "Oh, I see. May I ask your name?"

"I am Miss Green of the *Morning Express* newspaper." I

retrieved my visiting card from my carpet bag and gave it to him.

"Very good, ma'am."

He disappeared through a door at the back of the wood-panelled room and I seated myself on a plush cushioned bench to await his return. A pamphlet lying on an occasional table next to me outlined the services of W. Barnes and Son. I glanced through it and saw that there were several classes of funeral available. Special Class offered a hearse drawn by four horses, with four superior carriages each drawn by a pair. Once other provisions were included, such as the satin-lined, French-polished coffin and mourning attendants, the cost amounted to sixty pounds: almost ten times my monthly salary. By contrast, an eighth class funeral with a simple hearse and a pair was just four pounds. I wondered how someone earning two or three shillings a week could possibly pay for even the lowest class of funeral. It was no wonder that so many were forced to settle for a common burial.

"Miss Green?"

I looked up to see a smartly presented man with a pale, clean-shaven face, dark hair and light grey eyes standing before me. He examined my card closely.

"I see that you're from the *Morning Express*. What can we do for you?"

"I'm trying to solve a bit of a puzzle," I replied.

Mr Barnes listened intently as I told him about the Connolly family, who had been unable to find out where their family member was buried. His brow furrowed as he listened.

"I understand your company is the contracted undertaker for Shoreditch Workhouse," I stated.

"My company is a funeral furnisher rather than an undertaker," he replied. "We have contracts with a range of institutions."

"But you carry out the common funerals for Shoreditch Workhouse?"

"I contract undertakers to perform the common funerals."

I frowned as I tried to fathom what he was saying. "Your company has a contract with Shoreditch Workhouse?"

"Among others, yes."

"It's Shoreditch Workhouse that interests me because that's where Joseph Connolly died. His funeral would have been performed by one of the undertakers you have contracted, would it not?"

"Yes, that's right."

"And may I ask who that might be?"

"Let me see now." He raised his eyes to the ceiling as he gave this some thought. "For Shoreditch I think we have Finlay and Hicks."

"Is that the name of a single undertaker? Or two separate ones?"

"Allow me to write down their details for you." He said this hurriedly, as though he wished to be rid of me as soon as possible, and disappeared behind the wood-panelled door.

I sat down and perused the pamphlet again. A short while later Mr Barnes returned with two neatly written addresses on headed notepaper.

"Finlay is in Columbia Road and Hicks is in Harman Street."

"Thank you very much, Mr Barnes. Have you ever known this sort of thing to happen before?"

"What sort of thing?"

"A confusion with the burial records?"

"Oh yes, it happens quite often. It usually amounts to a mistake with the record-keeping. "His face assumed a sombre expression, which I imagined was routinely used for mourners. "I do hope his relatives receive answers to their questions."

. . .

My walk to Columbia Road took me through a series of narrow, cobbled streets lined with terraced red-brick houses and furniture workshops. An acrid smell from the nearby chemical works lingered in my nose, and two men loitering outside a public house made coarse comments as I passed.

George Finlay and Co. Funeral Service was a smaller establishment than Mr Barnes'. When I arrived I could hear sawing from an adjacent workshop, which I guessed was where the coffins were made.

Mr Finlay had a careworn face that didn't quite match his smart attire.

"You are contracted by Mr Barnes to bury the deceased workhouse inmates, is that right?" I asked.

"The paupers. Barnes does the ones with all the feathers and attendants and carriages with four 'orses an' the suchlike. I do the paupers."

I told him about the Connolly family, and he scratched his stubbled chin as he listened.

"I'll 'ave a look in the book," he replied as he walked over to a small desk and began leafing through records. "Just before Christmas, yer say?"

"Yes. The twenty-third of December."

"Joseph Connolly?"

"That's right. Or possibly Joe."

"He ain't 'ere."

"Are you sure?"

"Yeah. If 'e'd died on the twenny-third I would of picked 'im up on the twenty-fourth, earliest. For that day I got Mr Coleman, seventy-six, Mr Barrett, fifty-one, Mrs Allen, eighty-two, and Miss Redmond, thirty-six."

I wasn't sure why he had felt the need to tell me their ages.

"Four people in total?"

"Yeah, four of 'em. And no Connolly."

"Is it possible that you might have picked him up on the twenty-fifth?"

"I takes a day off Christmas Day. For the twenty-sixth I got three of 'em but none of 'em's named Connolly."

"It seems that quite a few are buried each day."

"I'd say between three and five."

"Is it possible that Mr Hicks buried Mr Connolly?"

Mr Finlay huffed as he closed the book shut. "He might've."

"How common is it for burial records to be inaccurate?"

He scowled. "None of my records is wrong."

"I don't understand why the workhouse says Mr Connolly was buried when there is no corresponding burial record."

He shrugged his shoulders. "I'm blowed if I knows."

At Hicks and Son on Harman Street the younger Mr Hicks informed me that his father was currently taking a consignment of paupers' coffins to Tower Hamlets Cemetery. He looked through the firm's records and confirmed that Joseph Connolly had not been listed there.

Harman Street was only a short walk from Shoreditch Workhouse. As I left the undertaker's I felt rather despondent as there was little I could do to help the Connolly family with news of their loved one. I paused at the corner of Harman Street and Kingsland Road and looked in the direction of the workhouse. The only other course of action I could think of was to return to the place from which I had been told to steer clear.

CHAPTER 25

I approached Shoreditch Workhouse via the administrative building; a large red-and-cream edifice on Kingsland Road. It was in this building that I had met with the board of guardians.

The porter at the reception desk fetched Mr Lennox for me, and I braced myself as the bald, grey-whiskered clerk descended a flight of stairs with a stern look in his eye. I prayed that Mr Hale was busy in the main part of the workhouse and wouldn't discover me here.

"Miss Green?"

The clerk did not invite me into an office to speak. Instead, he stood obstructively in the hallway waiting for my explanation. I kept it as brief as possible and told him what I had learned about Joseph Connolly.

"The police have been informed," I added slightly menacingly. The clerk seemed to concede that it was too sensitive a subject to dismiss out of hand.

"It sounds as though there has been an error in the record-keeping," he said.

"That seems most likely," I replied. "But I'm sure you can understand that the Connolly family will need to know what has happened to Joseph."

"I remember them enquiring here, and my recollection is that they weren't notified of his death as he hadn't given us their details. But before I check our records again, may I ask why you've involved yourself in this matter, Miss Green? It feels as though you're pursuing some sort of vendetta against the workhouse, and I can't for the life of me think why."

"There is no vendetta, Mr Lennox. Please let me assure you of that. I'm simply investigating because at the present time this doesn't seem to be a serious enough matter for the police to pursue and I'm not sure who else would be willing to look into it."

"Perhaps the poor law inspector, Mr Weyland, would?"

"Well, I shall certainly contact him if there appears to be a problem. But at the present time it may have been nothing more than a misunderstanding."

"And if there is a problem you'll be writing about it in your newspaper, no doubt."

"If it's a big problem then yes, I shall. But it's difficult to say at this stage, Mr Lennox. My hope is that it can be cleared up easily."

"Let me show you the records we hold for Mr Connolly," he replied, leading me up the staircase to his office.

The glass-fronted cabinets there housed countless leather-bound volumes. He noticed me surveying them.

"Over a hundred years of records," he stated proudly.

"Really?"

"A workhouse first opened on this site in the year 1778," he said. "The current buildings are modern, of course; they're only about twenty years old. But despite the changes that have taken place over the years, the administrators of this workhouse have always prided themselves on their record-keeping."

"In that case it's rather unfortunate that there appears to have been a mistake in them," I said.

"But it may not be *our* mistake, Miss Green. In fact, I'm tempted to lay the blame with the undertakers."

"There seems to be a complicated arrangement between them," I said. "I understand that your contract is with Barnes, but there are two others who are contracted to him."

"That's quite typical, I'm afraid," he replied, gesturing toward a seat positioned at the front of his desk. He sat opposite me and placed a pair of half-moon spectacles on his nose. "It's no wonder there is a bit of confusion at times. Let me show you the admissions forms, which are copied from the admissions book each day."

He leafed through a pile of papers and presented me with a sheet with Joseph Connolly's name on it.

"There you can see all the details he gave us when he was admitted to the workhouse on the tenth of December last year. You can quite clearly see that under the heading 'Name of family or friend' there is written the word 'None'."

"Yes, I do see that," I replied, "but I don't understand. Mr Connolly has a large family who care about him very much. Why would he say that he had none?"

The clerk shrugged. "Perhaps there had been a disagreement between them? Or perhaps he didn't want anyone to know that he'd had to fall back on the workhouse for help?"

"But his family knew that he had stayed here a few times," I said. "That's what prompted them to come here looking for him when they hadn't heard from him for a while."

"Then who knows?" he replied. "We could probably spend all day speculating on the whys and wherefores. The fact of the matter is that he didn't leave any details of anyone we could contact in the event of his death."

"And what of the record of his death?" I asked. "Do you have that information correctly entered?"

"Of course." He lifted a book from the far side of his desk, placed it in front of him and opened it up. "You'll have to remind me when he died."

"On the twenty-third of December."

It didn't take him long to find the entry. "He's here all right."

He turned the book round and pushed it toward me so I could read the record for myself. I saw that it stated his name, age and date of death. The cause of his death was given as heart failure.

"And I believe I told his family that he had been a patient in the infirmary for a week leading up to his death," added the clerk. "Dr Kemp keeps detailed records in his infirmary. Does this answer your query?"

"The records here certainly seem well kept, Mr Lennox."

"They are indeed."

"It says here on the record of Mr Connolly's death that he is buried in the Tower Hamlets cemetery," I said.

"That's correct."

"Can you be certain that he is buried there?"

"The workhouse doesn't oversee burials, Miss Green. That's down to the undertaker. When inmates die they're placed in the dead house. If the family can pay for the funeral they make the necessary arrangements with whichever funeral service they wish to use. In the case of a pauper, the contracted undertaker collects and buries them."

"And the fee is paid by Shoreditch Union."

"That's correct."

"But Tower Hamlets cemetery has no record of Joseph Connolly."

"That is rather unfortunate."

"And neither do the undertakers."

Mr Lennox gave me an open-handed gesture. "That's something which is beyond our control I'm afraid, Miss Green. You've seen for yourself how rigorous we are here with our record-keeping. If only other agencies followed suit!"

"I cannot understand what's happened to him," I said. "How can a dead man simply vanish?"

CHAPTER 26

I returned home on the omnibus, puzzling over the supposed disappearance of Mr Connolly. *He and his family had been failed by someone, but by whom?*

"A parcel has arrived for you, Miss Green," said Mrs Garnett as I stepped into the hallway. "For some reason it's been wrapped in newspaper."

She handed me the small parcel, which was tied up with string, and I recognised the newspaper from that morning's edition of the *Morning Express*. My heart gave a thud. The parcel appeared to be the size and shape of a book.

"There's nothing on the label to say who it's from," my landlady continued. "All it has is your name on it, not even an address. Someone must have delivered it by hand. I heard a knock at the door, and when I answered it no one was there, but this had been left on the top step."

"How strange." I felt a prickle at the back of my neck. "Thank you, Mrs Garnett." I turned to walk up the stairs.

"Aren't you going to open it to find out who it's from?"

"I will when I'm in my room."

I noticed a flicker of disappointment pass across her face.

"Oh, all right then, Mrs Garnett. I'll open it now so you can see who it's from. But it wouldn't surprise me if the sender has chosen to remain anonymous."

"Why so?"

"Because I have already received a gift rather like this. It was a book, and the person who gifted it left no name."

"But why not?"

"Because it isn't a nice gift; it's a threatening one."

Mrs Garnett gave a nervous laugh. "A threatening gift? You're the only person I know who could possibly receive a threatening gift, Miss Green. You do get yourself caught up in some odd business!"

I untied the string and carefully unwrapped the newspaper, hoping there would somehow be a clue somewhere as to the identity of the person who had left the book on the step.

The book was entitled *The Art of Prose,* and I turned to the title page to see my name written there in the same handwriting that had been inscribed in the previous book.

"They've put your name in it but not theirs," stated my landlady.

"That's correct. It's all rather strange."

"It looks like a useful book," said Mrs Garnett. "Quite instructional."

"Yes, but the implication is that I am not a particularly accomplished writer."

"So the anonymous person has given you this book to imply that you need to improve your writing."

"That's right."

Mrs Garnett sucked her lip. "How puzzling."

"It is rather, isn't it?"

"Perhaps it's from an admirer."

"This person is no admirer, Mrs Garnett."

"You never know; he might be."

"It's highly unlikely. You will let me know if you see

anyone acting suspiciously outside the house, won't you? It unnerves me that the sender of this 'gift' has discovered my address."

"If I see anyone acting suspiciously I shall call the police!"

"Good idea, Mrs Garnett."

"Are you expecting someone to be hanging about out there then? I can't say I would like that at all. I can't be doing with any suspicious strangers loitering outside my house."

"I certainly hope there won't be. But someone left this book on the doorstep, and it would be extremely useful to find out who it was. They may do the same thing again. Are you sure you didn't see anyone when you answered the knock on the door?"

"No one. There was a carriage passing by on the street; I suppose the driver might have seen someone. But I didn't think to ask him at that moment as I was too busy looking out for whoever might have called at the door. There were two people in the street but both appeared to be going about their usual business. They didn't look at me and neither of them was running. The person who knocked at the door must have run away very quickly."

"Either that or they hid down the side of the house."

"Oh, do you think they might have done that? I suppose they could have done, couldn't they? I didn't think to look down there."

"If it happens again it's probably worth having a quick look, but be careful as we don't know who it could be."

"The cowardly sort, I'd say, if they're leaving threatening gifts on your doorstep and then hiding so no can see who they are. If it happens again I'll look down the side of the house, taking the poker from the fireplace with me."

"I'm only interested to know what the person looks like. There would be no need for a confrontation, Mrs Garnett."

"If they're down the side of my house I shall confront them. They shouldn't be hanging around there!"

"Be careful. If you did happen to encounter anyone it would be enough just to ascertain what they look like and call the police. It wouldn't be wise to get involved in an altercation."

"There's never a dull moment with you, is there, Miss Green? We've had a few funny types around here over the years. I wish that I fully understood what it is you do to upset these people."

"I simply try to write the truth, Mrs Garnett. Not everyone appreciates that."

"Strange. You'd think that would be a good thing, wouldn't you?"

I went up to my room and let Tiger in through the window. She rubbed her cold head against my hand, then took up her favourite position in front of the little stove at one end of the room.

I sat at my writing desk and leafed through *The Art of Prose,* hoping that it might somehow contain a clue about the person who had delivered it to me. But, unsurprisingly, there was nothing.

Surely this person was known to me. He or she clearly knew where I worked and where I lived.

I locked my door, ensured that the window was locked and sat down at my desk again. I tried to reassure myself that this person had no wish to harm me physically, but was merely trying to intimidate. I wished that I knew the reason why.

I tucked the book into a drawer and tidied away some papers on my desk. Among them were the notes I had made on *Gray's Anatomy*. The detailed anatomical pictures within the book sprang to mind, followed by an unwelcome thought regarding Mr Connolly. I dismissed it as I had no wish to dwell on it. Then I rolled a piece of paper into my typewriter and began typing a letter to the poor law inspector, Mr Weyland, about the missing burial records.

CHAPTER 27

I told James and Eliza about my attempts to discover the fate of Joseph Connolly as we met in the foyer of the Steinway Hall that Saturday night. We had tickets to see a piano recital starring Mr Clifford Harrison.

"Undertakers are a strange bunch," Eliza commented. "And they're never at risk of going out of business, are they?"

"It seems one of them has taken the body of Mr Connolly from the workhouse dead house and failed to bury him," I said.

"He was a pauper, wasn't he?" asked James.

"Yes."

"And his body was unclaimed by his family because he hadn't provided the workhouse with their details," continued James. "You do know what happens to unclaimed bodies, don't you?"

"Yes, and you have mentioned something which is really beginning to bother me. Unclaimed bodies become the property of the Poor Law Union, which will either pay for a common funeral or..."

"Or what?" queried Eliza.

"Sell the corpse for dissection."

"Oh, don't say such things, Penelope!"

"Students of medicine have to learn their profession somehow," I said. The detailed pictures from *Gray's Anatomy* appeared in my mind once again.

"I thought the days of Burke and Hare were long behind us!" protested Eliza.

"They are," said James. "But these days unclaimed paupers' bodies are sometimes sold to schools of dissection. Perhaps the medical schools' dissection records need to be checked."

"Oh, how awful!" said Eliza.

"If Joseph Connolly's body was sold to a school of dissection the workhouse has falsified its records," I said. "The workhouse records state that he was buried at Tower Hamlets cemetery."

"Maybe that's what the superiors at the workhouse believe," said James. "They may have instructed the undertaker to bury Mr Connolly at Tower Hamlets cemetery, but perhaps he decided to make a little more profit."

"What a morbid conversation," said Eliza. "Is the suggestion here that the workhouse paid the undertaker to bury the chap and that he took the money – funded by our rates, I might add – and then made more money by selling the poor fellow to a medical school?"

"It's a possibility," I said.

"How terrible. I think the medical school should be held to account! They shouldn't be purchasing mortal remains from those shameless individuals! If there was no market for corpses these awful undertakers would never do such a thing. Surely it must be illegal! Can you not arrest the undertaker, James?"

"Only if we can prove that he has committed a crime."

"Of course he has! He's sold the corpse of a man he was paid to bury!"

"It's only a theory at the moment," said James, "and a case that certainly requires closer examination. You've informed the poor law inspector, haven't you, Penny?"

"Yes, I've written to him."

"He has the power to summon an inquiry," said James. "And if he finds evidence of wrongdoing he will be able to act. If a crime has been committed we can also get involved."

"I'd say that a crime has undoubtedly been committed!" protested Eliza.

"We can't yet be certain that this is what happened," I said. "And even if it did, we would need to find out which undertaker sold the corpse. At the moment there are two potential undertakers, or possibly even three. Although I can't be sure of exactly what has happened, I feel sure that at least one of the people I've spoken to over the past few days was lying to me."

"That wouldn't surprise me," said Eliza. "When there's money to be made people can be very economical with the truth. What's most upsetting, though, is that money appears to be being made from people who are too impoverished to influence their own destiny; not only in life, but beyond it as well! No one would wish to have a common funeral, but instead to be cut up into lots of little... oh goodness, I can't bear to consider it." Eliza held a handkerchief up to her mouth.

"I understand the dissected remains are given a respectful burial," said James.

"*Bits*," retorted Eliza bitterly. "Just little bits and pieces. Can you imagine that happening to a loved one of yours?"

"I can't, and we must consider ourselves fortunate in that respect. Although Penny made a good point when she said that medical students must have some examples to learn from."

"Why can't they just learn from books like everyone else?"

"Surgeons need to practise somehow," I said. "I just wish there was a better way because it doesn't seem at all fair that the unclaimed bodies of paupers are being used. People should have a say in the matter."

James sighed. "I must say that I'm looking forward to a little bit of Brahms this afternoon to lighten the mood."

"Me too!" agreed Eliza.

"I haven't told you yet that I received another book," I said.

"Oh no! Where was it left this time?" asked James.

"What book?" asked Eliza. "Is this another subject to dampen our spirits, Penelope?"

They listened as I began to tell them about the *Art of Prose*. I was interrupted by an instruction for us to take our seats.

CHAPTER 28

"**D**oes my letter give you cause for concern, sir?" I asked the poor law inspector. Mr Weyland was a plump-featured man with grey whiskers and thick wavy hair parted on one side. He had a languid manner about him, as if his job bored him and he would rather be doing something else. His office at the local government board in Whitehall was smart but small, and I wondered whether he had aspirations of a more important role and a bigger office from which to conduct it.

"I can't say that I'm overly concerned," he replied. "This incident may have been little more than lax record-keeping. I visit Shoreditch Workhouse once a month and am always reasonably pleased with what I see there. There is room for improvement, of course, but then there always is."

I told him briefly about my experience of staying on the casual ward. "It's not right that vulnerable women and children must endure those conditions, Mr Weyland."

"I agree that it's not right that anyone should live in poverty, Miss Green. The workhouse is the very last resort for people, and I understand why a lady such as yourself, from a comfortable, middle-class background, would find the conditions there quite distressing. In fact, I would have advised against you ever going anywhere near the place, as sudden exposure to such harsh realities can be extremely upsetting to someone who is unaccustomed to such hardships."

"My profession has taken me to many interesting places, sir, and while I realise I have been fortunate enough never to experience the difficulties of living in poverty, I also have a basic instinct for what seems right and fair. In an ideal world, nobody would live in poverty, but sadly at the current time it's a reality, and I believe there could be an improvement in conditions for everyone who is forced to spend their days in these places."

"Conditions have improved quite immeasurably over the past thirty years or so, Miss Green. I realise you are too young to fully appreciate that. But when my career began twenty-eight years ago, workhouses really were dreadful places to be. They are much better establishments these days.

"Now, with regard to your specific concerns, I would say that you have raised an issue which I suspect to be an isolated case. The workhouse is not always run perfectly of course, but I'd say that this particular issue falls within an acceptable margin of error."

"Would Mr Connolly's family accept that explanation, sir? That the disappearance of his body falls within an acceptable margin of error?"

"Of course not, but then families are always emotional about these matters."

I bit my tongue, trying my best to suppress a rude retort.

"And besides, the error may lie with the undertaker," he continued.

"Can you investigate the undertaker?"

"I have the authority to check that undertaking services

covered by the contract between the undertaker and the board of guardians meet the necessary standard."

"It's rather a confused situation because the undertaker, or funeral furnisher as he calls himself, who is contracted to the Shoreditch Workhouse has two undertakers to whom he contracts the day-to-day business of paupers' funerals."

"That's not so unusual."

"But it means that accountability becomes rather diluted."

He gave a shrug. "So what do you suggest, Miss Green?"

"Will you visit the undertakers involved?"

"If it can be demonstrated that their record-keeping is consistently poor I could raise the issue with them."

"So will you do that?"

"I can only act if I receive a sufficient number of complaints about a particular undertaker."

I felt a ball of frustration growing in my stomach. "So in the meantime, one or more of these undertakers can continue with their poor record-keeping and nothing will be done!"

"I only have your word for it that there is any poor record-keeping, Miss Green. And while I don't doubt what you have told me, the case of a single burial not being written down when it should have been falls within—"

"An acceptable margin of error?"

"Yes, I would say so."

"And what of the workhouse's claim that the deceased was buried at the Tower Hamlets cemetery when neither the undertaker nor the cemetery warden have any record of it?"

"Investigating individual cases is rather time-consuming, Miss Green—"

"But they must be investigated nonetheless, don't you think? I'm particularly concerned for the relatives of Joseph Connolly, who were not only distraught that the workhouse hadn't informed them of his death but that they also found no burial record at the cemetery."

"The poor record-keeping may also have been the fault of the cemetery, you know."

"So what can be done about it?"

Mr Weyland gave a sigh, picked up his pen and dipped it into the ink pot. "I shall write a memorandum to all concerned and remind them of their duty to keep detailed records."

I had to hold my breath for a moment to prevent myself from exploding with anger. His indifference was infuriating.

I decided to provoke him. "Perhaps Mr Connolly ended up on the dissection table," I suggested.

Mr Weyland started. "Good grief, Miss Green! What makes you say that?"

"If the body of a pauper lies unclaimed in the dead house for more than two days, it's sold to the medical school. Isn't that right?"

"Not exactly." He lowered his voice as if we were discussing a secret. "Bodies that remain unclaimed after a period of forty-eight hours pass into the possession of the relevant poor law union. The pauper may be buried or the body may be taken to a medical school."

"And sold for dissection."

"That is entirely at the discretion of the poor law union, and I must add, Miss Green, that the board of guardians at Shoreditch Union has decided against any such arrangement with the medical schools."

"So Shoreditch Workhouse does not sell bodies for dissection?"

"No."

"Do you know how widespread the practice is? How many bodies do the poor law unions sell to medical schools each year?"

"I really have no idea, and I must say this is rather a ghoulish topic to discuss so openly."

"Do the poor law unions derive an income from the sale of paupers' bodies?"

"Only a nominal amount, Miss Green, and it can then be spent on relief for the poor. Now, I really don't see why we're discussing this topic. It's quite obvious that Mr Connolly's body has not been sold to a medical school, and we are merely talking about a mistake to do with record-keeping."

Mr Weyland's assurances did little to placate me. I thought of Bill, the young man who had died suddenly from heart problems the night Eliza and I had stayed on the casual ward, and the mysterious deaths of Mr Patten and Mr Walker.

"Do you think there are more deaths at Shoreditch Workhouse than at other workhouses in London?"

"We are in the grip of winter, Miss Green. The death rate among paupers is high at this time of year. As I have already said, when a person is used to a comfortable, middle-class standard of living the number of pauper deaths can come as quite a shock."

"But what do the figures tell you?"

He dropped his pen onto his desk in agitation and leaned forward. "Which figures, Miss Green? Do they tell me *what* exactly?" He was clearly growing tired of our conversation.

"The numbers of people who have died at Shoreditch Workhouse compared with those at other workhouses. You receive reports with these figures in, do you not?"

"Yes I do, but I won't receive the figures for winter until March, so until then I will be unable to comment. Do you intend to publish this news story? It doesn't contain any real news as far as I can tell."

"And what of the deaths of Mr Patten and Mr Walker?"

"They have already been dealt with by the police and the coroner."

"But doesn't the incident concern you?"

"It's a sorry tale, that's for sure. And tragic events such as this do occur in workhouses. There really isn't anything for me to add."

I told him about Bill, and he scratched his brow impatiently while I spoke.

"Another sorry tale, Miss Green, and I extend my sincere condolences. Now, will that be all?"

I realised that any further attempt to challenge the poor law inspector would only antagonise him. I couldn't hope to achieve anything further.

"Yes. Thank you for your time, Mr Weyland."

CHAPTER 29

I arrived outside St Monica's in Hoxton Square at sunrise the following morning and surveyed the church's narrow facade with its tall, arched window. The bare trees in the square were white with a heavy frost.

I stepped inside the church and prepared what I was about to say. No one seemed interested in investigating the deaths of Mr Patten and Mr Walker any further, but I couldn't simply forget about them. I remained convinced that a third person had been involved, but if I couldn't freely wander about the workhouse asking questions then I had to track down someone who could.

The interior of the church was long and narrow with a high ceiling supported by a timber frame. Light filtered through a round stained-glass window above the altar and incense clouded the air.

I sat in a pew and bowed my head, as if in prayer. I hadn't been raised in the Catholic religion but it seemed like a reverential thing to do while I waited for someone to appear.

Before long, a nun stepped out of a small door and started tending to the candles on the altar. I got up from my seat and walked quietly over to speak to her. I kept my voice as low as possible, but I still managed to startle her when I spoke.

"Excuse me. Could you please tell me where I might find Father Keane?"

She took a moment to recover herself. "I didn't see you there!" she replied in a whisper. I noticed that she had large, owl-like eyes. "Father Keane, you say?"

I nodded.

"May I ask who you are?"

I introduced myself and rummaged around in my carpet bag to find one of my cards which she examined closely.

"I met him briefly at Shoreditch Workhouse while I was on a tour led by one of the guardians, Mrs Hodges. He might recall me, though our introduction was a brief one."

She appeared to relax slightly in response to this revelation. "I shall fetch him for you now, Miss Green."

I sat back down to wait, and a few moments later Father Keane stepped out through the small door. He wore a long black coat that was buttoned up and a lengthy black collar edged with white.

"Miss Green?"

I rose to my feet. "I was hoping that you might recall me from our brief meeting at the workhouse, Father Keane."

"I do indeed. I believe you're the lady they call 'the troublesome reporter'."

I felt my heart sink. "Oh dear, do they? Did you hear that description from Mr Lennox? Mr Hale? Or perhaps Mrs Hodges? I think I've managed to upset a few people there."

A smile spread across his boyish face. "Please don't worry, Miss Green. I read your article about the casual ward and it concerned me greatly. You are only considered troublesome because you are quite rightly questioning the way the workhouse is being run. I agree that there is a real need for certain conditions to improve at the workhouse, and my colleagues and I will do what we can to bring them about."

"Thank you, Father."

"Now, how can I help you?"

"I have some concerns I'd like to discuss with you."

Father Keane patiently listened as I explained my theory about the deaths of Mr Patten and Mr Walker. I stated that I was concerned about the fate of Mr Connolly and mentioned that Bill's sudden death also seemed rather odd. Father Keane occasionally nodded as I spoke. To my relief, there was nothing about his demeanour to suggest that he thought my theories were baseless nonsense.

"Do you think I'm right to be concerned?" I asked him.

"There may be cause for concern. The workhouse is quite well run, but I'm all too aware that it is not without its problems."

"I should like to investigate a little further, Father Keane. However, I have already annoyed the staff and it is unheard of for reporters to roam freely around the workhouse; especially lady reporters. How often do you visit the workhouse?"

"I'm quite a regular visitor. I go twice or even three times a week."

"I should like to establish whether any other inmates saw anything suspicious at the scene of Mr Patten and Mr Walker's deaths, or in the surrounding areas. I think Horace in the storeroom could potentially be a useful witness. Have you encountered him?"

"The simpleton, you mean?"

"I believe that he knows what he heard, even if he is of limited intelligence."

"It's possible, isn't it? I gather you would like me to ask around."

"If you wouldn't mind doing so I'd be very grateful indeed, Father Keane. You may need to be careful about the way you ask. If anyone on the board of guardians suspects that you're asking questions on my behalf they'll take a dim view of the situation."

"I can understand why they wouldn't want their authority questioned or undermined in any way, Miss Green, but I can assure you that I shall be completely discreet. People usually trust a priest, and we have the freedom to walk about the workhouse without anybody challenging our presence. We're there to help, of course, and I understand that you also wish to help. If untoward events are occurring then something needs to be done. I know that those on the board mean well, but sadly the lives of the poor are not afforded the same level of respect as the likes of us. And the poor, unfortunate individuals lack the education to speak up for themselves. They need people like us to help them."

"Thank you for being so helpful and understanding, Father Keane. I have found these past few weeks quite difficult, and I wish now that I had spoken to you sooner!"

"The door is always open here at St Monica's, Miss Green."

"My next request may seem rather odd to you, Father, but would you mind keeping this arrangement a secret for now? If people find out that I am still continuing with this work, I fear they would try to put a stop to it."

"Of course. You have my word."

CHAPTER 30

"**S**o you've enlisted the help of a priest who fancies himself a detective, have you?" asked James as we walked along the Embankment to meet Kit the shoeshine boy at Temple station. Clouds of smoke from a passing steam barge on the river drifted through the cold air.

"He seemed rather pleased to be of help," I replied. "He feels my concerns are justified and said he would be happy to ask around and find out if anyone else saw a man near the murder scene."

James took a sharp intake of breath. "He must be careful about that. If the master, clerk or board of guardians learn what he's up to they won't allow him to visit the workhouse any longer. That would be a great shame as I'm sure the priests do good work with the inmates there."

"He understands that he needs to be careful."

James shook his head again. "He's a priest though, isn't he? He's not a detective. He needs to know how to ask the right questions in the right way. We don't want him putting ideas into the inmates' heads and creating a whole host of sightings of this possible other culprit."

"But we want sightings of him!"

"We want *proper* sightings, not something the men come up with because they think it's what the priest wishes to hear. We don't even know if this alternative culprit exists."

"Then we need more witnesses, don't we? I don't know how else we're supposed to go about it, with the police refusing to co-operate—"

"We're not refusing, Penny. We've already carried out some investigative work, but it's complicated by the fact that the case is considered to be resolved and that the only possible witness is a man who some might consider unreliable."

"Then you must surely agree that if Father Keane can find out something more, it will give you the opportunity to have the police involved as they should be. Father Keane is perfectly positioned to carry out some careful investigations and he's extremely keen to do so."

James sighed. "Let's hope he'll be able to help, but if the board hears about it I fear something could go terribly wrong."

"Good mornin', Inspector," said Kit as we arrived at Temple station. He stood with his hands stuffed into the pockets of an oversized scruffy overcoat, his shabby wooden shoeshine box sat by his feet.

"Good morning, Kit. How did you get on with the blacksmith in Shepherd Market?"

"I sawed a lady go in there, sir, like as you said she would."

"How was she dressed?"

"Nuffink fancy, jus' a bonnet and shawl."

"How old would you say she was?"

"I ain't too good with ladies' ages. Twenny or thirty, I reckon."

"And how many times did you see her visiting the blacksmith?"

"Twice."

"And was she carrying anything with her?"

"Yeah, she 'ad a bundle under one arm."

"When she was arriving or leaving? Or at both times?"

"She 'ad it all the time, I fink."

"Thank you, Kit," James handed him some coins. "That sounds like an extremely useful piece of information. I'll visit the blacksmith again and ask him a few more questions. If he proves uncooperative I shall apply for a warrant to search his premises."

After leaving Kit we paused on the embankment above Temple Pier, where a steamboat had just called in. We watched the passengers disembark.

"I've been thinking about the two books you were sent," said James. "I wish I knew who they were from."

"Inspector Ferguson?" I suggested. "Mr Lennox? Mr Hale? Miss Russell?"

"It's rather cowardly, isn't it? If they have something to say to you they should write you a letter or pay you a visit. They should be able to talk about the matter sensibly rather than leaving books about the place. It's rather ridiculous behaviour."

"Similar things have happened to me before," I said. "I'm used to it."

"You shouldn't have to get used to intimidating behaviour!" fumed James. "It simply shouldn't happen. These people should be addressing their own wrongdoings rather than wasting time threatening you."

"It's not particularly threatening on the face of it, is it?" I said. "There are far worse things they could give me than a couple of books."

"But as you've said yourself, Penny, the manner in which they were left on your desk and doorstep suggests someone is watching you. That thought is far more menacing than the books themselves."

"I can live with it if they do nothing more than leave books for me to find."

"You can live with someone watching you?"

"Well, perhaps you could find out who is responsible if you think it necessary. This is something I could ask the police to look into, is it not?"

"It is."

"Only I'm sure they won't be overly bothered as presumably I have in some way asked for this by angering someone?"

"I would never take that view, Penny."

"But many of your colleagues would."

James sighed. "Yes, sadly they would. However, I shall ask a few of my men to do some reconnaissance and see if we can find out who is behind this."

"I'm sure there's no need, James. The police have far more important matters to deal with. For the time being this doesn't worry me too much. I'm sure it won't be long before the mysterious book-giver leaves a clue. And although it isn't entirely pleasant, this sort of behaviour suggests to me that I must be doing something right. If someone wishes to intimidate me it's because I've come a little closer to revealing their secret."

"That's one way of looking at it, I suppose. But what if this situation becomes something more threatening than the sending of books?"

"Then we shall have to worry about that if it happens."

"I'd rather prevent it from happening altogether."

"I feel sure that if someone could get to the bottom of

what has been happening at Shoreditch Workhouse this intimidation would naturally come to an end. Once the culprits are uncovered they will have no way of threatening me anymore, will they?"

"But what exactly do you think is happening at Shoreditch Workhouse?"

"I don't know, but something isn't right, is it? Two men supposedly fought to the death and the body of another man is missing. And I can't help thinking about Bill, who seemed fine when I saw him that evening when I stayed on the casual ward, yet he was dead by the following morning. I had hoped Mr Weyland would have been interested in doing more, but he seems like rather a waste of space to me.

"Unfortunately, it seems few people share my concerns. Sometimes once I have convinced myself of something, I begin to wonder whether I'm fooling myself. Perhaps I'm missing an obvious explanation or could it be that I've talked myself into thinking about this in a certain way?"

"Don't start to doubt yourself, Penny." James turned away from the river to face me. "I think there may well be something in this."

"You're not just saying that to humour me, are you?"

"No. I think there could be something untoward happening, and I think these two books are indirect evidence of that. You've unnerved someone, Penny."

"I want to learn a little more about dissection."

He gave a snort of surprise. "Why on earth?!"

"How much do you know about the industry of selling bodies for dissection?"

"I quite doubt that it is an *industry*, as such."

"Do you know anything about it?"

"Very little, Penny."

"I wonder if Dr Macpherson could help."

"Who is he?"

"I attended his anatomy lecture at the School of Medicine for Women. Do you remember?"

"Yes, I do now."

"I'm sure he could explain it to me."

"Do you think it might have something to do with the deaths at Shoreditch Workhouse?"

"With Mr Connolly's death, perhaps. The poor law inspector told me that the Shoreditch Union does not sell unclaimed bodies to the medical schools, but perhaps someone is doing so in secret."

"I doubt that Dr Macpherson would know anything about that."

"He won't. But he should be able to explain how the system works. And I want to understand how much demand there is for corpses. If there is a high demand, unscrupulous people will be looking to exploit it, won't they?"

"They will. But are you sure about this, Penny? The days of bodysnatchers are long gone, and that sort of business is highly regulated these days."

"At least, that's what we like to think, isn't it?"

CHAPTER 31

I had last visited the medical school at St Bartholomew's Hospital while reporting on the murder of Richard Geller at the museum the previous summer. It was difficult to imagine how warm the weather had been that day as I walked through the frozen quadrangle of the hospital buildings toward the entrance of the medical school.

As soon as I stepped into the lobby, I was reminded of my reason for being here. To my left I saw a door labelled 'Dissecting Room', while the door to my right was marked 'Anatomical Theatre'. An odd smell lingered in the air. It was the scent of carbolic soap mixed with the undeniable odour of a butcher's shop.

The diminutive Dr Macpherson greeted me warmly in his second-storey office, the large window of which overlooked the elegant spires of the neighbouring Christ's Hospital school. Beyond it rose the dome of St Paul's Cathedral.

"I see that you appreciate the view from here, Miss Green."

"It's certainly an interesting one." I walked up to the window. "It's rather intriguing to be able to see Newgate from this vantage point." The notorious prison, with its forbidding granite walls, gave me a chill whenever I passed by it.

Dr Macpherson joined me at the window. "I like to keep an eye out to ensure that none of the inmates are attempting to climb out over the walls! Actually, if you and I had stood here just a few hundred years ago, Miss Green, we'd have been looking at the Great Wall of London."

"Would we indeed?"

"Yes. Once upon a time this location was just beyond the city walls. They ran just in front of us here." He gestured the direction with his hand. "The more recent school buildings were constructed on top of it, which is a bit of a shame. However, I don't think the wall was in a great state by then." He walked back to his desk. "Now then, I've forgotten what you came here to speak to me about. Do I rightly recall that you attended my talk at the Women's School of Medicine?"

"Yes, that's right. I wrote about it for the ladies' column in the *Morning Express*."

"Excellent. There is no doubt that many more members of the fairer sex are taking an interest in medicine these days." He gestured for me to take a seat opposite him. "Do please remind me why you're here."

"I should like to understand how the anatomy trade works," I said.

The smile on Dr Macpherson's face remained fixed, but his brow furrowed. "I'm sorry?"

"The anatomy trade."

"Is there a trade?"

"I'm not sure quite how to refer to it. What I mean is the sale of corpses for dissection."

His expression suddenly grew more serious. "Oh, I see. That's not something I am at liberty to discuss, I'm afraid."

"But why not?"

He cleared his throat. "It's rather a political subject, and a controversial one too. We simply aren't serving ourselves if we discuss these matters in public."

"In public?"

"I'm assuming that everything I say will be printed in your newspaper."

"Not necessarily, Dr Macpherson."

"That is why you're here though, is it not?"

"I'm here to expand my own personal understanding. I have no intention of publishing an article about it."

"I see."

His shoulders relaxed slightly and I took the opportunity to share my fruitless attempts to discover the whereabouts of Mr Connolly's remains.

"If I had a better understanding of how the arrangement between the medical schools and the workhouses worked, perhaps I could make some progress with this particular mystery," I added.

"Indeed. I am more than happy to explain it to you, Miss Green, but only if you promise not to write a single word of it down."

"I see."

"Do I have your word?"

"Yes."

"I really must have your word, because whenever this matter finds its way into the public arena we end up with protestors at the door. It's a topic the man on the street has strong opinions about but very little understanding of the reasons behind it. Now, if I have your word, Miss Green, I am more than happy to explain it all to you. You'll soon realise that the system isn't half as gruesome as you are probably imagining."

"Thank you, Dr Macpherson. You have my word."

"Good. Now, you're aware of the Anatomy Act, which was passed a little over fifty years ago?"

"The act that put an end to the resurrectionists?"

"That's exactly what it did: no more bodysnatching. The act not only prevented it but also allowed licensed teachers of anatomy legal access to unclaimed corpses. That was very important."

I gave a reassuring nod.

"Have you heard of the Medical Act of 1858?"

"No."

"This act established the General Medical Council, which maintains the register of qualified doctors. Since then, the number of students wishing to study medicine has soared, and among those numbers are many women, as you well know. Properly qualified doctors are desperately needed in this country, and dissection is the only way for them to learn anatomy and surgery."

"What about learning from books?"

He gave a laugh and sat back in his chair. "Believe me, Miss Green, I would be delighted if books could provide all the education our future doctors needed! Unfortunately, books do not allow a student to learn everything for himself. They do not permit him to practise his discipline slowly and regularly, as he gradually learns the idiosyncrasies of each individual patient. Would you like a surgeon who had never touched a human body before to attend to you?"

I shook my head and he smiled in response. Then he opened a notebook on his desk. "These are the notes I have made for the forthcoming term. You're welcome to read them yourself. I take it you are not a lady with a nervous disposition?"

"No."

"Good, I didn't think you would be. Now then, let me read some of these notes to you. I currently have seventy-one students, and between them they need twenty-four heads."

"Heads?" I felt my stomach turn.

"Yes. Twenty-four heads for dissection. There are three classes a day and I need eight for each class. That's one head between two or three students. For the coming term I also need eighteen arms, fourteen legs and twenty abdomens. The list goes on from there. You may look at it in more detail if you wish, and you can see my class plan here. Winter is an excellent time for dissection because the cadavers remain fresher for longer. There are chemicals for preserving them, of course, but the general rule is that the fresher they are the better.

"Now, between you and me, Miss Green, procuring cadavers for dissection is not an easy task. We predominately rely on unclaimed corpses, some of which come from the workhouse, while others are released to us by coroners when bodies have been found in the river or on the street. We pay the hospital porters for amputated limbs, and occasionally we might get a brain from a post-mortem. But if I don't have sufficient cadavers for dissection, I end up losing students to these new night schools that are now appearing across town. This institution was founded in the twelfth century, and we take great pride in our long history of teaching. Imagine if we were to lose out to these new schools?

"Matters haven't been helped by the enthusiastic work of the new chair of human anatomy at Cambridge. He spends most of his time greasing the palms of the workhouse masters, coroners' mates, hospital porters, dead house staff, midwives and undertakers. And he doesn't just do it in Cambridge; he has bodies brought in via the railway lines from as far away as Hull and Brighton, not to mention London! Three times a week an express train leaves Liverpool Street Station with windowless carriages. What do you suppose is inside those carriages? For those in the know, it's the *dead train,* and its route to Doncaster conveniently takes it through Cambridge. Now, I don't consider it fair that Cambridge is able to take bodies from London. I acknowledge that the medical school there is twice the size of ours, but there should be rules in place about certain boundaries."

I could scarcely believe what I was hearing, having previously had no idea that corpses were still so prized. "Is it fair to say, then, that medical schools are battling one another over the unclaimed bodies of the poor?" I asked.

"I don't think the word *battle* quite describes it, but there's no doubt that there is a little treading on one another's toes. And all it does is push the prices up, of course."

"How much do you usually pay for a body?"

"About three pounds for an elderly man, rising to twelve pounds for a young adult and more for a woman or child."

"Why is there such a difference?"

"There are certain features of a woman's anatomy that are of particular interest to students and are extremely important for learning about childbirth and the suchlike. I'm sure there is no need for me to explain any further. Children make extremely interesting subjects, and abnormalities and deformities are also in high demand. Some of these remains aren't buried but are preserved in our medical museum."

"I've seen some of them."

"Fascinating, aren't they?"

"They are for medical students, no doubt."

"We pay a good price, and when we purchase a body from a poor law union there is no need for them to pay cemetery fees or to fund a coffin, carriage or undertaker. This presents significant savings for ratepayers, of course. In fact, the argument that lies behind this entire system is that the poor are paying society back for the welfare they have received in life. These people are not typically ratepayers, and public money has been spent on their poor relief, whether it has taken the form of outdoor relief, medical relief or accommodation in the workhouse. If a pauper is dissected after death his debt to society is repaid."

This comment left me speechless for a moment. "No one *chooses* to be poor," was all I could manage after a brief silence.

"Indeed not."

"So if someone is destitute they not only have no choice about where they live and work, but are also given no choice about what happens to them after their death!"

"You're beginning to sound like one of those protestors we get at the door, Miss Green. I've explained how it all works as clearly as I possibly can. I realise the subject can stir up a little emotion, but imagine if your son wished to become a doctor, or perhaps even your daughter? Would you deny your children the proper education and training required?"

"I haven't ever given it any thought. I don't have children, Dr Macpherson."

"But if you had children and, God forbid, one of them fell dangerously ill, wouldn't you wish for them to be attended to by a properly qualified doctor at the earliest possible moment?"

"Well yes, I would."

"Of course you would. It's what everyone would wish for. Sometimes there are no easy solutions."

CHAPTER 32

C lose to the medical school was a shop called Marshall & Hawes, which sold supplies to medical students. I had passed it a few times before, but on this occasion the two skeletons grinning at me in a macabre fashion from the window caught my eye.

A thought occurred to me that had never crossed my mind before. *Where had those bones come from?*

The long, narrow shop was cluttered, and for some odd reason it stocked magic and party tricks alongside the surgical instruments and medical supplies. A crooked staircase led up to a gallery above my head, and a musty smell hung in the air.

"How can I help you?" asked a dry-looking man with prominent yellow teeth. He had long grey hair and wore a faded velvet fez on his head.

"I'm interested in the skeletons you have for sale here," I said.

"Ah yes. A lady medical student are you?"

I was about to correct him but quickly decided to play along. "I am, yes."

"The Women's School of Medicine, I presume?"

"The very same." I gave a sweet smile, hoping he wouldn't ask me any questions about the institution. "What is the price of a skeleton?" I asked.

"We call them osteology sets," he replied. "You're a new student, are you? I take it you haven't owned one of these before?"

"No indeed. I'm quite new."

He gave a nod as if this was already clearly apparent to him.

"Prices start from five pounds and five shillings, then increase incrementally from there. The most superior sets are ten pounds and ten shillings. Many of the cheaper ones are second-hand. They will have been owned by former students who have sold them back to us. The more expensive ones are a little newer. And fresher, I should say." He grinned, displaying more of his discoloured teeth and gums.

"They have been recently procured, then?" I asked.

"Indeed they have." He led me to the back of the shop, where a number of wooden boxes were stacked on top of each other. He removed one, which was about twenty inches long and eight inches wide. He opened it to reveal a pile of bones upon which a skull had been placed.

"This is one of the superior osteology sets, and as you can see it includes the study notes."

He pointed to a small booklet. A label stating 'Marshall & Hawes: Dealers in Surgical Instruments and Osteology' had been pasted to the interior of the lid.

He picked up the skull, which had a clean cut between the upper and lower half. The two pieces were held together with little hooks and pegs. The skull was stamped 'Marshall & Hawes' where I imagined the left ear had once been. The proprietor checked the side of the box, where something had been pencilled on it.

"This is a young male, and one of good stature as well.

We've had some excellent-quality sets in recently. This is quite a significant investment but we would gladly buy it back from you once you had finished with it."

"For how much?"

"Three or four pounds for this one if you look after him well."

"Where did he come from?"

The shopkeeper gave me a bemused smile. "I've no idea, ma'am. The man's life is far behind him now."

"Where did you obtain him from, I mean?"

"We source our osteology sets from a number of places. Sometimes from overseas."

"And this one?"

"You wish to know the provenance of this particular set?"

"It's a superior-quality set, as you say."

"Yes, well I can't be certain where we got this chap from."

"Might it have been one of the medical schools?"

"Sometimes, if they haven't been too chopped up, that is. I must say you're quite interested in all this, ma'am."

"I am indeed. Each of these osteology sets was once a person."

He gave a nod of agreement. "When you look at it that way, I suppose you're right. I can't say that many of the medical students who come in here give quite so much thought to the provenance of these bones. However, as a member of the fairer sex you are perhaps more likely to consider these things."

"I'm interested to know how a young man of good stature, as you describe him, came to have been reduced to a box of bones in your shop."

He gave a laugh. "An interesting thought indeed!"

"Might he have been a pauper?"

The shop owner scratched his chin as he considered this. "Yes, I suppose that would be quite likely. Anyone with means would have been buried in the usual way, wouldn't they? It's the unclaimed bodies that find their way to the medical schools."

I laughed inwardly at his description, which made it sound as though the unfortunate cadavers somehow transported themselves onto the dissecting table.

"Well, it's getting on," he said, checking his pocket watch. "I'm closing for lunch soon. What do you think to this chap here at ten pounds and ten shillings? He'd be a good investment for your years of study."

"I shall have to give it some thought."

"Of course. And you'll need to discuss it with your father, as he'll be the one paying for it, no doubt!"

CHAPTER 33

"I have a feeling that the missing remains of Joseph Connolly may have been dissected," I said to Mr Sherman in the newsroom the following day.

"Really?" His eyes widened with interest. "Have you any evidence, or is this just a suspicion?"

"It's just a suspicion at present, but having spent some time with Dr Macpherson at St Bartholomew's Medical School I now realise how valuable bodies are to those within the medical profession."

"They are indeed. My brother would know about all that. I recall that we published a piece called '*In the Dissecting Room*' several years ago, and I think it's high time we did something similar again. How about we report on the School of Medicine for Women this time? You could visit the dissecting room there and write an account of what you see the female medical students doing."

"I really don't think I'd be up to the task, sir."

"You don't have the stomach for it?"

"I never thought I would find myself saying this, but I'd rather write fashion tips for the ladies' column!"

Mr Sherman laughed. "I understand. Fish! Fancy a visit to the dissecting room?"

"No thank you, sir."

"Potter?"

"I really couldn't, sir."

"Well, that is a shame. I think a report of some sort is necessary if we can prove that poor Mr Connolly ended up there."

"I hope he didn't," I said.

"Well, someone's got to end up there, haven't they?" replied the editor. "How else will our doctors learn?"

"That's what Dr Macpherson said. But I think people should have a say in whether their bodies are dissected or not. To deny people a choice because they happen to be poor is unconscionable."

"You can't go giving people a choice!" scoffed Edgar. "Everyone would say no if they were asked. No one wants to be dissected, do they? Otherwise, what will happen on the Day of Judgement? One can hardly stand before the Lord cut up into small pieces, can one?"

"Doctors should be dissected," said Frederick. "If each doctor offered himself up to be dissected after his death, demand would most likely be satisfied."

"I don't think there are enough doctors for that," said Mr Sherman.

"I could check the dissection registers at the medical schools for a record of Mr Connolly," I said.

"You are not to spend your time doing that, Miss Green. If any wrongdoing has occurred, it's up to the poor law inspector to investigate."

I gave a derisory snort. "I can't imagine the poor law inspector doing anything about it."

"All the same, it's not your job to locate Mr Connolly's remains."

I thought of his family and felt saddened that I would be unable to bring them any good news.

"Let's get on with the reports on General Gordon's death at Khartoum," said Mr Sherman, rubbing his hands together. "That's the only news people want to hear about at the moment. Two days! If the relief force had arrived just two days sooner, he'd have been saved. What a disgrace. I need your article as soon as possible, Miss Green."

"I shall get right on with it, sir."

"Good. And I'm pleased that you're no longer bothering the police about those deaths at Shoreditch Workhouse. Your attention is needed elsewhere."

"Indeed, sir."

I decided it was best to pretend that I was no longer interested in the case at Shoreditch for the time being.

※

"Liverpool Street Station, Penny?" asked James as we met on the cold street outside it. "Why here?"

"This way," I replied, striding off in the direction of Bishopsgate Street.

It was early evening and the light was fading fast. The gas lamps were being lit, and around us smartly dressed clerks and bankers were hurrying through the cold to the train station and their journeys home.

"Dr Macpherson told me something interesting, so I wanted to come and see it for myself."

"And you've invited me here to keep you company?" James asked, matching my stride.

"That was foremost in my mind yes," I replied with a smile, "but I also thought it would be interesting for both of us to see who might be involved in this."

"Involved in what?"

"I'll show you. These people don't want to be seen, so my guess is that they'll use the back entrance to the station rather than the main entrance on Liverpool Street."

"I'm intrigued," replied James.

We continued along Bishopsgate.

"I obtained a warrant to search Mr Brook the blacksmith's premises," said James. "And what do you suppose we found?"

"Some of the items that had been stolen from Lord Courtauld?"

"Exactly that. Along with a quantity of melted down silver."

"I presume he is under arrest now, then."

"Yes, but there is still no sign of Maisie Hopkins, unfortunately."

"But she sold the items to Mr Brook?"

"Yes, and I think she must have made some good money from the things she sold to him, as well as the items she pawned."

"Perhaps if the Courtaulds had paid her more she wouldn't have considered it necessary to steal from them."

"She has to take responsibility for her actions, Penny."

"Yes, she does. But Mrs Hodges explained to me that Lady Courtauld's scheme to help girls from the workhouse become maids affords them a much lower wage than other maids would be paid. While I realise that Maisie shouldn't have turned to stealing as a result, that must have caused her to develop great animosity against her employers. Anyone who works as a servant should be paid a fair and equal wage."

"Depending on their age and experience."

"Yes, that's right. The fact that a maid has come from the workhouse shouldn't give her employers an excuse to pay her less. And the Courtaulds are hardly short of money! I reported on their daughter's birthday party, and it was abundantly clear that there was no hardship among their circle."

"I have visited their home a few times and can concur with that."

"And that's just their London home. No doubt they have one in the country too."

"I believe they do."

We turned left into a narrow lane just beyond a large public house.

"I have no desire to condone what Maisie did," I continued, "but I actually have more sympathy for her than for the Courtaulds."

"Crime is never the answer, Penny."

"No, but if you are unable to arrest her I won't feel too upset about it. In my mind, the real criminals are those who exploit the poor and vulnerable. They profit from their misery by paying them as little as possible for their long days of hard work. You see it in factories and you see it in wealthy townhouses. And even when the poor souls are dead people continue to make money from them!"

"Are you sure it was a good idea to find out more about dissection?"

"Of course! And I'll tell you what else I've discovered. Once the medical schools are finished with the paupers' corpses, some are sold again to businesses that supply medical students. Some poor individuals are doomed to be a pile of bones in a box for ever, eventually accompanied by a set of study notes! Would you wish that fate upon your loved ones, James?"

"No, I wouldn't."

"And yet it happens."

"I suppose medical students and doctors must have skeletons to aid their study."

"Yes, they must. But must those skeletons always be

supplied by the poor and the destitute? By those who have no say in their destiny?"

The lane opened out onto Skinner Street, which took the form of a long bridge over the many railway lines leading in and out of Liverpool Street Station. A train passed beneath us, covering us with plumes of smoke.

We paused for a moment and surveyed the vast iron and glass structure that covered the platforms. It was lit with the warm glow of gaslight, and beyond it we could see the dark silhouette of the new station hotel, which was under construction. A covered cart passed by before turning left into a narrow roadway that led down to the platforms.

"That looks interesting," I said, beginning to follow.

"I hope it is," replied James. "When are you going to tell me what's going on?"

"You'll see for yourself in a moment."

We followed the cart down the roadway and watched as it moved onto the platform and halted beside a row of carriages. I quickened my step so we could get a better look.

"Carriages without windows!" I exclaimed. "Just as Dr Macpherson described them."

"And what are they transporting?" James asked. Two men uncovered the cart, and we saw that it was loaded with long wooden chests. "Are those coffins?"

"This is the dead train," I replied.

I explained to James what I had learnt from Dr Macpherson about the anatomy trade as we watched the men unload the coffins.

"Can you be sure that these coffins are being taken to Cambridge?" he asked.

"Why don't we ask the men who are unloading them?"

We walked down to the platform and saw that the train had three plain, windowless carriages.

"These are destined for the medical school at Cambridge

are they?" I asked two startled men who had just unloaded another coffin.

"We ain't at liberty ter say," one of them replied curtly.

We continued on our way and soon came across a second cart. One of the men unloading it looked familiar. It was a few moments before I realised that I could put a name to the careworn expression.

"That's Mr Finlay!" I whispered to James excitedly. "He's one of the undertakers I spoke to about Mr Connolly. Now that we've seen him he can't possibly deny that he's involved in this trade. Perhaps he sold Mr Connolly's remains?"

"He may not have done, Penny. From what you've told me there is nothing criminal about what these men are doing here. The only reason for the secrecy is that passengers would likely be upset by the sight of coffins being loaded onto a train."

"Let's go and speak to him."

"You're not expecting me to make an arrest are you, Penny? There's no obvious crime being committed, and we're also within the jurisdiction of the City of London Police. I'll need to tread carefully."

"I just want to hear what his explanation is."

I introduced myself and James once we had approached Mr Finlay.

He gave me a cautious smile and then glanced at James. "I've got all the official papers, Hinspector."

"I'm sure you have. I'm not here to question you."

"Do you know the chair of human anatomy at the University of Cambridge Medical School?" I asked Mr Finlay.

"As a matter of fact I do, yeah. D'you know 'im too?"

"Not personally, but I hear he's kept extremely busy sourcing bodies for his medical school."

"Yeah."

Mr Finlay looked distractedly around him. He clearly didn't want to be drawn any further into the conversation.

"The missing body of the man I asked you about," I ventured. "Is it possible that it was taken to Cambridge?"

"Only if I 'ad a record of 'im, and I ain't got no record of 'im. I got all the papers, though. I'm careful with me papers."

"So you've no idea what might have happened to him?"

"None. Yer asked me that afore, and I still ain't got no idea."

"Where did you get these bodies from?" I asked, gesturing toward the coffins on the cart.

"Finchley. They send a fair few up to Cambridge. You can ask 'em yourself. There ain't no funny business 'ere. They got their papers, I got my papers and everythin's in order."

"Good," I said. "Thank you for speaking to us, Mr Finlay."

He doffed his cap and continued with his work.

We walked along the platform toward the main entrance of the station. The crowd thronged busily, unaware of the macabre cargo being loaded onto one of the express trains.

"We can't allow them to get away with it," I said.

"I know it's an unpleasant business, but these undertakers aren't breaking the law."

"I realise that, but some will be. I just know that they will be! The medical schools pay good money for corpses, and that's why Joseph Connolly's body is unaccounted for. How many others have vanished the way he did? Please will you do something for me?"

"Yes, Penny. Am I likely to regret saying that?"

"Would you please speak to the poor law inspector, Mr Weyland? I don't think he took me seriously, probably because I'm a woman. But he'll have to listen to an inspector from Scotland Yard. Please, James, will you ask him to investigate?"

CHAPTER 34

"Scandalous, that's what it is," I overheard Mrs Garnett saying as I arrived home that evening and climbed the steps to the front door. "You can't trust anyone with anything these days."

She was talking in the doorway to her friend Mrs Wilkinson, a stout woman with a gleaming white bonnet and a thick woollen shawl.

"What's Mr Torrance done now?" I asked with a smile as I reached them.

"Mr Torrance? What do you mean, Miss Green?"

"I heard you mention the word *scandalous* and that no one can be trusted these days."

"Oh, that had nothing to do with Mr Torrance," replied my landlady. "Mrs Wilkinson has just told me the awful news."

"What awful news?" I asked, swiftly forgetting my rather poor quip about Mr Torrance.

"The coffin with the sand in it."

"Sand*bags*," corrected Mrs Wilkinson. "*Two* sandbags, ter be exact."

"A coffin with sandbags in it?" I asked. "Where was it discovered?"

"In the dead 'ouse at the work'ouse. The bodysnatchers 'ave taken 'er."

"*Her*? Who do you mean?"

"The young lady what was in the coffin! They've taken 'er out and put sandbags in so as no one'd be any the wiser."

I readied myself to head back down the steps and return to the newsroom to report on the story.

"Where did this happen, Mrs Wilkinson?"

"Down Shoreditch Work'ouse."

I gave a sigh. "Thank you, Mrs Wilkinson."

A man in a dark blue porter's uniform stood on the work-house steps in front of a crowd of people and reporters in The Land of Promise.

"I ain't never known nuffink like it!" he stated. "We brought 'er over to the dead 'ouse in a shell and then we put 'er in the coffin. Chalked 'er name on it an' nailed the lid down like we always does."

"So someone has pulled the nails out, removed Miss Lloyd's corpse, placed bags of sand in the coffin and nailed the lid down again?" asked a reporter.

"Yeah! That's what they done!"

"Bodysnatchers, Mr Plunkett?"

"Yeah, they'd 'ave ter be!"

"When would someone have had an opportunity to get into the dead house, Mr Plunkett?" I called out.

"They must've got in durin' the night!"

"Was there any sign that the door had been forced open?" I asked.

"Nah. They must've picked the lock or got 'old o' the key."

"Who keeps the key?" asked another reporter.

"The master 'as one and I got one. No one else 'as 'em."

"And where do you keep yours?" someone else asked.

"On me belt, and I keeps it on an 'ook in me room night-times."

"Could someone have taken it from your room?"

"I dunno 'ow, but I s'pose they could of!"

Following the many questions and answers between the reporters and Mr Plunkett, we were able to establish that Miss Sarah Lloyd's body had been taken to the dead house at half-past six the previous evening. Mr Plunkett had placed her in the coffin and nailed the lid closed. He had locked the dead house up at seven o'clock in the evening, and he presumed that it had remained locked until half past three the following morning when he was awoken to admit the body of a man into the dead house. Once this was done, the door was locked again at four o'clock, and Mr Plunkett was certain that all had remained quiet there until he returned to the dead house at seven o'clock.

Having been notified of the death of their daughter, Miss Lloyd's family had arrived at the dead house at four o'clock that afternoon. Prior to their arrival, two more bodies had been brought to the dead house, and the undertaker's cart had arrived to take away five other coffins for burials. Mr Plunkett had supervised this activity without anything having raised his suspicions. The coffin of Miss Lloyd did not appear to have been disturbed in any way. He stated that there was no chance that any coffin might have been confused with another because the name of the deceased was chalked upon it.

Mr Plunkett said that Miss Lloyd's family members had been greatly distressed that the coffin lid was nailed down and that they would be unable to see their daughter one last time. When the family returned at half past seven that evening, Mr Plunkett had no idea what they planned to do. He had assumed that they wished to spend a little more time with their daughter and had left them alone with her while he walked around the yard smoking his pipe.

Just ten minutes later he heard screams and ran to the dead house, where he found the family in great distress. He was horrified to see that the lid had been removed from the coffin, and even more horrified when he saw that the woman's body was missing. He checked that the name he had chalked onto the side was correct, and it was. Mr Plunkett's first thought was that the wrong coffin had been opened, but even if it had he couldn't imagine how or why bags of sand should have been placed inside.

The other coffins in the dead house at the time were opened and checked, and were found to contain the bodies of the appropriate people. The police at Commercial Street had been summoned, and Inspector Ferguson and his men were making enquiries at the workhouse.

"It weren't nuffink ter do wiv me!" protested the dead house porter. "I didn't know nuffink abaht it!"

As the reporters clamoured around him with more questions, confusion reigned outside the entrance of the workhouse. I was expecting Mr Lennox or Mr Hale to appear and impose some sort of order, but when they weren't forthcoming I surmised that they were probably busy speaking to the police officers.

I pushed my way through the crowd to the entrance and tentatively headed into the hallway. With no other staff about I continued, unchallenged, along the covered walkway. As I walked, I tried to comprehend what had happened. I wondered where Miss Lloyd's relatives were and how they must have been feeling. She appeared to have been a young woman, and I was interested to know what the cause of death had been.

Might her death have been suspicious?

CHAPTER 35

The dead house was a windowless brick structure at the far end of the yard from the infirmary. It seemed I wasn't the only person to have wandered in, for a large group of people had gathered outside the little building, some of them holding lanterns. In the flickering light I could just make out the grey uniforms of the inmates and the blue uniforms of the police constables. There was also an assortment of onlookers and a few reporters hanging around with their notebooks. I joined the crowd, hoping to hear more about this sad occurrence.

There was a lull in the noise around me as the door of the dead house opened and out stepped the bushy-whiskered chairman of the board of guardians, Mr Buller. He was accompanied by Mr Hale, Inspector Ferguson and James.

"This is a despicable outrage!" fumed the chairman in response to the questions the reporters shouted at him. "What sort of world do we live in when the remains of our dead cannot be respected? Sealed coffins are kept under lock and key, yet we must suffer such atrocities!"

"Where do you intend to start looking for Miss Lloyd's body, Mr Buller?" someone asked.

"That is a matter for the police now, and I trust that Inspector Ferguson and his men will do all they can to assist with the inquiry, with the help of Scotland Yard, of course. I trust that the remains of the poor woman will soon be found and returned to her family."

Mr Buller pushed his way through the crowd and strode over to the walkway that led to the administration block. Most of the reporters and some of the onlookers followed him. Other people tried to access the dead house door, which was closely guarded by two constables.

James hadn't yet seen me in the gloomy yard, so I slowly approached him.

"Penny!" he said with a weak smile. "It's an unpleasant business this, don't you think?"

"I wonder whether poor Miss Lloyd's body was being loaded onto that train at Liverpool Street station," I replied.

"You think Finlay could be behind this?"

"It's possible. Has he been here today?"

"Apparently Mr Hicks, another undertaker, visited at midday today."

"I spoke to his son about Mr Connolly a matter of days ago. Is he the undertaker who took away the five coffins?"

"Yes, I believe so."

"But there was no sign of Finlay?"

"Not that we know of yet."

Inspector Ferguson joined us, giving me a brief nod of acknowledgement.

"What are your thoughts on all this, Inspector?" I asked him.

"I believe someone has stolen the corpse in order to benefit financially," he replied. "My concern at the present time is that this could already be a common practice. It just so happened that the Lloyd family decided to prise the lid off the coffin in this instance."

"There's only one way to find out," said James. "And that's to exhume all of the workhouse's recent burials."

I gave a shudder.

"Most of them are in Tower Hamlets cemetery," replied the Inspector. "I'll have to ask the coroner's permission."

"But how many will you exhume?" I asked. "The undertaker, Mr Finlay, told me there are between three and five burials from the workhouse each day."

"It sounds as though quite a few will need to be exhumed," said James. "Just a fortnight's worth of burials could number... let me see now." He paused to make the calculation. "Between forty and seventy coffins! And I'd say that you would need to exhume more than just the past fortnight. You'd probably have to go back a few months."

Inspector Ferguson wiped his brow. "Good grief! What a thought. There'll be hundreds of them! And it will all be a thorough waste of our time if we don't find any more bags of sand."

"But a necessary endeavour all the same," said James. "We need to establish whether what has happened to Miss Lloyd was an isolated case or part of a wider pattern."

"What a horrible job," said Inspector Ferguson with a tut and a shake of his head.

"I'm sure the cemetery staff will be able to help your men," said James. "Meanwhile, what of the medical schools? We should have each school of dissection checked for the body of Miss Lloyd."

"We should indeed."

"I'd be happy to enquire with the medical colleges if you're busy overseeing the exhumations, Inspector Ferguson," James volunteered.

The inspector gave a dry laugh. "I wonder who's got the rum job there!"

"How many schools of dissection are there in London, I wonder?" said James.

"Dr Kemp, the medical officer, might know," I suggested.

Dr Kemp told us more about the young lady whose body had been stolen.

"Miss Sarah Lloyd was a young lady of twenty-two. She was admitted to the workhouse two weeks ago," he said. "She was suffering from bronchitis when she arrived, and sadly her condition worsened. She was admitted to the infirmary three days ago, and we treated her as well as we could. However, her constitution had already been greatly weakened and unfortunately she died early yesterday evening.

"I certified that her death had been due to bronchitis, and the porters arrived with the shell, which they used to transport her to the dead house." He wiped his brow. "We followed the usual routine when someone dies, and I really can't understand how this has happened. How could someone just take her? And when I think of that girl's poor family... They shouldn't have removed the coffin lid, of course, but we should be grateful that they disobeyed our orders and did so, otherwise we never would have found this out, would we?"

"There's a possibility, then," I ventured, "that this has happened before?"

"Good grief, Miss Green, I would hope not! But when the coffin lids are nailed down as they are, and a bodysnatcher has the audacity to break into the dead house and open the coffins in that way... Yes, I suppose it could have happened before and we would have been none the wiser!"

The senior nurse, Miss Turner, joined us. Her eyes were

red, as if she had been crying. "It has upset us all deeply," she added. "Everybody who works here, and the inmates too."

"So despite the coffin lid being nailed down," said James, "the coffin was actually opened twice. Once by the person who took Miss Lloyd's remains and once by the family."

"That appears to be the case," replied Dr Kemp. "I must say that the family members of the deceased are usually a little upset that they are unable to see their loved ones for a final time, but the coffins have always been nailed shut for sanitary reasons. There is a large population of people here in a confined space, and I'm sure you don't need me to explain to you how swiftly disease can spread in such conditions, especially when many of the inmates are already in poor health. They're much more susceptible to it than other people. We have insisted on the coffins being sealed shut for some years now, but this is the first time I have ever known a family remove the lid themselves."

"A bodysnatcher, Dr Kemp, would have to be in league with a school of dissection, wouldn't you say?" I asked.

"No reputable medical school would conspire with the likes of bodysnatchers these days," he replied. "There's simply no need. An arrangement is in place to supply the medical schools, and I should add that this workhouse does not partake in it. Everyone receives a proper funeral and burial here."

"Is there any reason, other than dissection, why someone would steal a body?" I asked.

"I can think of no reason at all why anyone would wish to steal this poor woman's remains. But clearly someone had a reason, and it is the job of the police service to find it out."

"We'll need to check the records at the medical schools," said James. "Are you able to tell me how many there are?"

"I can't recall the number off the top of my head, but I can certainly list them for you," replied the doctor. "There's

St Bartholomew's, St Thomas's, Guy's, London Hospital College, St Mary's, Westminster, St George's, Charing Cross, Middlesex, King's College and University College. Not forgetting the Women's School of Medicine, of course."

"That's twelve altogether," said James once he had written them down. "We'll need to send officers to each of them."

"Aren't there also night schools?" I asked. "I'm sure Dr Macpherson at St Bartholomew's mentioned them."

"That's a good point," said the doctor. "I know of one in Holborn, which is run by Dr Clayton, but there may be others I don't know about. Do excuse the bluntness of what I'm about to say, Inspector, but your men will need to be quick if the body of Miss Lloyd is to be recovered in one piece."

"What about Mr Hicks, the undertaker?" I said to James once we had left the infirmary. "He visited the dead house and took away five coffins. Perhaps some of them were swapped around without Mr Plunkett realising."

"But the coffin with the bags of sand in had Miss Lloyd's name chalked on the side."

"Then the undertaker must have swapped her body for the bags of sand."

"You think the undertaker may be behind this?"

"He might be. If five coffins were removed that day there would have been some toing and froing, and general confusion. Perhaps the swap was carried out while that was going on? They could have removed Miss Lloyd in one of the coffins and those in charge would have been none the wiser. Do we know whether Mr Plunkett was present for the entire time the undertaker was there?"

"I can only assume that he was, but maybe he wasn't. He may have simply unlocked the door for the undertaker and then left him to it. After all, he presumably knows the undertaker and his men well as they visit the place every day."

"Which makes it more likely that he would have left them to get on with the job unhampered, doesn't it? If they turn up and do the same job every day, they would hardly require any supervision. I can imagine there are records to cross-check with each other, but nothing more than that."

James nodded. "It's the most likely explanation we have as to how Miss Lloyd's body was removed from the dead house. Any other form of removal would have aroused suspicion. It means that the undertaker would need to have brought a coffin with him to put Miss Lloyd in."

"Perhaps he did? And presumably it had the bags of sand inside which he swapped with her body."

"He was supposed to take away five coffins, and yet he left with six," pondered James. "It's possible isn't it?"

"An alternative method would be to have stolen her in the middle of the night."

"Working under the cover of darkness would have helped, but how did the culprits gain access to the dead house?"

"Perhaps they stole a key," I suggested.

"There are only two keys, apparently, and neither has been stolen."

"Perhaps Mr Plunkett colluded with the bodysnatchers."

"That's a possibility, isn't it?"

"He could have agreed to meet them at the dead house in the middle of the night and opened the door of the dead house for them. Or if she was taken by the undertaker, he could have overseen the swapping of her body for the bags of sand."

"He's certainly suspicious," said James. "And everything he has told us could be a fabrication. We'll need to question him further, along with Hicks and his men. They and Mr Plunkett were best-placed to carry out this crime."

CHAPTER 36

"The bodysnatchers have returned!" announced Edgar, his eyes opened dramatically wide. "I knew this would happen again someday."

"I don't believe there are any bodysnatchers," replied Frederick.

"Then who stole the body from the coffin?"

"Someone who wished to play a prank."

"What sort of prank?" asked Edgar.

"Oh, I don't know. Perhaps he planned to seat the poor deceased woman in a chair at his home, announcing to visitors that his wife is uncharacteristically quiet and asking whether they can spot anything the matter with her."

Edgar gave a laugh while I felt my stomach turn.

"That's a horribly disrespectful comment," I said.

"Stealing a woman from her coffin is disrespectful, Miss Green!" retorted Edgar. "Potter is only trying to make light of the situation. What I don't understand is how the chap got her out of there. Did he carry her out like a sack of potatoes? Surely that would have raised a few eyebrows?"

"Not if the theft was carried out at night," said Frederick. "Few people would have seen anything in the dark."

"I think she must have been removed in a coffin," I said, "in which case no one would have become suspicious."

"Who could get away with carrying a coffin out of the workhouse?" asked Edgar. "It's no easy task, and the perpetrator would have needed a horse and cart to transport it away. And not just any old cart either; it would have had to be a covered one or he soon would have been questioned by someone if he'd been travelling along Hoxton Street with a coffin bouncing about in his cart."

"The only person who could remove a coffin without being challenged is an undertaker," I said.

"Goodness, what a thought! Does that mean none of us is safe? It makes you wonder, doesn't it? How many undertakers are snatching away our bodies and replacing them with bags of sand?"

"Hopefully very few," I said.

"This is the problem with these new mortuaries they're building everywhere," said Edgar. "Once you're put in there, you're not safe, are you? One is far better off under one's own roof."

"And that is the usual practice for most people," I said. "It's only the poor and destitute who have no homes to rest in who end up in the dead house."

"And the undertaker helps himself to them," said Edgar, "like a hungry spider!"

"I would agree that the undertaker is a likely suspect," I said, "but there is no concrete evidence as yet, and we will have to let the police investigate. There's a good deal of work for them to do. The pauper burials in Tower Hamlets cemetery are being exhumed to find out whether any more coffins contain bags of sand. The staff at the workhouse are being questioned, as are the undertaker and his men. And the medical schools are also being visited by the police."

"Those doctors must take responsibility for this," said Edgar. "They demand bodies and feed on them like ghouls!"

"The students need to learn about anatomy," I said, "and they need to practise surgery. I can't say that I agree with the way the system operates, but I do recognise that doctors need to be properly trained. Even if Miss Lloyd's body happens to be discovered at one of the medical schools, it doesn't necessarily mean that the school is in the wrong. They may have bought her remains in good faith that all the correct procedures were followed."

Miss Welton entered the room and handed me a small parcel wrapped in newspaper. I felt a sinking sensation in my chest.

"I don't know who delivered this," she said, "but one of the compositors found it just inside the doorway downstairs. It has your name on it."

"I thought it might," I replied.

"Well, open it, Miss Green!" said Edgar excitedly.

"There's no need. It will be yet another malicious gift."

"Better than no gift at all!" joked Edgar.

"You do talk a lot of nonsense," I retorted.

"I don't understand," said Miss Welton. "A malicious gift?"

"Yes. Here, let me show you," I said, tearing off the paper, which happened to be from the previous day's *Morning Express*. "This will be an instruction book on the art of writing or journalism. The anonymous sender wishes to suggest that my skills in those areas are somehow deficient."

"That isn't particularly nice," commented Miss Welton.

I examined the green, leather-bound book in my hand. "*A Guide to the Profession of Writing*," I said. "Just as I thought."

"It's a nice-looking book," said Miss Welton.

"I suppose I should be flattered that my tormentor likes to spend his money on me."

I opened the book to see my name written on the title page, just as it had been in the previous two books.

"And you don't know who it's from?" said Miss Welton. "How very odd!"

There was a knock at the newsroom door and James walked in.

"Inspector Blakely!" announced Edgar. "What can we do for you? I'm assuming it's me you've come to speak to," he added with a wink.

"Of course, Mr Fish," replied James. "I've come to ask whether you've heard anything from the detective priest."

"There's a detective priest now? How exciting!"

"Have you heard anything from him?"

"Erm, no. I can't say that I have."

"I assume you're asking about Father Keane, James," I said with a smile.

"I am indeed, Penny."

"I haven't heard anything from him either, but we could call on him together and find out what he has learned."

I tucked the book into my carpet bag.

"The priest is actually a detective?" asked Edgar with a puzzled expression on his face.

"Not exactly," I said. "He's someone I asked to help with asking a few questions down at the workhouse."

"Fancy asking a priest to do your dirty work for you!" replied Edgar with a laugh. "Why haven't I thought of that before? I wonder whether I could ask Father O'Hallaghan at St Dominic's to write my dull article on the Afghan Boundary Commission!"

"How's the investigation progressing?" I asked James as we

climbed into a hansom cab on Fleet Street.

"Mr Plunkett, the dead house porter, has been questioned, as have all the staff in the workhouse. There was an interesting absentee, however."

"Who?"

"The workhouse clerk."

"Mr Lennox?"

"Yes. He hasn't been seen since the drama of yesterday evening, and when the constables called at his home this morning his wife informed them that he'd left town to attend to an aunt with a sudden illness."

"You know where he is, then?"

"Wales, it's believed. A telegram has been sent to a local police station, and we have two men journeying there as we speak."

"He must have had something to do with it! I never did like the man."

"It may just be coincidence that he's run off, Penny. But it's an interesting coincidence all the same. The facts we know so far are that Miss Lloyd died on the women's ward in the infirmary shortly before six o'clock that evening, then the porters placed her body in a shell and took her to the dead house. Mr Plunkett assisted them by placing her body in a coffin, which was nailed shut, and her name was chalked on the side. Mr Plunkett swears by his story, and there have been no inconsistencies in his retelling of events. If he is lying, he's quite accomplished at it."

"And the undertaker, Hicks?"

"Ferguson's men have spoken to him, and he seemed just as horrified as everyone else. He's incredibly upset by the suggestion that he might have had anything to do with it."

"Though that is exactly what a guilty man would say. The only way Miss Lloyd's body could have been removed from the dead house was in a coffin."

"We can't be sure about that. There appears to be a genuine horror among everyone we've spoken to about this terrible event. I think this is the action of just a select few; maybe only one or two people."

"And what of the medical schools?"

"Officers have visited five of the twelve so far, and unfortunately there has been no sign of Miss Lloyd's body nor a record in the dissection registers. There are seven more to visit, so there is still some hope that the body will be found. However, the medical schools are adamant that they operate within the formal agreements set up between the poor law unions and coroners for each district."

"There is also the possibility that Miss Lloyd's body is in Cambridge."

"I haven't ignored that possibility. I sent a telegram to the medical school there but haven't received a reply as yet."

"It's interesting, don't you think, that Shoreditch Poor Law Union has voted not to sell unclaimed bodies to medical schools? Yet having spoken to Dr Macpherson I know that there is plenty of competition among the medical schools for supply. Someone, perhaps Mr Lennox, has clearly been selling bodies regardless of the board's decision."

"Whether it's Mr Lennox or not, I think there can be little doubt that someone at Shoreditch Workhouse has struck up an arrangement with another party. Perhaps the arrangement hasn't been established with a medical school directly. It could have been set up with an undertaker. The men involved are effectively body dealers."

"Shoreditch Workhouse appears to be having more than its fair share of problems," I said. "They have to be connected, don't you think? There is no doubt in my mind that the bodies of Mr Connolly and Miss Lloyd have suffered the same fate. And then there are the murders of Mr Patten and Mr Walker."

"How can their murders be connected to the theft of corpses?"

"I'm not sure yet, but I feel certain that there has to be a link somewhere. Perhaps one or both of them knew something and the murderer wished to silence them."

"That's assuming your theory of a third person being involved is correct. At the moment there is little evidence to suggest that the two men did anything other than fight each other to the death."

"Perhaps the third person murdered them so their bodies could be sold?"

"I'd say that would be extremely unlikely. Don't forget that in the case of a suspicious death there is an inquest, which also involves a post-mortem examination. I cannot imagine the medical schools being interested in a body that has undergone a post-mortem."

"I see. Well, I also keep thinking about poor Bill, the young chap who died suddenly of heart problems in the night. I wonder what his fate was. Perhaps his body was unclaimed and subsequently sold."

"I suppose we would need to find out what the records say about him."

"Did you speak to that hopeless poor law inspector, Mr Weyland?"

"Yes I did, and he agreed to look into what had happened to Mr Connolly."

"Oh good! Thank you, James."

"And I should think his ears have pricked up even more now that we have the case of Miss Lloyd to investigate. There can be no doubt that there's something fishy going on. Did I see you with a book in your hand when I entered the newsroom? It's not another one of those anonymous gifts is it?"

"I'm afraid it is." I pulled the book out of my carpet bag and handed it to him. "Yet another mystery to solve."

CHAPTER 37

J ames and I disembarked from the cab outside St Monica's Church in Hoxton Square.

"What are you hoping Father Keane can tell us?" I asked.

"I'm just interested to hear whether he has come across anything useful. You asked him to find more witnesses to the murders in the stone-breaking yard, did you not?"

"Yes. I hope he's found someone who saw something."

"Maybe he can also help us with this latest incident."

Father Keane greeted us both with a wide smile as I introduced James. The priest led us into the vestry, which consisted of a small desk, a few chairs and a large mahogany wardrobe. He arranged the chairs in the centre of the room and we sat down.

"When we last spoke, Miss Green, we couldn't have possibly foreseen the dreadful incident that has occurred this week!" exclaimed the priest. "Horrific, isn't it? That poor woman and her family."

"It really is awful, and there is a great deal of work for Inspector Blakely and his colleagues to carry out now," I replied. "We wondered whether you'd found out anything that could help the investigations. I know I specifically asked you about the deaths of Mr Patten and Mr Walker, but it's possible that you may have uncovered something else as well."

"Possibly. Until now I have mainly been concentrating on the deaths in the stone-breaking yard, and I've had some interesting conversations with several inmates."

"What did they tell you?"

"Well, a few names were mentioned." Father Keane went to fetch a notebook from his desk and sat down again as he leafed through it. "There's no doubt that a few people passed that way at around the time of the men's deaths, which is rather unusual, don't you think, given that they failed to come forward as witnesses at the inquest?"

"I think Inspector Ferguson rushed his investigation a little," I commented.

"And sometimes people feel wary about speaking to police officers," added James. "They may consider a familiar friendly face such as yours, Father Keane, as more approachable."

"Thank you, Inspector," he replied with a smile. "I'll take that as a compliment."

"So who was near the stone-breaking yard at the time?" I asked.

"I found a man who said that he crossed the stone-breaking yard on his way to the coal store at about nine o'clock. His name is John Price."

"And what did he see?"

"Nothing."

"Did he have a lantern with him?"

"Yes, I believe so. He would have needed one to find his way across the yard in that darkness."

"And he presumably returned to the main block shortly afterwards," said James.

"Yes. He went to fetch a pail of coal."

"So Mr Price crossed the stone-breaking yard twice that evening," summarised James. "The first time at nine o'clock and the second time, walking in the opposite direction, a short while later."

"Yes. I suppose I should have asked him what time it was when he returned to the main block," said Father Keane. "I can only imagine that it was a short while later."

"So he didn't see anything out of the ordinary," said James, "but he must have passed quite close to where the men's bodies were lying by that stage."

"Fairly close, but the most direct route from the main block to the coal store is along one side of the yard. The two men were found on the other side of the yard, and Mr Price's route wouldn't have taken him near them. Had he diverted and searched about with his lantern a little he would have found them, I suppose. But he didn't because there was no need to, was there? He was merely there to fetch some coal, and it was a route he had taken many times before."

"The lanterns intrigue me," I said. "Mr Patten took a lantern out into the yard for him to work by, and Mr Walker also took a lantern with him. But by the time Horace looked out of the storeroom there was no sign of either lantern. He said that it was completely dark in the yard."

"And it was still dark in the yard at nine o'clock when Mr Price crossed it," added the priest.

"Mr Patten's lantern would presumably have had enough light in it for at least three hours, which was the amount of time the labour master had ordered him to work," I said. "Therefore, someone purposefully extinguished his lantern."

"He might have put it out himself," said Father Keane.

"But why would he do that?" asked James. "The man expected to work from eight o'clock until eleven o'clock that evening; that was what he had been instructed to do. If he did extinguish the lantern himself then we will need to consider why he would do such a thing."

"Mr Walker was seen entering the stone-breaking yard at a quarter past eight o'clock," I said. "And he also had a lantern with him. Did anyone see where he went after he left the main block?"

"I can't find anyone who saw him after he left the men's day room and stepped into the yard," replied the priest.

"But at ten minutes past eight the yard was in darkness," I said. "That's what Horace told me, at least."

"He may not be correct," said James.

"Let's assume for a moment that he is," I said. "It suggests that Mr Patten's lantern was extinguished within ten minutes of him beginning his work in the yard. Did he extinguish it because he knew Mr Walker was about to venture out into the yard?"

"How would he know that Mr Walker was about to appear?" asked James.

"Perhaps the two men had arranged to meet," I replied.

"It doesn't explain why Patten's lantern was extinguished," said James, "unless he somehow knew that Walker was going to be in the yard and was preparing to ambush him."

"Why would he do that?" I asked.

"I've no idea, Penny. I'm simply trying to weigh up all of the possibilities."

"I have found no evidence that Mr Patten and Mr Walker knew each other," said the priest. "In fact, I cannot find any suggestion of a friendship between the two men, and neither can I find any proof of a disagreement between them. So I can see no reason why they would arrange to meet in the stone-breaking yard, or why they would come to such severe blows with one another that they would both lose their lives."

"That's interesting to hear," said James. "An altercation as supposedly violent as theirs is likely to have followed a period of antagonism. Can no one bear witness to the fact that they might have had even a slight disagreement over something a few days previously? Is there no evidence that one bore a grudge against the other?"

"Nothing at all," replied Father Keane. "And I'm speaking from my own experience, too. I have witnessed a great number of disagreements during my visits to the workhouse, and I can tell you the names of the men who are most likely to cause trouble. Neither of these men struck me as violent or troublesome individuals. I'm aware that Mr Walker took to drink from time to time, but I cannot understand how or why he met his unfortunate end."

"So, we know that Mr Cricks, the labour master, left Mr Patten to get on with his work in the stone-breaking yard at eight o'clock," said James. "And by ten minutes past eight his lantern, for whatever reason, had been extinguished. Five minutes later Mr Walker set foot in the yard, and that was the last time anyone saw him alive. We know that his lantern was extinguished by nine o'clock, otherwise our new witness, Mr Price, would have seen it when he crossed the yard to visit the coal store.

"There is a possibility that some of the witness accounts are slightly inaccurate. Horace may have looked out a little later than he said and Mr Walker may have stepped into the yard a little earlier. This would allow for the possibility that the two men's lanterns were extinguished at the same time."

"By a third person," I said.

"A third person lurking in the yard without a lantern?" asked the priest.

"It's possible, I suppose," I replied. "But would he have extinguished the lanterns before or after he killed the men?"

"I struggle to believe either possibility," said James. "If he extinguished them before killing the men, how would he have done so without them being highly suspicious of his intentions? And how could he possibly have overpowered two men and murdered them using different methods in pitch darkness? Alternatively, would he have left two lanterns lit while he murdered both men and put himself at risk of being seen?"

"Perhaps there was more than one assailant," I suggested.

James sighed. "That might explain it, but I would prefer not to have to consider a second suspect. The coroner ruled that there were no suspects!"

"The coroner was mistaken," I said.

"If the men fought each other to the death," said the priest, "why would they have extinguished their lanterns? Surely their tempers would have been raging too much to concern themselves with whether the lanterns were lit or not."

"You're right," said James. "A man in a fit of temper would not have given it a moment's thought."

"And the witnesses who saw Mr Walker before he went out into the yard have told me that his mood was quite calm," said Father Keane. "He wasn't angry, and neither was he drunk. He must have had a very quick temper indeed to strike up such a quick and fatal argument with Mr Patten. Perhaps a strong gust of wind blew out the lanterns."

"We shouldn't dismiss that idea," said James. "Can anyone recall whether it was particularly windy that night?"

"There was a heavy frost the following morning," I said. "Am I right in thinking that frost doesn't settle so easily when there's a strong wind?"

"I think you're right, Penny. I believe a heavy frost is indicative of still conditions overnight. And I cannot recall any strong winds recently, though I could check that with the meteorological office." He opened his notebook and made a note of this.

"While I'm extremely grateful for all the help you've given

us, Father Keane," I said, "I feel that we are still no closer to the truth."

"Our conversation has convinced me that foul play was involved in the deaths of Mr Patten and Mr Walker," said James. "I have been wary of considering a third suspect for a while, but I'm more convinced of it than ever now, especially when we consider the other strange recent events at the workhouse. Something is very wrong indeed, and we need to find the people behind all this."

"Which is presumably why Mr Lennox has fled," I said.

"Has he?" asked Father Keane with surprise.

"He is ostensibly caring for an unwell aunt in Wales," said James, "but his disappearance does seem to be something of a convenient coincidence."

"It is," said Father Keane thoughtfully. "It very much is."

"Do any members of the workhouse staff strike you as suspicious, Father?" James asked him.

"Well no, they don't. Some have their foibles, of course, and I can't say that I have warmed to the master, Mr Hale. That's strictly between us, you understand. But I cannot imagine any staff member murdering inmates in the stone-breaking yard or stealing the bodies of poor, deceased inmates. That is truly barbaric, isn't it?"

"Well, someone is evidently doing it," replied James. "The question is, who?"

CHAPTER 38

"The whole business is simply dreadful," commented Eliza after I had updated her with recent events at Shoreditch Workhouse. "Mind you, we knew the place was dreadful, didn't we? It's so terribly sad that the poor are not being looked after properly."

We were sitting in Eliza's drawing room at her Bayswater home. We had both finished work for the day and a maid had just brought us a glass of sherry each.

"Anyway," continued Eliza, "I have decided that I should like to try to do something with regard to these places."

"Good for you, Ellie."

"The Paddington Union is about to elect its new board of guardians and I have applied for election."

"That's excellent news!"

"Well, I haven't been appointed as yet, and I'm not quite sure what I'm letting myself in for, but the West London Women's Society will be voting in my favour."

"As will I!"

"You don't live in the Paddington Union district, Penelope, so sadly you won't be able to vote."

"Oh yes of course. I do hope you get enough votes, Ellie!"

"My employer, Miss Barrington, has been extremely encouraging about it. As it's a role she has held in the past, she has plenty of advice to offer me."

"I'm sure you will do very well at it."

"Well, we shall see. I know that it can be a difficult job."

"Especially if Paddington has its own versions of Mr Buller and Mr Hale."

"I'm sure it will. But if I don't do something, nothing will ever change will it?"

"Very true, Ellie. I think it extremely admirable of you. Now, I must ask..." I lowered my voice in case any of the maids were in a position to overhear. "Have you found anything incriminating among George's letters and diaries?"

"Something that suggests infidelity you mean?"

"Yes! Was there anything of that nature?"

"Nothing." She gave a sigh. "Absolutely nothing at all. It appears that he has been wholeheartedly devoted to me throughout our marriage."

"Oh dear. Although that must have been nice to discover, it doesn't particularly help in terms of your divorce."

"It doesn't at all."

"I'm sure he would petition for divorce if you committed adultery."

"Oh, Penelope!" My sister's face flushed red. "We've already discussed this. It's unthinkable that I could conduct myself in such a manner!"

"If you say so, Ellie."

"But of course it is. What nonsense! Now then, have you received any more of those strange books?"

"Yes. I've had one more since I last saw you."

She shook her head in dismay. "James should do some-thing about it."

"I'm sure he would if I asked him to, but I think his time

is better spent trying to discover exactly what is happening at the workhouse."

"But this person's behaviour is sinister!"

"The very worst the culprit has done is gift me a few books. And I'm quite sure they won't send any more, because I think it must be someone from the workhouse. Mr Lennox, the clerk, is now in Wales and Mr Hale, the master, is now more preoccupied with saving his own skin than with trying to intimidate me."

"Well, I hope it's the end of it in that case, Penelope, but you must be careful. This whole affair could become quite malicious."

"Not if this person is a coward, and I suspect that he is. Anyway, I'm quite sure that I'll hear no more from him."

"I shall tell you whom I wish to hear from, and that's Francis. I am eager to hear whether he has recovered well and whether or not he has met with this European orchid grower. I feel as though we have been waiting years for news, and I'm beginning to worry that his mission to find Father has failed."

"I'm quite sure it hasn't failed, Ellie. We just have to be patient."

"But we've been patient for long enough!"

"He only left five months ago, and that really isn't long at all, especially when you consider that it takes a month for his letters to reach us."

"Telegrams are almost immediate, though, aren't they?"

"The cables have only been laid in the west of Colombia; you know that, Ellie. How can he possibly send a telegram if he's not in the west?"

"Oh, I don't know. He could despatch a messenger, perhaps."

"I'm sure he'll do so as soon as he has something significant to tell us."

My sister sighed. "Yes, you're right. I know he will. I

suppose I'm just waiting for something good to happen. It's rather silly of me, isn't it?"

"You're already making something good happen. You're about to be elected as a member of the board of guardians at the Paddington Union!"

She gave a coy smile. "Only if I get enough votes."

"You will, Ellie. I feel sure of it."

CHAPTER 39

A sullen Mr Hale admitted me and James at the workhouse door.

"May I respectfully remind you, Miss Green, of our last conversation?" he asked

"I recall it, Mr Hale," I replied. "You said that if you saw me here again you would make a complaint to the editor of my newspaper."

"I did indeed."

"In light of what has happened here, Mr Hale, I think the press are fully entitled to report on the matter," said James sternly. "Can you please take us to the stone-breaking yard? I should also like to speak to a man here named John Price. Do you suppose you could find him for us?"

"Of course," replied Mr Hale with a jut of his jaw.

The atmosphere at the workhouse seemed even more subdued than usual. Grey-uniformed inmates stared at us as they shuffled past.

"And once we've finished in the yard, we would like to look at the records in the clerk's office. Has there been any news on the whereabouts of Mr Lennox?" James asked the master as we strode along the covered walkway.

"Not yet, sir. But he has nothing to do with any of this business, I'm quite sure of it."

"His disappearance is purely coincidental, then?"

"He hasn't disappeared, Inspector. He is merely visiting his aunt."

"Well, our colleagues in Wales haven't been able to locate him yet."

A number of inmates were hard at work in the stone-breaking yard when we arrived.

"Can you please ask Mr Crick to halt work for a short while, Mr Hale?" asked James.

"Halt work?" the master retorted. "There are strict rules with regard to the hours the men must work!"

"I'm sure there are, Mr Hale, but a police investigation is currently being carried out at this workhouse, and we must ensure it is done as thoroughly as possible."

Mr Hale glanced around the yard then lowered his voice. "If your interest is in the deaths of Mr Patten and Mr Walker, that sorry incident is thankfully behind us," he hissed.

"There are some new developments to take into consideration, Mr Hale."

"Such as what, may I ask?"

"I'm sure you'll agree that it is a poor use of our time to be standing about here bickering, you are no doubt as keen as I am to understand what has been happening here over the past few months. Shall we just get on with it?"

I had to hide my mirth as Mr Hale opened his mouth to argue and then thought better of it.

"Right!"

He marched over to Mr Crick to pass on the instruction.

"The man cannot abide being told what to do, can he?" whispered James with a grin.

The order for an unscheduled break was accepted quite happily by the inmates, who strolled into the men's day room with a spring in their step. One of the men remained in the yard and was marched over to us by Mr Hale.

"This is Mr Price, Inspector," he said.

Mr Price was a dark-skinned gentleman with a lined face. Sporting thin grey hair and whiskers he looked to be about fifty, but I conjectured that he might have been younger.

James briefly introduced us. "I understand you crossed this yard on the night that Mr Patten and Mr Walker died."

"Yeah, but I ain't seen nuffink! And I didn't do nuffink."

Mr Hale gave a laugh. "I don't think this man will be of much help to you, Inspector."

"Actually he already has been," replied James. "Because the fact that he didn't see anything means that the lanterns must have been extinguished by the time he crossed the yard. What time did you walk through the yard, Mr Price?"

"Nine o'clock."

"And it was dark out here, was it?"

"Yeah."

"Did you have a lantern with you?"

"Yeah."

"But you didn't see anyone in this yard?"

"Nope."

"Not even Patten and Walker?" interjected Mr Hale.

"Interesting point, Mr Hale," said James. "Can you please show us where the bodies of Mr Patten and Mr Walker lay?"

Mr Hale walked off across the yard and we followed. Hammers and blocks of stone lay scattered on the ground in front of the iron grill. To the left of the grill were some smaller heaps of stone. Mr Hale stopped beside them.

"These are the stone heaps we use for the punishments,"

he said. "The inmate must shovel all the stone from one pile into another and then back again if necessary." He gave a smug smile.

"And where were the men found?" asked James.

"Here," he pointed at the ground.

"Where did Mr Patten lie?"

"Along here."

"And which way was his head facing?"

"Towards the stone heap."

Guided by James, Mr Hale went on to show us where Mr Patten had been lying on his back and where Mr Walker had lain close by on his left side. He also showed us where the shovel, empty pail and two extinguished lanterns had been found.

We surveyed the yard and could see that the coal store lay at the far corner. The door to the men's day room was in another corner on the same side of the yard as the coal store.

"Could you show us the route you took that evening, Mr Price?" asked James.

The inmate pointed to the door of the men's day room. "I came outta there an' walked along there." He gestured toward the side of the yard on which the coal store and storeroom lay. "Then I wen' in the coal store there."

"So your route took you nowhere near the location where we are standing now?"

Mr Price shook his head.

"Even with a lantern I don't think Mr Price would have been able to see Mr Patten and Mr Walker lying here," said James. "It's on the other side of the yard completely."

Mr Hale gave a shrug. "You'd have to visit again when it's dark and find out for yourself, Inspector."

"Indeed I could. The most interesting point, however, is that the yard was in darkness, and that means someone must have extinguished the lanterns of Mr Patten and Mr Walker.

Did you return to the men's block via the same route, Mr Price?"

The man nodded.

"Thank you for your help," said James. He stooped down to a crouch and began to examine the stone flags on the ground around him.

"What are you looking for?" I asked.

"I don't really know. Anything that looks out of place, I suppose. Am I right in thinking, Mr Hale, that most of the stone-breaking takes place in front of the iron grill?"

"That's right."

"So this area of the yard we're in now is mainly reserved for those serving out a punishment."

"That's right."

"And how often does someone have to serve a punishment here?"

"Every few days or so."

"Then I'm hoping the ground here wouldn't have had as much footfall as, let's say, the area of the yard where the stone-breaking takes place."

"No, not as much."

"I hope that means, then, that if something had been dropped during the struggle on that fateful night it might still be here."

"Surely Inspector Ferguson's men would have retrieved anything that had been dropped," I said.

"Ferguson told me nothing else was found, but I'm not sure how thoroughly they searched," replied James.

"I'm quite sure anything left here would either have been picked up or trodden into the dirt by now," I said.

"I suppose you may be right, Penny," he replied with a sigh. He edged forward and gently swept his gloved hand across the stone. "I can't see anything at all. Is this yard regularly swept, Mr Hale?"

"It's swept during the drier months when we don't want the dust to be blown about, but not usually at this time of year."

"So the yard hasn't been swept since the two men died?"

"No."

James rose to his feet and looked about him. "But it seems rather tidy," he commented.

I glanced around the yard and the storeroom caught my eye. It was then that I recalled seeing Horace pick something up from the ground.

"The windowsill in the storeroom," I said. "It's covered in all sorts of odds and ends. Things you might just find lying around."

"Is that so?" said James with interest. "Let's go and take a look."

"I wouldn't count on Horace being of any use," scoffed Mr Hale.

Ignoring this comment, James and I began to walk toward the storeroom.

"Can the inmates resume their work now, Inspector?" he called after us.

"Of course," replied James over his shoulder. "And thank you for speaking to me, Mr Price!" Then he turned to face me. "Now you mention it, Penny, I can remember a good deal of clutter on that windowsill. The trouble is, even if Horace picked up something that happened to be connected to these deaths, how can we prove such a thing?"

"Let's see what he has and take it from there."

The storeroom door was closed. James knocked and we waited until we heard the slide of a bolt. The door opened slightly and the young man's cross-eyed face appeared in the gap. He looked James up and down, then opened the door wider, as if worried that he would find himself in trouble if he failed to comply with a police officer.

"Hello again, Horace," said James. "Do you remember me?"

Horace nodded.

"Miss Green and I wondered whether you picked up anything in the yard after Mr Patten and Mr Walker sadly lost their lives there. Do you remember finding anything?"

Horace shrugged.

"I can't help but notice all the things you have on the windowsill here," said James. "Are these the items you've picked up from the yard?"

"Yeah." Horace gave a faint smile, as if he were proud of his collection.

"Is there anything among them that you picked up from the yard after the two men died?"

Horace shrugged again, and I felt my teeth clench with frustration.

James managed to maintain his patient demeanour. "Would you mind if Miss Green and I took a look at these items?"

Horace gave another shrug, which did nothing to indicate whether he objected or not. James and I stepped further into the room and began to look at everything it contained.

Dust, deceased insects and cobwebs gave an indication of how long some of the items had been sitting there, but others appeared to have been added more recently. A round brass snuff box caught my eye, as it appeared to have been set slightly apart from the other items and was completely free of dust. I picked it up and rested it in the palm of my hand.

"Where did you find this, Horace?" I asked.

To my disappointment he shrugged again. I wondered if Mr Patten or Mr Walker had owned it, and whether it had fallen out of a pocket. *Or perhaps it had belonged to their assailant.* I turned the snuff box over to see whether there were any initials inscribed upon it. There were none, but as I turned it I felt something moving about inside. I opened the box.

I hadn't in any way been prepared for what I found inside. There were countless miniature vials, except they weren't made from glass. Instead, they were soft to the touch.

"Gelatine capsules?" said James, sounding puzzled. "Do they have anything in them?"

"Some are a little crushed, so it's hard to tell," I replied. "Others have broken, but some have what appears to be a brown powder inside them."

Some of the light brown powder had collected at the bottom of the snuff box.

"Do you know what these are?" James asked Horace.

"No," he replied.

"You don't know what the powder they contain might be?"

"I dunno."

"A type of medicine maybe?"

"Don't touch them, Penny," instructed James. "We need to find out what that powder is first. Where did you find these, Horace?"

"All over the place."

"In the yard?"

He nodded.

"Elsewhere in the workhouse?"

He nodded again.

"So not just in the yard, but in other parts of the workhouse too?"

Horace gave another nod. I closed the snuff box and passed it to James.

"We're just going to borrow this for a short while," said James. "I'll return the snuff box to you when we've finished with it. Is that all right?"

Horace nodded. Then he reached over to the windowsill

and picked up a small button and gave it to me. It looked to be made of black glass and appeared fairly unremarkable.

"Thank you, Horace," I said. "From the size of this I would guess it has come from a cuff or a waistcoat. What do you think, James?"

"It may well have done. It's interesting because, given that the inmates wear a uniform, I imagine this must have once belonged to a member of staff. Where did you find this, Horace?"

"In the yard."

"Thank you. We'll look after this as well for now. Is that all right?"

Horace nodded once again.

CHAPTER 40

"This goes some way to solving the mystery!" proclaimed Dr Kemp as he examined the gelatine capsules inside the snuff box.

"What mystery?" I asked.

"We had some medicines stolen from the infirmary about six weeks ago."

"What sort of medicines?"

"A bottle of chloroform, another of morphine and some aconitine capsules."

"These are the aconitine, are they?"

"Yes. Where did you find them?"

"On the windowsill of the chap who looks after the storeroom in the stone-breaking yard."

"So he's the thief, then!"

"No, I don't think he is, Dr Kemp," I said. "Horace appears to collect things he has picked up from the ground. Some of the capsules in this snuff box are crushed and broken, which suggests that he found them lying around. There was no sign of a jar of capsules in the storeroom; nor did I see a jar of chloroform or morphine."

"Neither did I," added James. "Although they might be hidden in there. We weren't really looking for them, were we? I think we should search the storeroom properly."

"I don't think Horace can be the thief," I said. "I should think the only capsules he has are the ones he has found. It seems that not only did someone steal your medicines, Dr Kemp, but that they have also been using them."

"What is aconitine used for?" James asked.

"I put it in a liniment and apply it to the skin," replied the doctor. "It's extremely effective in treating neuralgia and rheumatism. A very small amount can also be used to cure a fever."

"But why would anyone steal it?" James asked.

"I have no idea. If the thief had no medicinal knowledge, which is quite likely, I expect they simply saw an opportunity to take it and did so. Though someone with a knowledge of medicines might have had a more specific purpose in mind."

"The fact that Horace found the capsules suggests that the medicines have remained within the workhouse," I said. "But there can't be many people in the workhouse with medical knowledge, can there?"

"I suppose there is always the possibility that someone who has worked as a physician and fallen on hard times could have been admitted to the workhouse," said Dr Kemp, "but that would be uncommon. I should think it more likely that someone has stolen the medicines without understanding their purpose."

"But what might they be using them for?" asked James. "Treating neuralgia?" He gave a laugh.

"There is a more sinister side to aconitine, I'm afraid," said Dr Kemp. "You may have heard of its other names: monkshood or wolfsbane. It's a deadly poison."

"Oh dear," replied James. "Then we don't want it falling

into the wrong hands, do we? Though it's possible the thief hasn't realised that it can be used as a poison."

"But what about the broken capsules?" I said. "Someone could be poisoned by accident."

"There has been no word of such a thing as yet," replied the doctor.

"What are the symptoms?" asked James.

"They begin with a burning sensation on the tongue," replied Dr Kemp, "which is followed by a numbness of the throat and mouth. The victim then becomes dizzy and weak, and struggles to breathe."

"How horrible." I gave a shudder.

"Does the person ever recover?" asked James.

"I'm afraid not. Death inevitably occurs within a few hours."

"Goodness," I said. "Then it is fatal every time?"

"With a dose of a certain size it is, yes. And the dose doesn't have to be large. I use only a very small amount when treating fever, and I'm extremely careful with the liniment, too."

"So when aconitine finds itself in the wrong hands it can be very dangerous indeed," commented James. "Weren't you extremely concerned when you discovered that your aconitine was missing?"

"Yes, very! I alerted all members of staff here at the workhouse, and thorough searches were carried out, but there was no sign of it until you discovered these capsules. We didn't tell the inmates about the theft as we were concerned that someone with malicious intent might lay ahold of them."

"Thankfully no one has been poisoned yet," I said, "but all the missing medicine must be found as a matter of urgency."

James gave a deep sigh. "Along with everything else we have to do."

"It is a worry, Inspector," said Dr Kemp. "The staff and I

will keep looking for it. The fact that no one has been poisoned yet suggests that the jar may lie undisturbed somewhere, hidden away."

"But what of the capsules Horace found?" I asked.

"There aren't too many of them, fortunately. Perhaps the jar was dropped somewhere and some fell out."

"Right, well, thank you for your help, Dr Kemp," said James. "We had better continue with our investigations. I'll ask Inspector Ferguson and his men to keep an eye out for the stolen medicines as they continue to search the workhouse."

We looked through the admissions records for the casual wards in the clerk's office.

"I see the entry for you and Eliza here, Penny," said James with a smile. "So who are we looking for? Bill?"

"Yes. I'm sure that's what his friends said his name was."

"There's a William Sawyer recorded as having stayed that evening," stated Mr Hale. He pointed a bitten fingernail at the record.

"I suppose that must be him," I said. "Is there no one named Bill listed for that evening?"

The master shook his head.

"No one by the name of Billy? Or another William?"

Mr Hale shook his head again. "I can't see one. Mr Sawyer is most probably the man you're enquiring about."

I examined the record. William Sawyer was listed as a single man born in 1860, and his calling was that of a labourer. Under the column for the nearest relation was written the word 'none'.

"No known family," I commented, "just like Joseph Connolly. And Lawrence Patten, too. Do you have Mr Sawyer's death record, Mr Hale?"

"That would be written in here," he replied sullenly, pushing a book across the desk to us. It was the same book Mr Lennox had shown me when I had asked to see the record of Joseph Connolly's death. The record for William Sawyer stated that he had died of heart failure and was buried in Tower Hamlets Cemetery.

"Exactly the same as Joseph Connolly's record," I said. "But can we be certain that William Sawyer was buried at Tower Hamlets Cemetery? Or might his remains have vanished as well?"

"You'll have to enquire with the cemetery," replied the master.

"I'd like to enquire with your clerk," said James. "The man who writes down these records and is currently in Wales."

"I'm happy to do all that I can to help, Inspector," replied Mr Hale. "But if Mr Lennox is otherwise engaged, I'm afraid there isn't a great deal I can do about it."

"You will let me know as soon as you hear from him, won't you, Mr Hale?"

"But of course."

We were interrupted by a knock at the door, whereupon Inspector Ferguson and two of his men entered.

"Apologies for the interruption, Inspector Blakely," Inspector Ferguson said.

"We've just finished making our enquiries here," replied James.

I had hoped to examine the workhouse records in more detail but realised the police had urgent work to be getting on with.

"Good. Then hopefully Mr Hale can answer a few questions for me."

The beleaguered-looking workhouse master slumped into the clerk's chair and gave a weary sigh.

"The master seems absolutely ready for you," said James with a smile.

"Good. You're more than welcome to remain present, Inspector Blakely, while I speak to Mr Hale. In fact, you might be interested to hear what my men have discovered at Tower Hamlets cemetery."

"Which is what?"

"Ten empty coffins!"

"*Ten?*"

"Not completely empty, I should add."

"Sandbags?"

"Yes. Two in each one. It's rather an interesting operation you're running here, Mr Hale."

CHAPTER 41

T errible Scandal at Shoreditch Workhouse

Allegations are circulating that the bodies of paupers who have died at Shoreditch Workhouse are being disposed of for the purpose of dissection. The board of guardians had previously claimed that all bodies, whether unclaimed or not, are buried in Tower Hamlets Cemetery.

The recent theft of the corpse of Miss Sarah Lloyd, a woman aged twenty-two who died in the workhouse infirmary, prompted the police to investigate the possibility of further wrongdoing.

It has previously been reported that the family of another deceased inmate, Mr Joseph Connolly, had been unable to find a record of his burial at Tower Hamlets Cemetery. There is a growing suspicion that Mr Connolly's corpse has also been stolen.

Shocking scenes were witnessed at Tower Hamlets Cemetery this week as police constables, working under the direction of Inspector

Ferguson of Commercial Street station, assisted with the exhumation of a great number of paupers' coffins. Upon examination, it was discovered that ten of the exhumed coffins contained sandbags in place of bodies. The total number of paupers' bodies unaccounted for currently stands at twelve.

Two arrests have been made: the first is undertaker Mr Harry Hicks, who is suspected of conveying the bodies to a school of anatomy instead of to the burial ground. The second is Mr Simon Hale, the master of the workhouse. The clerk of the workhouse, Mr John Lennox, who is believed to have made a sudden departure to Wales, is currently being sought. It is suspected that all three men have received payment in exchange for the supply of corpses for dissection. An inquiry is to be opened by the poor law inspector, Mr Arthur Weyland.

"It's all a bit of a shambles, isn't it?" commented Mr Sherman as he read through my latest report.

"Ten empty coffins!" exclaimed Edgar with a grin. "Who'd have thought that? And there must be more, mustn't there?"

"I truly hope not," I said glumly.

"Ten missing bodies," said Frederick. "And all sold for dissection, we presume? Someone's been earning some decent money."

"Eleven missing bodies if you include Miss Lloyd," I added. "And twelve if you include Mr Connolly, who remains unaccounted for. There was no record of him at the cemetery, so he probably wasn't even honoured with a sandbag-filled coffin."

"I don't understand, though," said Edgar. "Why fill a coffin with sandbags?"

"Because the body's been taken," replied Frederick, "so the weight of the body is replaced by the sandbags. An empty coffin is likely to arouse suspicion when lifted, isn't it?"

"But there's no record of the Connolly chap being buried, so why wasn't he gifted a sandbag-filled coffin?" asked Edgar.

"They presumably didn't bother because he apparently had no close relatives," I said. "There was no one to miss him, so they didn't even perform a common funeral."

"Except that his family did miss him."

"Yes. In Mr Connolly's case it just so happened that they did. And despite Shoreditch Union agreeing not to sell unclaimed bodies, I suspect someone at the workhouse has been doing it anyway. In those cases the bodies have most likely been taken directly to the medical school, and a misleading note has been entered into the workhouse records that the individual was buried at the cemetery."

"And the sandbags?" asked Edgar.

"I think they have only been used in instances when the deceased had known relatives. The funeral will have been carried out with the family's involvement, and no one will have been aware that the body was replaced with sandbags. That's obviously what has happened with poor Miss Lloyd. I feel terribly sad for the families of those who were supposed to have been buried in the cemetery but have found that the coffins were empty."

"Do they even know who's who? The coffins are piled on top of each other in those common burials, aren't they?"

"The names are chalked on the side of each coffin. I'm not sure how long the chalk remains there; perhaps it fades once the coffin has been in the damp ground for a while. It's possible that the police have been able to make a note of all the names on the coffins."

"But why take the risk of replacing the bodies with sandbags?" asked Edgar. "Surely the scheme was bound to be discovered before long."

"Plain old greed," I replied. "The medical schools are competing with one another for bodies. Someone at the workhouse clearly saw an opportunity to make a bit of money for themselves."

"Some people have no scruples," said Edgar with a sigh.

"I'm afraid they don't, Fish," said Mr Sherman. "Laws were put in place to prevent this sort of thing from happening, but the unscrupulous always manage to find a way round these things."

"Except this time their actions have been discovered," I said.

"And they've been rightly arrested," added Edgar. "The case is resolved!"

"I only wish it were that simple," I replied.

⚜

"Miss Lloyd's body has been found," announced James when I met him at the workhouse.

We were standing in the administration block where I was hoping to examine the workhouse records more closely.

"What excellent news!" I felt my heart lift. "That's the best news we've heard in a long time. Where was she found?"

"At St Bartholomew's Medical School."

"Really?"

"We assumed she had been taken to a school of dissection, didn't we?"

"Yes, but could Dr Macpherson have been involved?"

"Hicks the undertaker relented in the end. He told us he had taken her body and sold it to Dr Macpherson."

"But the doctor doesn't seem the type to do business with that kind of man. Dr Macpherson is a perfectly pleasant gentleman. He probably trusted Hicks for some reason. I don't know why he would, but he must have done."

"Miss Lloyd's body has been returned to her family now. I

can see that you're feeling uneasy about asking your next question, Penny, but I can reassure you before you ask it that she is still in one piece."

"Goodness, that's fortunate."

"Apparently, she had been admitted under a false name that Hicks had devised. Her parents were taken to see the body and confirmed that it was that of their daughter."

"Her poor family," I said. "So when Hicks visited the dead house he must have brought a coffin containing two sandbags in with him, then switched Miss Lloyd's body with the sandbags."

"He must have done. Ferguson's men are still questioning him, so hopefully he'll be able to explain how he has gone about it all."

"So Plunkett, the dead house warden, had nothing to do with it?"

"He claims not to have, though there is a distinct possibility that he was paid to turn a blind eye."

"It's dreadful, it truly is. And to think of all the people who knew about it! Mr Hale and Mr Lennox are surely involved, too."

"We can't be certain of that yet. Ferguson has arrested Hale, as he feels certain that this simply cannot have taken place without him knowing about it. And Lennox has implicated himself by running away. He'll be arrested as soon as he's found, but there's always a slim possibility that he's innocent."

"Who is in charge of the workhouse now?" I asked.

"I understand that Mrs Hodges is acting as both master and matron. Mrs Hale is said to be too upset about her husband's arrest to continue in her role as matron for the time being."

"I cannot say that I ever warmed to the Hales or to Mr

Lennox, but discovering that Dr Macpherson had something to do with this came as quite a surprise."

"There's no evidence that he has done anything wrong just yet, Penny. He may have bought Miss Lloyd's body from Mr Hicks in good faith."

"I wonder whether he has bought many others from Hicks."

"That's a good question. Whether the other missing corpses ended up there or elsewhere is something we will need to uncover."

"I should like to look at the records in a moment and make a note of all the people without any known relatives who have died at the workhouse recently. I think it will be interesting to get an idea of the numbers."

"Here comes Father Keane," said James.

I turned to see the boyish-faced priest approaching us. He greeted us solemnly.

"The inmates are terribly upset about this business," he said. "Many of them are understandably worried that they'll be headed for the dissection table the moment they die!"

"You can reassure them of the fact that it won't be anyone's fate from now on," replied James. "We've made arrests and all of the burials should take place just as they should in future."

"I shall do my best to tell them that," he replied, "but I sympathise with them."

"I sympathise too," I said. "Many of the people here have so little control over their destiny."

"What else can I do to assist with the investigation?" asked Father Keane.

"Now that there's a proper police investigation underway we have a good few men to assist," said James. "Thank you for the help you have given us. It has served to convince me that a third person is behind the deaths of Mr Patten and Mr Walker."

"Did you speak to Mr Price?"

"We did indeed."

"And we are no closer to discovering what happened to them," I added.

"There is, perhaps, another mystery you can help us with, Father," said James. "Dr Kemp told us some medicines were stolen from the infirmary approximately six weeks ago. I don't suppose you've come across them or heard anyone talking about them?"

"No, I can't say that I have. What sort of medicines?"

"Chloroform, morphine and a jar of aconitine capsules. Apparently, aconitine can be dangerous if it falls into the wrong hands. It's a deadly poison."

"Oh goodness." His eyes widened. "And you think it's somewhere here in the workhouse?"

"Horace from the storeroom picked up a few capsules he had found," I said. "They were mostly damaged and contained little of the powder."

"It's fortunate that he hasn't poisoned himself, in that case."

"Indeed. And thankfully it seems no one else has been poisoned either," I said. "But the medicines do need to be recovered."

"We shall look for them, of course," said James. "But an extra pair of eyes would be a great help."

"I would be very happy to help, Inspector."

"Thank you, Father."

"I'll let you know as soon as I uncover anything."

The priest went on his way and James and I climbed the staircase to the clerk's office.

"Do the deaths of Mr Connolly and Mr Sawyer seem rather similar to you?" I asked. "They were both the same age and each died of heart failure. And neither claimed to have any relatives when they were admitted. And come to think of it, neither did Mr Patten! Doesn't that strike you as odd?"

"Mr Patten's death was quite different," said James. "The poor chap was strangled."

"Even if we consider only the deaths of Connolly and Sawyer, you must admit that there are similarities?"

"There certainly are."

"And heart failure as a cause of death? In a young man?"

"It's not unheard of."

"But it would be more common in an older man, wouldn't you say?"

"Yes, I would definitely say so, Penny. But if their deaths were suspicious there would have been a police investigation and an inquest."

"Can we be certain of that? We're discussing the lives of the destitute here, and they are simply not considered to be as important as you and me."

"Even if that's the case, Penny, there can be no doubt that the police and the coroner take as much interest in the death of a poor man as a rich man."

"If someone died suspiciously in a workhouse," I ventured, "who would alert the authorities?"

"The master, I suppose. That's what Mr Hale did when he found Patten and Walker in the stone-breaking yard."

"But what if the suspicious death wasn't obviously suspicious?"

"Then I suppose no one would be any the wiser! What point are you making here, Penny?"

"Someone could have murdered those men in a way that made it seem as though they had an illness. Dr Kemp would have admitted them to the infirmary none the wiser and done his best to treat them. He would have failed, of course, because the fatal act would already have been carried out."

"Poison?"

"Exactly! I think the aconitine may have been used after all but nobody has realised it until now."

"Apart from the murderer." James gave this some thought. "It's an interesting theory. And when the men were unwell in the infirmary, their symptoms would have been mistaken for something else. Heart failure in this instance."

"And there was no inquest or post-mortem because their deaths were never deemed to be suspicious."

"And then their bodies were sold to the undertaker." James shook his head. "This could be even more macabre than we first thought."

"And if Mr Hale is the murderer, he would never have alerted the authorities would he?"

"He did in the case of Patten and Walker, presumably because word had already spread about what had happened. It couldn't exactly be covered up, could it?"

"But he was able to convince the police that the men had killed one another in a fight," I said.

"Was it him who suggested it? We would have to check that with Inspector Ferguson."

"I certainly remember Hale stating so at the inquest. He said that he was sure the men had come to blows because he had warned Walker about fighting in the past."

"So you think that Hale influenced the outcome of the inquest?" he asked.

"A coroner who was doing his job properly shouldn't allow it, but you know how I feel about that particular inquest. And he probably convinced Ferguson the same facts, which explains why his men didn't carry out a thorough investigation. They were convinced that they knew what had happened there."

"At least Hale has been arrested now. It'll be interesting to find out how he has been answering Ferguson's questions. It's even more important that the aconitine is found as soon as possible now, as it could lead us straight to the murderer. I'll make sure we have enough men assisting Father Keane."

CHAPTER 42

A police constable sat in the clerk's office looking through a pile of papers.

"Good afternoon," said James. "Miss Green would like to have a look at some of the records."

The constable nodded in reply.

I found the workhouse admissions book and sat down opposite the constable as I started leafing through it.

"You intend to write down the name of every inmate with no apparent relatives?" James asked.

"Yes, and then I plan to check the list against the death records. Anyone who died without any known relatives may have been sold."

James grimaced. "Well, I'm off to locate Ferguson to find out how his work is progressing. Oh, good afternoon, Mrs Hodges."

The poor law guardian marched into the room and stood staring at me, her eyes narrowed above her pointed nose.

"It is not appropriate for a news reporter to be in this room," she said.

"This is the third time I've visited this room," I replied

breezily. "I'm making a note of the names of all the inmates who died with no known relatives, as it is highly likely that their bodies were sold."

"Highly *un*likely, I should say! The board of guardians voted to—"

"I realise that," I interrupted. "But bodies have been sold regardless of what the board of guardians agreed upon. I'd say that the board has been completely undermined, wouldn't you?"

"What nonsense. And as I said, you have no business being here!"

"What do you know of Dr Macpherson, Mrs Hodges?" asked James.

His unexpected question left her turning her head back and forth between us. "Why would you ask that? What does he have to do with anything?"

"Do you know who he is?" James continued.

"I'm not sure. I think I've heard his name before, but I can't seem to place it."

"You've heard of the medical school at St Bartholomew's Hospital, have you not?"

"Of course I have, Inspector, there's no need to patronise me."

"Dr Macpherson instructs the students there in human anatomy."

"Oh yes. I know who you mean now."

"Have you ever seen him at this workhouse?"

"Why would he be visiting this workhouse?"

"Please answer my question, Mrs Hodges. We're asking the same question of Mr Hale, and we shall ask it of Mr Lennox when we finally catch up with him. If all the staff members answer truthfully your replies will be consistent, don't you agree?"

Mrs Hodges wavered a little before replying, as if she

were trying to avoid being caught out. "Yes, I think he has visited this workhouse before."

"You *think* it, or you know it for sure?"

"I have seen him here, yes."

"Did anyone accompany him?"

"Mr Hale, who I'm sure will be able to tell you much more."

"Have you ever spoken to Dr Macpherson yourself?"

"Once or twice as a passing greeting, but never more than that. I have never held a conversation with him."

"Thank you, Mrs Hodges. I think I had better go and see what the doctor has to say for himself. Would you like to come along, Penny?"

"Yes I would. I shall look at these records again later."

❦

"To say that I am completely horrified would be a huge understatement," said Dr Macpherson when we reached his office.

A heavy shower of sleet lashed against the large window-pane and obscured the view.

"And as soon as we realised the poor young lady was on our premises here at the medical school we did all we could to have her body returned to her family."

"Thank you for being so cooperative," said James. "I know that the recovery of Miss Lloyd's body has been of great comfort to her family. Can I ask how long you have been dealing with Mr Hicks the undertaker?"

"Well, let's see. It must be a few years now," replied the doctor, gesturing for us both to take a seat at his desk. "It was Mr Barnes that I first spoke to about acquiring corpses for our school of anatomy." He sat down behind his desk.

"Mr Barnes is an undertaker?"

"A funeral furnisher," I corrected.

"Ah yes, I remember you saying now," said James. "And Mr Barnes introduced you to Mr Hicks, Dr Macpherson?"

"He did indeed. I must say, Inspector, that this entire system is clearly laid out in the Anatomy Act, and we follow it to the letter. And while dissection is an essential part of a medical student's education, I am only too aware that the topic does not sit well with the minds of the general public. It would be most foolish of me to risk the purchase of stolen corpses. And there is no need to, in fact, as we are well provided for by the Anatomy Act."

"The right to dissect the bodies of unclaimed paupers?" said James.

"That's correct. And Miss Green is well acquainted with how it all works, as per our previous conversation." He gave me a smile.

"You say that your medical school is *well provided for*," I said, "but is that actually true? In our previous conversation you implied that acquiring corpses for dissection was quite difficult, and that there is significant competition between the medical schools for them. So much so, in fact, that the chap at Cambridge has bodies brought to him from a number of locations on the so-called dead train."

Dr Macpherson cleared his throat as he considered this. "It's true that we could benefit from a greater supply of bodies, Miss Green, but when I state that we are *provided for*, I mean that the Anatomy Act makes provision for us."

"What do you know of Mr Hicks?" James asked.

"The man profits from the dead," replied the doctor with a bemused smile. "That fact is not likely to win him much admiration from anyone, is it? But it's the same tale with all these men, whether they're lofty funeral furnishers or lowly coffin makers."

"Have you ever heard that he might be guilty of stealing corpses?"

"No, of course not! Do you think I would continue to deal with such a man, Inspector?"

"We've discovered more empty coffins," replied James. "They contain sandbags and were buried at Tower Hamlets cemetery. Hicks is currently under arrest and is not only being questioned about the theft of Miss Lloyd's remains but also the theft of many others. Are you quite sure you had no idea that this was taking place?"

"I've heard of this sort of thing happening, if that's what you mean, Inspector. But I would certainly never be involved in any such thing myself. I have the reputation of one of the finest medical schools in the country to protect! I cannot deny that these nefarious corpse stealers exist, but I would have nothing to do with them. The purchase of Miss Lloyd's remains was an extremely regrettable incident, and I can only hope that the medical school has redeemed itself by co-operating with the police so promptly. I should add, Inspector, that Mr Hicks had all the necessary paperwork in place, just as he always did. I have since learned that he changed Miss Lloyd's name, and I must say that the manner in which the fraudulent paperwork was produced is really rather clever."

"Is it possible that he had sold you stolen corpses before without you being aware of it?" asked James.

"I should hate to think so! But could I lay my hand on a Bible and swear that he hasn't? Unfortunately, I don't think I could. As I have already stated, Mr Hicks provided impeccable paperwork when we conducted the transaction regarding Miss Lloyd's corpse, and I only suspected that something was awry when we heard the story of her missing body. I am only too glad that we were able to rectify the situation.

"You and your men are quite at liberty to examine everything we have here. You may explore our records and visit the dissecting room if you so wish. We have nothing to hide, and my only regret is that I ever trusted Mr Hicks. That is also my greatest crime."

I thought of Connolly and Sawyer, and how their supposed deaths from heart failure could actually have been a product of poisoning.

"If someone had died of poisoning and been sold to your medical school," I asked Dr Macpherson, "would the cause of death be obvious when the body was dissected?"

"It would depend on what the poison was, Miss Green," he replied. "Some poisons leave more of a trace than others. On the whole, however, I would say that signs of poisoning would not be strikingly obvious to our students. Most of the cadavers are dismembered quite soon after being admitted here, and the students tend to concentrate their study on particular body parts."

"So it's possible that a victim of poisoning could go unde-tected in a school of dissection?"

"I sincerely hope that a victim of poisoning would not find its way here, and would instead be subject to a thorough inquest, including a post-mortem!"

"But if it did," I ventured. "The cause of death wouldn't necessarily be noticed, would it?"

"It might not be, but this is becoming rather a hypothet-ical conversation."

"Not necessarily," I replied. "I can think of two men who may have been poisoned whose bodies were sold for dissection."

"Well that is dreadful indeed! I sincerely hope that the men behind this vile act will soon be caught. Do you have proof that this has happened?"

"Not yet," replied James. "It's a theory we're working on at present. Have you ever visited Shoreditch Workhouse?"

"Oh yes, a number of times."

"May I ask why?"

The doctor gave a sigh. "For the same reason that I visit all workhouses. We have to do what we can to acquire cadavers for the medical school. I'm only too aware that the Shoreditch Union chooses not to sell unclaimed bodies and to bury them instead. I'll freely admit that I have visited on one or two occasions and politely requested that the policy be reviewed, but the poor law guardians are quite steadfast and I respect their decision. Please rest assured, Inspector, that all of my work is carried out to the letter of the law."

CHAPTER 43

"We're within the jurisdiction of the City of London police here," said James as we left the medical school. "I need to call in at Old Jewry to request their help in examining the records at the medical school and in ascertaining whether Dr Macpherson has committed any wrongdoing."

"Do you think that he has?"

"I struggle to believe that he had no idea Mr Hicks was up to no good. Just a quick glance at that undertaker suggests that he is capable of criminal behaviour, don't you think?"

"Oh, I don't know, I prefer not to judge whether someone is a criminal or not based on their appearance," I said with a smile.

James laughed. "How worthy of you, Penny! As do I, as a rule. A police officer cannot be too quick to judge or make up his mind about someone. However, Dr Macpherson is an intelligent man, and I think his proclaimed innocence has more to do with turning a blind eye than anything else. Your impression, when you first spoke to him, Penny, was that he was quite desperate to source unclaimed corpses, was it not?"

"Yes. It seems as though all the medical schools are."

"Before I go to Old Jewry, then, I should like to take a quick detour."

We walked north through the hospital grounds, sheltering from the sleet beneath James' umbrella. We passed Smithfield market and then turned right into the pleasant green of Charterhouse Square, beyond which lay the Tudor Charterhouse buildings with their pointed gables and mullioned windows. Once a medieval priory, the site was now home to a school.

Once we had crossed Goswell Road, however, we found ourselves in a very different place from the peaceful cloisters of Charterhouse. Tall, narrow buildings cast their shadows over a maze of narrow streets, where a layer of white sleet was quickly turning a dirty brown. The sound of hammers and saws from the workshops joined the cacophony of shouts from street traders and dirty-faced children, all of whom were keen to encourage passers-by to part with their precious coins.

"I've been meaning to ask," said James. "Have you received any more of those books wrapped in newspaper?"

"Thankfully, not since the *Guide to the Profession of Writing* was delivered to the office. I think Mr Lennox must have been behind it, as I don't think I've received one since he ran off to Wales."

"Are you quite sure of that?"

"Yes. I think the sender must have other things to worry about now."

"Let's hope so."

We stopped at a lodging house that was advertising a night's stay for a mere sixpence. Inside, a rough-faced woman greeted us with a puff of tobacco smoke from behind her desk.

James introduced himself, then said, "If one of your

lodgers were to pass away while staying here, what would you do?"

"I'd get the boy to fetch sawbones."

"The doctor?"

"Yeah. But if it's a murder I'd send the boy ter the p'lice."

"And a natural death?"

"Sawbones'd deal with it an' tell the coroner as 'e sees fit."

"And if the body remains unclaimed? Say, for example, that the unfortunate individual has no friends or family. What happens then?"

"The coroner'd see to it."

"Have you ever been visited by Dr Macpherson of St Bartholomew's Medical School?"

"Oh yeah, we gets 'im in 'ere."

"And what is the purpose of his visits?"

"'E's always after the bodies, but I tells 'im the coroner's seein' to it."

"Has Dr Macpherson ever removed any bodies from this lodging house?"

She narrowed her eyes, puffed out another cloud of smoke, then lowered her voice. "A few of 'em, yeah."

"Recently?"

"Nope, not recent. 'E's allowed to, though, ain't 'e?"

"If the body is unclaimed he has some permissions, yes. Has he ever given you any money in return for the bodies?"

"Jus' summink for me trouble. It's a lotta trouble when someone's gone an' died. I gotta get 'em moved an' then fetch sawbones."

"How much does Dr Macpherson give you?"

"Just nuff for the trouble, as I says, Hinspector. But I know as some people make harrangements direct."

"With Dr Macpherson?"

"Yeah, or the undertaker. They gets sixpence. If a family

can't get no poor relief they sells 'emselves. Some of 'em don't mind it. I've knowed some women as would sell littluns."

"Really?" I was sickened by this thought. "Their babies?"

"They ain't got no poor relief."

I took a deep, smoke-filled breath and was unable to focus on the remainder of James' conversation with the lodging house owner. Instead, I dwelled on the desperation of a destitute mother who might be forced to sell her deceased child to a school of dissection because she had no money for a funeral.

"Are you all right, Penny?" James asked once we had stepped back out onto the street.

"No," I replied. My throat felt tight and tears were spilling out of my eyes.

"Here." He pressed a clean handkerchief into my hand.

I removed my glasses and wiped my face, but the tears kept coming.

"Sixpence." My voice cracked. "They get sixpence! And what does that give them? A night's stay in a miserable lodging house. And yet a medical school will pay an undertaker or workhouse up to twelve pounds for a young woman or child! A *child*, James! Or even a *baby*!"

He put his arm around my shoulders until my sobs began to subside.

"I'm sorry I brought you here," he said. "I should have thought better of it."

"Don't apologise," I snapped. "I need to be aware of these things."

"I'm not sure you do, Penny."

"I'm a reporter! I need to understand what happens and why."

"Only to a certain extent."

"I shall be fine; it was just a shock."

I thought of the rough-faced woman and how calmly she

had informed us about the people who sold themselves and their children directly to the medical school. She had clearly experienced enough hardship in life to be unfazed by such things.

"Perhaps you need to work on something else for a day or two, Penny. Investigations like this can take their toll after a while."

"We need to find out who is behind all this, James."

"We do indeed."

"So I can't stop working on it. Not now that I've put so much effort in already. I should still like to go back and examine the records at the workhouse."

"How about you do that tomorrow? This case is not an easy one, Penny. Surely you'd like a bit of time to work on something different. Perhaps Mr Sherman has tasked you with something suitably superficial for the ladies' column this week?"

I finished drying my eyes. "He has, actually."

"Then work on that for now. I shall remain here for a little while longer and make some more enquires before speaking to the City of London police at Old Jewry. Would you like me to hail you a cab?"

"No, I shall walk to the office. It'll only take me fifteen minutes from here."

"Are you sure you'll be all right Penny?"

"Yes, of course. I'll be fine."

"Take my umbrella with you."

"Thank you, James."

Writing about the stage costumes of actress and socialite Lillie Langtry for the ladies' column that afternoon proved to be a welcome distraction. As I described a white velvet ball dress with large gold leaves on the skirt teamed with a pale pink bodice and train, I pictured what I might look like in such a garment. Then I pictured how James' face would look if he saw me wearing such a dress, and I smiled.

"Are you all right over there, Miss Green?" asked Edgar.

"I'm fine thank you, Edgar. Did you know that Lillie Langtry has a green velvet dress trimmed with Impeyan pheasant feathers?"

"That would make me sneeze terribly," he replied. "If Mrs Fish decided to wear a gown like that, our evening would be ruined."

"All because of a few feathers?" said Frederick.

"Yes, just one is enough. Mrs Fish has a hat with an ostrich feather in that has to be kept in a hatbox in the attic. If I get even just a sniff of it, I'm finished."

Frederick laughed. "You clearly need to be made of stronger stuff."

"Feathers are my only weakness."

"Are you sure about that, Fish?" queried Mr Sherman, who had just marched into the newsroom. "What about your weakness when it comes to failing to complete articles by deadline? Your article on the school board budget was due in five minutes ago."

"I have it right here for you, sir."

"Five minutes late!"

"It was ready on time."

"Then why didn't you hand it to me on time?"

"Miss Green distracted me, sir, with her talk of feathers."

"Then there is another weakness of yours, Fish. You're easily distracted." Mr Sherman turned to face me and dropped something onto my desk, "A telegram has arrived for you, Miss Green."

"Thank you, sir."

The telegram was only brief:

I have news. Please visit me tomorrow at St Monica's.
    Father Keane

CHAPTER 44

I arrived at St Monica's shortly after eight o'clock the following morning. Inside, the nun with the owl-like eyes was tending to the altar beneath the rose window.

"Oh dear, I'm afraid he's been taken ill," she replied earnestly when I asked for Father Keane.

"When?"

"Last night."

I pulled the telegram out of my carpet bag. "He sent me this at about half-past four yesterday afternoon. He must have been taken ill after that."

"Yes, he was at the workhouse for much of the day yesterday and was due to lead mass at seven o'clock yesterday evening. We began to worry, of course, when he didn't arrive back in time, and then we had a nurse from the infirmary visit to tell us that he had been taken ill."

"Which infirmary?"

"The one at the workhouse."

"He was taken ill at the workhouse?"

"No, it was after he left. Father O'Callaghan knows more

because he went with the nurse to see Father Keane at the infirmary. I understand he was on his way here from the workhouse when he was taken ill in the street. He was clearly well enough to send you the telegram. I imagine he must have done that from the telegraph office on Hoxton Street, which would have been on his way back here from the workhouse. He was found collapsed outside the Bacchus public house at about five o'clock."

I considered this. "So he sent this telegram to me about half-past four, presumably on his route here from the workhouse. I cannot understand why he should suddenly be so ill." I felt a sense of alarm begin to rise. "I shall go and visit him now. Thank you, Sister."

"Tell him I am praying for him," she said in reply.

It was a brisk ten-minute walk along Hoxton Street to the workhouse. Shopkeepers were setting out their stalls for the day, and the pavement outside the Britannia Theatre was being swept clean following the previous night's performance.

I passed the Bacchus public house where poor Father Keane had been found, and about a minute's walk beyond it was the telegraph office from which the priest had no doubt sent his telegram the previous day.

Father Keane's sudden illness sounded extremely suspicious, and my worst fear was that he had been poisoned. The more I considered it, the more likely it seemed. He had clearly happened upon something important because his telegram had told me he had news. *Was it news that someone wished to keep covered up?*

My heart thudded from the exertion of striding along the street, but also from a serious concern that Father Keane had been fatally harmed. *Had I put him in danger by enlisting his help?* I feared that I had.

I hurried on to the workhouse entrance and explained to the warden that I needed to visit a patient in the infirmary as a matter of urgency. When his face suggested that he was about to deny me permission I showed him the telegram from Father Keane and impressed upon him the fact that I knew Dr Kemp well.

The warden gave a low sigh. "You'll have to obtain express permission from Dr Kemp before entering the infirmary. We can't just let anyone wander in from the street."

"I realise that," I replied. I continued to explain why I was there, making sure to mention the names of James and Inspector Ferguson, and how I had been reporting on the recent scandal at the workhouse.

The warden soon became bored enough to admit me without any further trouble.

I found the senior nurse, Miss Turner, outside the medical officer's office in the infirmary.

"Father Keane," I said breathlessly. "How is he? He sent me a telegram."

I was in no way reassured by her concerned expression. She stared at me as if she wasn't sure how to answer, then glanced around her as if looking for someone else who could help.

"He is here, isn't he?" I continued. "I was told he had been taken unwell yesterday evening. He was found by the Bacchus on Hoxton Street. Do you know who found him?"

Footsteps behind me announced the arrival of Dr Kemp. I turned around, but the relief I felt on seeing him was immediately tempered by his sombre expression.

"You bring bad news about Father Keane, Doctor?"

He nodded. "I'm afraid so. He passed away about two hours ago."

My eyes sank to the floor.

"Miss Green?" I heard someone speaking my name, but the voice sounded far away. "Miss Green?"

I felt a hand on my arm, and I was led into the office, where Dr Kemp seated me on a chair.

"Miss Green," he said again, crouching beside me so that his face was in view. "Are you all right?" I caught my breath and shook myself, as if trying to shrug off the news I had just been given.

"How did he die?" I asked. "He sent me this telegram yesterday afternoon." The piece of paper was quite crumpled in my hand. "I think someone may have harmed him. He found out something and someone has done something to him."

"I think you're right," replied Dr Kemp sadly. "I think he displayed signs of poisoning before he died."

"So you agree? Then we need to find this person urgently! Did Father Keane tell you what he had found out?"

The doctor shook his head. "He was quite insensible by the time he reached the infirmary."

"What were his symptoms?" I asked. "Do you think it might have been the aconitine?"

"He was struggling to breathe when he was brought in, and he was vomiting, which reflects the body's need to purge itself from the poison. I cannot expressly say at this moment that it was aconitine poisoning, but I have no doubt that it was poisoning of some sort."

"It must have been the aconitine," I said. "It's still missing, isn't it?"

"Yes, it is."

"Father Keane had agreed to help us find it, and I wonder now if he had done so, because his telegram told me he had news."

"Inspector Ferguson and his men are already investigating his death," replied the doctor. "And a post-mortem will no doubt be carried out, which will give us the answers we need."

"But not the most important answer of all!" I remonstrated. "Who is behind all this?"

CHAPTER 45

Father O'Callaghan, an elderly Irishman, was clearly distressed about Father Keane's death. James had arrived at the workhouse and the pair of us were sitting with Father O'Callaghan in the little chapel. He told us how he had sat by Father Keane's bedside and administered the last rites as his colleague approached death.

"Was he able to speak to you at all?" I asked.

"He could only say a little."

"What did he say?" asked James.

"It didn't make a lot of sense to me, to be honest with you. His breathing was laboured and he seemed to be trying to say something about a cake."

"The poison!" I said. "The poison had to be in the cake!"

"Poison?" asked the priest, raising his bushy grey eyebrows. "He was poisoned?"

"We cannot be certain yet," replied James.

"Of course he was!" I said vehemently.

"Let's await the results of the post-mortem before we jump to any conclusions," said James. "I know it looks like a case of poisoning, and I think we should treat it as such, but we must wait for it be confirmed before we tell anyone that was the cause."

"*Suspected* poisoning, then," I said.

"Well, it's a sad day indeed when someone decides to poison a priest," said Father O'Callaghan mournfully. "We can comfort ourselves with the knowledge that whoever did so will be forever separated from God and cast into the eternal fire."

"Once he is dead himself, perhaps," I retorted. "But what about now? He must be found right away!"

"We need to find that aconitine," said James, glancing at the crumpled telegram Father Keane had sent me, which he held in his hand. "Perhaps he found the source and then it was used against him."

"Put into a cake, by the sound of it!" I said. "That would have required quite a degree of planning."

"Did Father Keane tell you who gave him the cake, Father?"

"His words were quite jumbled, but I got the impression that it was a lady who gave him the cake, Inspector. He said the word '*she*' a few times, but I couldn't quite discern the other words associated with it."

"No names?"

"Not that I could discern. I wish I'd listened more closely to what he was trying to tell me now. If I'd known it was important..."

"Please don't blame yourself, Father," I said. "You did everything you could, and you must have been a source of great comfort in his final moments."

"I never suspected foul play. And because his words weren't making a lot of sense I just assumed it was some form of delirium. I'll keep thinking about what he said and try to remember as much as I possibly can."

"Thank you, Father," said James. "I realise how distressing

this must be for you. I know that you will have administered last rites many times, but presumably you have only done so a few times for someone you knew well. This must be an exceptionally sad day for you."

"The Lord will help me. He helps all of us in our hour of need."

"Indeed. It's possible that the information you've shared with us may be helpful to the investigation. I'll speak to Inspector Ferguson next and see what he makes of it."

We found Inspector Ferguson in the administration block.

"Fortunately, the sight of a priest tends to remain in a person's mind," he said. "We have located a number of witnesses who saw Father Keane as he left the workhouse and walked down Hoxton Street in the direction of Hoxton Square. He was seen entering and leaving the telegraph office, and the staff at the telegraph office recall him dropping in to send a telegram."

"Was he unaccompanied?" asked James.

"Yes."

"And the cake?" I asked.

"Odd as it sounds, Father Keane was seen to be eating something after he had left the telegraph office," replied Ferguson. "Witnesses believed it to be cake, and indeed a piece of fruit cake was found, partially wrapped in paper, close to where he was found outside the Bacchus."

"Was he seen with it before he entered the telegraph office?" I asked.

"We believe he had it with him when he entered, because the clerk we spoke to there said he placed an item – wrapped completely in paper and tied with string at the time – on the counter next to him."

"So someone in the workhouse could have given him that piece of cake," I said, "maybe as a gift."

"It could have been a gift. And I agree that it was probably given to him while he was at the workhouse. He clearly decided to eat it as he walked back to St Monica's. Dr Kemp believes that Father Keane displayed signs of poisoning, so the cake has been taken to an analytical chemist at the Royal Institution. I hope to receive the results from him tomorrow."

"And in the meantime there will be a post-mortem," said James.

"Yes, that is being carried out today. However it usually takes a few days to allow time for the relevant tests to be conducted in the case of a poisoning."

"I remember it well from the case of the Bermondsey poisoner," said James with a sigh.

"And while we wait, the culprit will have plenty of opportunity to cover his tracks," I said.

"Or *her* tracks," corrected James. "Remember that Father O'Callaghan mentioned Father Keane talking about a woman."

"We'll get every man we have searching that workhouse," replied Inspector Ferguson. "The poison will be hidden somewhere there, and hopefully we'll find the rest of the cake, too."

"Perhaps someone in the bakehouse would know about it," I suggested. "Cake isn't often served to the inmates, is it? Perhaps it's unusual for cake to be baked there."

"Possibly," replied Inspector Ferguson. "I think it is most often eaten by the staff."

"Has there been any word on Mr Lennox yet?" asked James.

"Yes, I have good news on that front. He was arrested last night near Merthyr Tydfil, so I shall be travelling to

Paddington Station later today to meet him and his accompanying police officers off the train."

"Excellent!" said James.

"There's an awful lot to unravel here," continued Inspector Ferguson. "Although Hicks has admitted to stealing Miss Lloyd's body, he is refusing to tell us anything more. He seems unwilling to implicate anyone at the workhouse, yet I'm sure at least one of them knew what was going on."

"Has Mr Hale told you much so far?"

"No. He continues to maintain his innocence."

"Perhaps he really is innocent," suggested James.

"I doubt it," replied Inspector Ferguson. "We'll have to persevere with him. In the meantime we have Father Keane's possible murderer to find, and from the sounds of it we're looking for a woman."

CHAPTER 46

James and Inspector Ferguson agreed on how the search would be conducted, then James and I made our way to the bakehouse. Inside, a group of women kneaded dough at one table while a group of men worked at another. A row of stoves covered one wall. Everyone in the room paused to watch us as we entered.

James introduced himself and asked who was in charge.

"That'd be me, Mrs Griffiths," replied a small, round-faced lady with steel-rimmed spectacles. She stepped forward and gave us an awkward smile.

"Please could you tell us who bakes the cakes here?" James asked.

Her face fell. "This is abaht the poor priest, ain't it? I heard 'e fell ill after 'e ate a bitta cake. I dunno what 'appened; it weren't nuffink to do wiv me!"

"Do you bake the cakes yourself, Mrs Griffiths?"

"Yeah. And Betty 'elps me."

"Betty?"

A young woman stepped forward and joined Mrs Griffiths, nervously twisting her apron in her hands.

"Have you baked a fruit cake recently?" James asked the pair.

"We bake fifteen of 'em each week," replied Mrs Griffiths.

"For whom?"

"Master and matron, an' the officers and clerks, and what-not. I dunno 'ow the priest got 'is 'ands on some of it."

"Then it's not baked for the inmates?"

Mrs Griffiths shook her head. "They gets the bread."

"Has anyone specifically asked you to bake an extra fruit cake this week?"

She shook her head again. "No, sir. We baked fifteen of 'em Monday, din't we Betty? That does us for the 'ole week, then."

"Did anyone give you any extra ingredients to put in one or more of them?"

"No, there weren't nuffink like that. We didn't put nuffink in as would 'arm 'im, and no one's told us ter put nuffink in, did they Betty?"

The girl shook her head.

"What did you put in the cakes?"

"Jus' the usual!"

"Can you list the ingredients?"

"Flour, eggs, sugar, milk, molasses, bakin' powder, currants, raisins, lemon, nutmeg and plenty o' spice."

"Enough to bake fifteen cakes in total, I assume."

"Yep."

"In one bowl?"

"There ain't enough room in one bowl, Inspector! Five bowls with enough mix for three of 'em."

"I see. So if something harmful had been added to one bowl three cakes would be affected."

"Nuffink 'armful was put in none o' the bowls. I was there meself the 'ole time."

I surveyed the earnest faces of Mrs Griffiths and Betty,

struggling to believe that either woman might have poisoned the cake mixture.

"Thank you for speaking to me," said James. "It's likely that either I or my colleague Inspector Ferguson will need to speak to you both again. In the meantime, please think about whether anyone else might have had an opportunity to tamper with any of the cake mixture you've made recently."

"We'll 'ave a think, sir."

"Where are the cakes stored once they're baked?"

"They're wrapped up in paper, tied wiv string and sent over ter the main block."

"The administration block?"

"Yes, sir."

"Whereabouts?"

"To a cupboard in the master's office."

We came across Mrs Hodges shortly after leaving the bakehouse.

"What's going on, Inspector?" she asked. "This workhouse is filled with police officers! It's very alarming for the inmates."

"I'm sorry that the inmates are distressed," he replied, "but it's important that we locate the cake and the poison that is likely to have killed Father Keane."

"I realise that, but couldn't it be done in a more orderly manner? There are constables everywhere!"

"It's a necessary precaution, Mrs Hodges. Did you happen to give Father Keane a slice of cake?"

"No, I did not! Are you trying to suggest that I poisoned him?"

"No. I'm merely asking whether you gave him a slice of cake."

"I find your manner quite impertinent, Inspector. I've a

good mind to ask every police officer on the premises to leave!"

"Have you no wish to find out who is behind the suspicious deaths that have taken place here, Mrs Hodges?"

"Are they suspicious?"

"Even if they're not, I'd say that ten empty coffins are certainly suspicious, wouldn't you?"

"That's something the undertaker was responsible for, and you've already arrested him."

"And there'll be more arrests to make before the day is out. Now please excuse me, Mrs Hodges, but I really must get on with my job."

"With a newspaper reporter in tow? What is the nature of the relationship between you, exactly?"

"Miss Green was the first person to realise that something untoward was happening within these walls. My only regret is that I didn't start listening to her sooner."

"I'm quite sure that there is no need for her to be here."

"And I'm quite sure that there is. Good day, Mrs Hodges."

James and I made our way to the master's office in the administration block.

"Perhaps Mrs Hodges is the woman Father Keane was referring to?" I said.

"She could be, I suppose. Her manner is defensive rather than helpful, so perhaps she has something to hide."

"If three cakes have been poisoned, someone else must surely have been affected by now?"

"It's quite likely, isn't it? Perhaps the poison was only added to the piece Father Keane consumed. If the cakes are stored in Mr Hale's office it would have been quite easy for him to poison one of them. However, given that he has been in police custody for the past few days it's difficult to see how he had anything to do with the poisoning. We need to find out who else has access to that cupboard in his office."

"Did you discover anything further about Dr Macpherson?" I asked.

"I made a few enquiries at the lodging houses of St Luke's and Cripplegate," he replied, "and a number of people have come across him. He and Hicks have an arrangement in place with St Luke's Asylum, and he is also known at the offices of the City of London coroner. He's not the only one, of course. The clerk I spoke to at the coroner's office told me a number of anatomy schools are in regular contact with them, some of which are from medical schools outside London."

"Such as Cambridge," I said. "Dr Macpherson told me that himself. They're all in dire need of corpses for dissection."

"And wherever there is demand people will see the opportunity to make money," he replied sourly. "I've informed Inspector Stroud at Old Jewry about our investigation, and he's arranging for the City of London police to look into this as well. We may yet discover some wrongdoing on Dr Macpherson's part."

We entered the infirmary block and made our way along the corridor that led through it. As we walked, we heard raised voices.

"There must be some mistake, Inspector!" came a shout from behind us.

We retraced our steps to the corridor that led toward the men's wards. We could see Dr Kemp and Inspector Ferguson locked in a heated discussion outside the medical officer's office.

"Is everything all right?" asked James.

"No!" replied Dr Kemp, wiping his brow. "They've found poison in Miss Turner's room, but it cannot be true!"

"I'm afraid it is," replied Inspector Ferguson, turning to

James. "The jar of stolen capsules and the remains of a fruit cake were found on top of a wardrobe in Miss Turner's room.

"The aconitine?" I asked, astonished.

"Dr Kemp has identified it as the missing jar of poison," replied Inspector Ferguson.

"And what of Miss Turner?" asked James.

"My men are looking for her at this very moment," replied the inspector. "She was last seen on one of the women's wards about half an hour ago, but there has been no sign of her since her room was searched."

"Then there is no time to waste!" said James. "We'll help with the search."

"My men have barred all the exits," replied Inspector Ferguson, "so we're hoping she is still somewhere within the confines of this building."

I thought of Miss Turner and how I'd seen her busy at work on the wards when I had come to help with reading to the patients. She had always seemed to be such a kind lady. *Could she really be a murderer?*

"She was last seen on the women's wards, you say?" James asked.

"Yes, but my men have already checked there."

"Have they questioned the patients on that ward?"

"They certainly haven't had time to question all of them as yet."

"Miss Green and I will go there now and ask each of them whether they have any idea where she may have gone," said James.

"What's goin' on?" Mrs King called out when we arrived on the first ward. "There's people comin' an' goin', an' comin' an' goin'."

James introduced himself to her and she gave us both a smile.

"You're the lady what does the readin', ain't you?" she asked me.

I nodded.

"What's goin' on terday, Hinspector?" she asked.

"Have you seen the nurse, Miss Turner, recently?"

"Not recent, no."

"Have you seen her at all this morning?"

"Oh yeah, she's been 'ere."

"Can you recall how long ago that was?"

"I'm blowed if I know."

"Was it within the past hour, do you think?"

"Like I says, I really dunno!"

My eyes rested on the door in the corner of the room and recalled Mrs King complaining that Miss Turner always seemed to be opening and closing it. I walked over and tried the handle, but it was locked.

"Where does this door lead?" asked James, who had swiftly joined me.

"I don't know. Perhaps it's just a cupboard, but apparently Miss Turner opens this door a good deal."

James knocked on the door. "Miss Turner?"

There was no reply.

"Does anyone know whether this door has been opened this morning?" James called out to the ward.

His question was met with a host of blank faces.

"I haven't seen it open today," said a young nurse, stepping forward. "It's Miss Turner's cupboard, sir, and we don't know where she is."

"Do you happen to have a key for this cupboard?" he asked.

She shook her head in reply.

"Then there's only one thing for it," said James.

He took a few steps back, then launched himself at the door, aiming his shoulder just above the lock. The door moved slightly on impact but remained steadfastly locked.

"Whatcha doin', Hinspector?" Mrs King cried out.

James launched his shoulder at the door twice more but the door refused to give way.

"I'll have to try this, then," he said, taking a larger step back.

"Try what?" I asked.

"This!"

He lifted his leg and kicked just below the lock with the heel of his foot. Some of the door frame splintered to a backdrop of gasps from the patients. After a few more kicks the frame gave way and the door opened wide into the darkness of the cupboard.

CHAPTER 47

I was half-expecting to find a startled Miss Turner hiding beyond the door, but when James and I peered in we saw nothing inside but a large, dingy cupboard filled with basic supplies.

"Do you have a lantern I could borrow, please?" he asked the nurse.

As she went to fetch one, I stepped into the gloom. I could see blankets neatly folded on shelves and bowls stacked according to size and shape.

A moment later, James shone the lantern inside. "Just nursing supplies, by the looks of things," he said, "and no Miss Turner."

"Perhaps the rest of the stolen medicines are in here," I suggested.

We both looked around but saw nothing that looked medicinal.

"This looks out of place," said James, shining the lantern on a dark sack at the back of the cupboard.

"I think they've found her!" exclaimed the nurse behind us.

We stepped out of the cupboard to see a number of patients gathered around the windows. James and I managed to get close enough to see that they overlooked one of the yards, where a small group of people stood.

"Come on, let's go," said James, handing the lantern back to the nurse.

"What about that sack in the cupboard?" I asked.

"Oh yes! It didn't look right, did it?"

I dashed back into the cupboard to fetch it, only just managing to make it out in the gloom. James was at the far end of the ward by the time I re-emerged, so I jogged to catch up with him.

"I'd like to hear what she has to say for herself," he said as we dashed down the staircase, two steps at a time.

Out in the women's yard, Inspector Ferguson and a group of constables had encircled the nurse, her white apron was a dazzling contrast to the blue of their uniforms.

A crowd of bystanders had already gathered around them, but Mrs Hodges swiftly appeared and ordered them all inside. I looked up at the windows overlooking the yard and saw faces peering out from every one of them. Dr Kemp strode out into the yard, his expression etched with concern.

"I haven't done anything wrong!" Miss Turner protested as James and I approached.

"I'd say that murdering Father Keane was wrong, wouldn't you, Miss Turner?" said Inspector Ferguson as a sergeant clapped handcuffs around her wrists.

"I didn't do it!" she protested.

"Did you also give pieces of cake to Mr Connolly and Mr Sawyer?" I called over to her.

Her brow furrowed, as if she had no idea what I was

talking about. The yard we were standing in reminded me of the stone-breaking yard, and consequently of Mr Patten and Mr Walker. *Surely she hadn't also murdered them?*

Miss Turner was a tall lady, but she was on the slender side, such that I couldn't imagine her overpowering the two men. Perhaps the murder of Father Keane had been resolved, but there were still questions to be answered.

"Take her to the administration block," Inspector Ferguson ordered his constables. "And bring the Black Maria to the Kingsland Road entrance."

As she was led away, Miss Turner locked eyes with Dr Kemp. Her look was a pleading one, as though imploring him to intervene.

He shook his head as he watched her being led away. "And to think that I trusted her," he said sadly. "And a nurse at that! You wouldn't think it of a nurse, would you?"

"It takes all sorts, Dr Kemp," said Mrs Hodges. "I never would have thought it either. What a foolish woman! She's thrown her life away."

"You'll question her about Mr Connolly and Mr Sawyer as well, won't you?" I asked Inspector Ferguson.

"I certainly will," he replied. "There's no doubt that there are more victims. We have already found ten empty coffins, but there may be more at Tower Hamlets cemetery. There's plenty of investigating to do yet on that score."

"So what's your working theory, Inspector?" asked James.

"Someone at the workhouse colluded with Hicks to sell the bodies of deceased paupers to the medical schools. Paupers who seemingly had no family members or friends to miss them," he replied. "I suspect Lennox knows something given the manner in which he took off when Miss Lloyd's coffin was found to be empty. I'm not sure as to the extent of Hale's involvement yet, but it seems quite certain that Miss

Turner was the one who carried out the despicable acts. She no doubt did so on the orders of someone else, possibly Lennox or Hicks. We'll continue to question these men until we are able to get the truth out of them."

"And Dr Macpherson of St Bart's Medical School?" I asked.

"We know that he bought Miss Lloyd's body from Hicks," replied Ferguson.

"In good faith, no doubt," muttered Dr Kemp.

"Yes indeed. Unpleasant as this whole business is, there is no suggestion that the medical school is guilty of any wrongdoing."

"When exactly did Miss Turner steal the aconitine, Dr Kemp?" I asked.

"I noticed it was missing about six weeks ago."

"Since that time she'd have had the opportunity to poison countless inmates," I said.

"As I've already stated, there is still quite a job to do at Tower Hamlets cemetery," said Inspector Ferguson. He strode off to join the constables who were standing at the far end of the yard with Miss Turner.

"I blame myself," said Dr Kemp, wiping his brow.

"Oh no, you mustn't!" said Mrs Hodges. "You trusted her. We all did! No one could have known that she would steal medicine and poison the inmates with it. And a priest too! It truly is the most despicable act I have ever encountered."

I noticed Dr Kemp's eyes resting on the sack I held in my hand, which I had quite forgotten about. A piece of string tied it closed. I examined the knot and saw that it had been drawn quite tight, so I started pulling at it with my fingernails.

"I should never have allowed her to have a key for the medicine cupboard," continued Dr Kemp. "Knowing how harmful those medicines were, I should have kept them safe.

And to think that we were caring for poisoned inmates in the infirmary! I should have spotted the signs, but I didn't."

Mrs Hodges offered him further platitudes as I struggled with the knot.

"Here, allow me," said James, taking out a small pocketknife and unfolding it.

He cut the string on the sack and opened it up. Several items of dark clothing appeared to be folded up inside it.

"What have you got there?" asked Mrs Hodges.

Dr Kemp stepped away to speak to a nearby constable.

James pulled the clothing out of the sack to reveal a dark grey woollen suit consisting of trousers, a waistcoat and a jacket. Wrapped within the jacket was a white shirt with reddish brown spots on it. A collar fell to the ground, and I saw that it also had dark red stains upon it.

"Good grief!" exclaimed Mrs Hodges. "Is that blood?"

When I saw the stains on the waistcoat and the jacket sleeves I instantly turned away, feeling sickened. As I did so, my eyes landed on Dr Kemp just as he was slipping through the door to the covered walkway.

"He's leaving!" I shouted.

"Where?" James looked up from the spot where he had stopped to retrieve the blood-stained collar from the ground.

I started running toward the door that Dr Kemp had stepped through.

James soon caught up with me.

"This way!" he shouted over to Inspector Ferguson. "We need to grab hold of Kemp!"

Once we were inside the covered walkway we could see Kemp's retreating form ahead of us.

James chased after him, and I did my best to follow as quickly as my skirts and corset would allow. A number of inmates stopped and stared.

"Police! Stop that man!" shouted James.

A brave man stepped in the direction of the doctor in a bid to apprehend him, but Dr Kemp responded by shoving him out of his way. The man fell against the wall.

"Are you all right?" I stopped to ask him.

"Yeah," he replied, bemused. "But why's the doctor runnin' away from the police?"

"Good question," I replied as I hurried on, following James and Dr Kemp inside the block. I could see Dr Kemp up ahead, running for the door that opened out onto The Land of Promise. Fortunately, the exit was still being guarded by a constable. Kemp swung around and changed direction, heading instead for the casual wards.

"Keep guarding the door!" called James to the constable before following the doctor through the door to the men's casual ward. I paused for a moment, unsure whether to follow them into the men's ward before deciding that James might need my help.

A short corridor led into a cold, spartan bathroom identical to the women's bathroom next door. Someone was sprawled out on the floor, close to one of the bathtubs. I saw that it was a man lying on his side.

James.

A shriek echoed around the stone walls, and I only realised that the sound had come from me once I was knelt by James' side. His eyes were closed and a trickle of blood ran out from a cut on his lower lip.

"James!" I cried out. "James! Wake up!"

I gently lifted his head from the cold, tiled floor.

"James!"

But there was no response.

An icy sensation ran through my chest, like the blade of a knife.

"Please, James, wake up!"

I gave his shoulder a shake, but his body remained limp. *Surely he would come round. Was he even breathing?*

I placed my fingers beneath his nose to check. Before I could find out either way, darkness fell and I knew nothing more.

CHAPTER 48

A harsh light stabbed at my eyes and my head throbbed with pain. My body felt crooked, and I realised I was lying face down on a tiled floor.

I heard a groan beside me, and then shouting from further away.

I managed to lift my head, and a face swam into focus.

"James?"

His blue eyes flickered open and I felt a grin spread across my face.

"You're all right!"

I reached out to him, and he pulled a puzzled expression as though he had no idea where he was.

A shout from behind me brought us both to our senses. James propped himself up on his elbow, then looked up over my head before trying to scramble to his feet.

"Careful," I said, attempting to help him. As I moved to get up, my head span with a dizzying pain.

"Are you all right, Penny? What happened?" He held out a hand to steady me.

"I'm not sure."

We both staggered to our feet, then James lunged past me in the direction of the raised voices. I turned to see three workhouse inmates hunched together on the bathroom floor. It was only when I looked closer that I saw a fourth man lying beneath them.

It was Dr Kemp.

I couldn't help but admit a loud laugh. With the weight of three men bearing down on him, the doctor had no chance of getting away.

One of the inmates, a young man with dark eyes, grinned at me. For a fleeting moment he reminded me of Bill Sawyer, the poor man who had supposedly died of heart failure the night Eliza and I had stayed at the workhouse.

"We got 'im for yer!" he said triumphantly. "Shame on the doctor for punchin' a lady like that!"

"He punched me?"

"Yeah, an' I saw the toerag do it! Tried to get away after, but we got 'im."

"Thank you," I said fervently.

Inspector Ferguson soon arrived with two constables in tow.

"Here you are!" he said breathlessly. "We didn't know which way you'd gone. Are you all right, Blakely?"

"Sawbones punched 'im," piped up one of the men, who I now recognised as Mr Price.

"Good grief! Dr Kemp's down there!" said the inspector.

"Thank you for your help," James said to the inmates. "We've got him now. I'm a little concerned about the fact that his lips appear to be turning blue."

Dr Kemp didn't look well at all. The inmates moved away from him, but he lacked the strength to struggle as James put the handcuffs on.

"I don't understand what Kemp has to do with all this,"

said Inspector Ferguson as the doctor was propped up into a sitting position against the wall.

"Did you not see what was inside the sack?" James asked him.

"No."

"The blood-stained clothing he was presumably wearing the night he killed Mr Patten and Mr Walker," replied James. "The clothes had been bundled into a sack, which was placed at the back of a cupboard that only Miss Turner was believed to have a key for. Either Kemp has his own or he asked her to put the sack in there on his behalf. You were hoping no one would ever find it, weren't you, Doctor?"

"You've no proof that it's mine," muttered Kemp breathlessly.

"I think the fact that you bolted as soon as we opened the sack is indictment enough," said James. "And although I didn't have much time to examine the clothing, I noticed there was a button missing from the waistcoat. A black glass button like the one Horace found in the stone-breaking yard. That's where the two men were murdered, isn't it?"

"Then Dr Kemp murdered 'em!" exclaimed the young inmate.

The doctor shook his head rapidly as he tried to recover his breath.

"I always thought sawbones was a good 'un," said Mr Price. "'E looked out for us, 'e did."

"In what way?" asked James.

"Givin' people med'cine when they needed it."

"Is that so?" queried Inspector Ferguson.

"Yeah, so's they didn't get no fever an' end up in the 'firmary."

"There's a medicine that helps to prevent fever is there, Dr Kemp?" James asked.

He gave a casual shrug.

"That's what 'e said," claimed the younger man. "Only I didn't want no pills. I don't trust 'em."

"Dr Kemp offered you some pills to prevent fever, but you refused to take them. Is that what you're saying?" asked Inspector Ferguson.

"Yeah. I didn't like the look of 'em."

"And what did the doctor say when you refused them?"

"'E told me I'd get sick an' die."

"Was he angry with you?" I queried.

"Yeah, a bit."

"Is this true, Dr Kemp?" James asked the apprehended man. "Did you get angry when certain inmates refused to take the medication you had offered them?"

"Not a bit of it," he muttered.

"Was it medication they actually needed, or was this the aconitine pills? Did you persuade Mr Patten or Mr Walker to take them, Dr Kemp?"

"I have no idea what you're talking about."

"The two men who were found murdered in the yard. As you know, we have already found the blood-stained clothing you wore that night. Did you see Lawrence Patten working alone in the stone-breaking yard that evening and attempt to persuade him to take the gelatine capsules filled with aconitine?"

The doctor gave a derisive laugh, as if the suggestion were entirely ridiculous.

"Was that why he was murdered? Because he resisted you?" continued James. "Did you then lose your temper with him? Perhaps you struck him, a struggle ensued and you lost one of the buttons from your waistcoat during the tussle. Am I right?"

The doctor shook his head, appearing bemused.

"And then you decided to teach him a lesson and strangle him, did you?" James probed.

"I suppose you had originally intended to poison him so that you could sell his body," I added. "A quick check of his admission record would have reassured you that no friends or family members would come looking for him. Perhaps you looked at the record yourself, but I'm more inclined to think that the clerk, Mr Lennox, would have done that part for you. He probably did the same thing with regard to Mr Connolly and Mr Sawyer."

"Young men whose bodies would remain unclaimed once they'd died," said James. "No family members to miss them. And presumably their youthful bodies would have fetched you a better price than the body of an older man."

"How many times did you commit this heinous crime, Dr Kemp?" asked Inspector Ferguson. "How many victims are there?"

"I've never heard such utter nonsense," he said scornfully.

"Quite a number of times, I'd wager," said James. "But your plan failed when it came to Lawrence Patten, didn't it, Dr Kemp? Once you had lost your temper with the poor man and strangled him you realised the murder would be quite obvious. Panic no doubt ensued as you desperately tried to cover your tracks. You needed to frame someone else.

"You waited for the next man to enter the yard and, unfortunately for Mr Walker, it was him. You must have summoned him over, perhaps under the pretence that you required some assistance. Somehow you persuaded him to join you and the deceased Mr Patten. Without warning, you hit him with the shovel until you were sure he was dead, then you placed the shovel next to Patten's body to make it appear as though he had struck the fatal blow."

"When did you extinguish the lanterns, Dr Kemp?" I asked.

He shook his head as if it wasn't even worth his time to reply.

"Perhaps you did so immediately after the death of each man," said James. "When Horace looked out into the yard at ten minutes past eight Patten's lantern had just been extinguished. Perhaps that was when you began lying in wait for someone to cross the yard, Dr Kemp. Once you had attacked Mr Walker and extinguished his lantern, you swiftly made your way back to your rooms. A number of inmates must have seen you hurrying away from the scene. Perhaps you told them you were on your way to or from a medical emergency."

"You know Dr Macpherson, don't you, Dr Kemp?" I asked.

"Of course I do. I studied with him." The mention of this name had provoked a stronger reaction from Dr Kemp. "But that doesn't mean I've had anything to do with supplying corpses to his medical school. Why don't you ask Lennox about him?"

"We will," replied Inspector Ferguson.

"The City of London Police are assisting me with an investigation into Dr Macpherson's involvement in this crime," James explained to Inspector Ferguson. "It's possible that he struck a deal with Dr Kemp here to supply certain corpses to the medical school. I wonder whether there was such a high demand from, dare I say Dr Macpherson, that Dr Kemp was sometimes unable to find suitable inmates without any family or friends. In those instances, relatives were given the coffins filled with sandbags to bury. Isn't that right, Dr Kemp?"

"That's something else you need to ask Lennox about."

"Did you and Lennox collude, Doctor? We will certainly be asking him that same question."

"Why should I collude with him? I never even liked the man."

"It will be very interesting to hear what he has to say about you. I should think the death of Sarah Lloyd would have earned you both a good sum. Perhaps as much as twelve pounds. You must have conspired with Hicks to switch her body for sandbags, and perhaps Plunkett, the dead house warden, was paid to look the other way when Hicks visited."

"I think it's time for this line of questioning to continue down at the station," said Inspector Ferguson. He instructed his constables to put the doctor in the Black Maria with Miss Turner.

"Can you be sure that she was involved in the murders?" I asked. "The only pieces of evidence against her are the supposedly stolen medicines and the cake found in her room. They could have been planted there."

"But there's the bloodied clothing found in the cupboard," said Inspector Ferguson. "She must have known about that."

I pondered this. "I suppose she must have," I replied. "I can't imagine Miss Turner assisting Dr Kemp with his dreadful crimes, but perhaps she did. The medicines, including the aconitine, were probably never even stolen," I continued. "Dr Kemp merely claimed they were so no one would suspect that he was behind the poisonings. As a medical officer he could treat his own poisoning cases as if the patients were genuinely unwell. And when they finally succumbed he was able to certify the deaths himself."

"I imagine Dr Kemp took one of the cakes from the master's office and laced it with aconitine," said James. "Then he cut a piece for Father Keane and asked Miss Turner to give it to him. She must have been the woman Father Keane mentioned to Father O'Callaghan."

"But why murder Father Keane?" asked Inspector Ferguson.

"He had obviously discovered something," I said. "His telegram yesterday afternoon told me that he had news.

Perhaps he had found out something that would incriminate Dr Kemp."

The doctor gave another contemptuous laugh.

"And was murdered in a bid to silence him," suggested Inspector Ferguson.

"Yes, I believe so. Why else should an innocent priest be targeted?" I said. "I had asked him to help with the investigation, something I now bitterly regret because he lost his life. Although I felt sure that there was a murderer lurking within the walls of the workhouse, I had no idea that he would be quite so monstrous as this."

"You couldn't have anticipated Father Keane's death, Penny," said James. "None of us could."

"Well, we must await the results of the post-mortem and the toxicology tests yet," said Inspector Ferguson. "I'm sure everything will become much clearer over the next day or two."

Dr Kemp was led away by the constables.

"Bye, Doctor!" said the young inmate with a broad grin.

"Thank you, Blakely, for all your work on this case," said Inspector Ferguson. "There's a fair bit to do yet, but I consider this a satisfactory outcome. At least the paupers in this place will be treated with more respect from hereon in."

"Miss Green is the person we should be thanking," said James. "If she hadn't persuaded me that a third person had to have murdered Patten and Walker, Kemp would still be roaming free now."

"I'm sure we'd have got him in the end."

"But after how many more murders?"

CHAPTER 49

"So what was the final death toll?" Edgar asked me in the newsroom a few days later.

"That's a very good question," I said. "There is overwhelming evidence now that Dr Kemp murdered Mr Patten and Mr Walker in the stone-breaking yard. The senior nurse, Miss Turner, confirmed the bloodied clothing was his and claims that Kemp asked her to provide an alibi for him should the police question her. She has confessed to Inspector Ferguson that she wasn't aware of his whereabouts at the time the two men died, and that he had asked her to lie."

"Was the nurse also involved?"

"No, she wasn't. She was bullied and intimidated by Dr Kemp, and he tried to frame her by hiding the poison and cake in her room. However, she has cooperated fully with the police. Now that he is in custody she has become brave enough to speak out."

"That's good," replied Edgar. "And the empty coffins?"

"Inspector Ferguson's men are to continue the exhumations, though I am sincerely hoping they won't find any more."

"They probably will, though, won't they?" said Frederick.

"Ten empty coffins so far," said Edgar. "And still a number of missing people. Presumably they've all been dissected?"

I gave a shudder. "Sadly, the bodies of Mr Connolly and Mr Sawyer remain unaccounted for," I replied. "They must have gone to the medical school under false names and I feel sure that they were poisoned by Dr Kemp. If the doctor has any decency at all, then he'll own up to what he's done so the loved ones of the two men will finally know what happened to them."

Edgar gave a snort. "Decency from Dr Kemp? He doesn't seem the type."

"Unfortunately he doesn't. But perhaps if he told the police everything he might escape the noose?"

"I should think the man's doomed," said Frederick. "I can't imagine him receiving any leniency after what he's done."

"Dr Macpherson of St Bartholomew's Medical School has now been arrested by the City of London Police," I continued. "The undertaker, Mr Hicks, implicated him. It appears that Dr Macpherson had been placing orders."

"Orders?" queried Edgar.

"He was instructing Mr Hicks and Dr Kemp on which bodies he needed for his medical school."

"Ugh!"

"And if there wasn't a suitable deceased inmate available, Dr Kemp simply took matters into his own hands."

"By using poison?"

"Yes. It was provided in capsule form to fool the inmates into thinking they were taking medicine to prevent fever."

"And he added it to a piece of cake to murder a priest."

"Unfortunately, yes. The toxicology tests have confirmed that now."

"Then the priest had discovered something?"

"He had, though we'll never be certain of what it was. Father Keane clearly came across something that could have incriminated Dr Kemp. Perhaps he had discovered the poison somewhere. I can only hope that Dr Kemp will do the right thing and enlighten us in time."

"It's not looking good for him, is it?" commented Edgar. "The chap should just confess and be done with it. It wasn't just him behind it all, though, was it?"

"No. The undertaker, Mr Hicks, has also confessed, and if he tells the police everything he knows the others will be in for it; not only Dr Macpherson, but also the clerk, Mr Lennox."

"The one who ran away to Wales?"

"Yes, I feel sure he knew something about Kemp's actions. Why else would he try to escape? The master, Mr Hale, was also arrested, but it's possible that he wasn't actually involved. Then there is also the dead house warden, Mr Plunkett, who may not have been directly involved but perhaps rather too readily accepted payments to turn a blind eye."

Edgar gave a low whistle. "There's still a lot of work to do, isn't there?"

"There is indeed. In theory, the poor law inspector, Mr Weyland, is leading an inquiry into everything that has happened at Shoreditch Workhouse, though I won't be holding my breath!"

"The entire board of guardians could perhaps be arrested!"

"I hope they will be asked to resign at the very least," I replied. "Someone should have spotted the fact that something was very wrong at that workhouse. But those who did know were either paid off or intimidated into keeping quiet."

"You were intimidated yourself, Miss Green."

"Was I?"

"Yes, with those books you were mysteriously given."

"I had almost forgotten about those, and my tormentor clearly has as well. I'm quite pleased that it never came to anything more than that."

"It was a job well done, Miss Green," said Mr Sherman as he marched briskly into the newsroom. "Here's a letter for you."

"Thank you, sir."

"There is a lot of reporting for you yet to do on this story, Miss Green. Will you still have time to write the ladies' column or shall I give it to someone else?"

"I was rather beginning to enjoy the ladies' column, sir. It helps to provide a little variety."

"Good. I think it would be rather fitting to write something on the theme of weddings this week. Current fashions for brides and bridesmaids, and for the bouquet, of course."

"That would be of great interest to Miss Green, I feel sure of it!" said Edgar with a grin.

"Why so?" asked Mr Sherman with a puzzled glance.

"Because she will soon be wed herself!" enthused Edgar.

"Is this true, Miss Green?" asked the editor.

"Far from it!" I snapped, trying to ignore the sudden heat in my face.

"Not true!" retorted Edgar. "And I do believe you're smiling despite yourself, Miss Green!"

"Only from embarrassment," I replied. "I have no desire for my marriage prospects to be discussed in the newsroom."

"Quite so, Miss Green," said my editor. "Leave her alone, Fish."

The letter which Mr Sherman had given to me was from Miss Russell, and I read it while travelling home on the omnibus. In it, she expressed her horror on hearing about the recent events at the workhouse and deep regret that she hadn't realised what was happening there. She apologised for suggesting that I had helped her and Mrs Menzies only to further my own professional interests, and expressed a hope that I would return to the workhouse to help them again in the future.

I could hear voices at the top of the stairs when I returned home. As I climbed the staircase, I could hear a man and a woman talking loudly, and the tone of their voices suggested an altercation of some sort.

Puzzled, I reached the top of the main carpeted staircase but could see no one hanging about there. Then I climbed the narrow wooden staircase to my room and wondered who could possibly be talking right outside my door.

Visible on the little landing at the top of the stairs was a man whom I instantly recognised as Mr Torrance. He was standing with his back to me conversing with a woman I could see little of, other than her mouse-grey velvet skirts.

"You should let me pass," she said in a voice I could easily recognise.

I felt my heart sink.

"And I say that you need to answer to Miss Green herself. You must explain to her why you were trying to gain access to her room."

Mr Torrance spun round when he heard my step on the stairs.

"Miss Green, you're here!" A vague smile was almost discernible beneath his thick moustache. "I found this lady trying to break into your room." He stepped aside so that I could get a proper look at her.

Her gaze was cool and icy when our eyes met, and her wide face was paler than I recalled.

"Charlotte?" I ventured. "Charlotte Jenkins?"

It was James' former fiancée.

"Oh, so you do know her, Miss Green," said Mr Torrance. "I suppose that's of some relief."

Charlotte was holding something in her hand. It appeared to be a parcel wrapped in newspaper.

"I see you've brought me another book," I said. "Were you brave enough to sign your own name in it this time?"

CHAPTER 50

"*An Instruction on Essay Writing*,'" said James as he examined the book in his hand. "I'm so sorry that you had to be on the receiving end of this, Penny."

"I should think it'll come in quite useful," I replied with a smile.

We were sitting in Eliza's drawing room, as she had invited us both for dinner that evening.

"And it was obviously also Charlotte who sent you those other books," continued James. "What a nuisance. She has taken recent events rather badly, hasn't she?"

"She clearly has nothing better to do," stated Eliza.

"I shall visit her and warn her to stay away," said James.

"Oh, don't waste your time," I said. "I should think she'll stop sending them now that we've discovered her identity. The act doesn't seem quite so menacing now, does it? Besides, I can understand why she still feels angry."

"I can understand it too, but attempting to frighten you was completely wrong of her."

"Did I ever seem particularly frightened?"

James laughed. "No, I suppose not. But you were a little unnerved."

"Yes, I was, there's no doubt that it affected me slightly. Nevertheless, I found myself in the unexpected position of being able to thank Mr Torrance for doing something helpful. If he hadn't detained Charlotte, I never would have realised that she was the one behind it."

"And she'd have continued with it, no doubt. It seems as though irritating neighbours have their uses after all."

Eliza's maid entered the room and informed my sister that there had been a disagreement between the housekeeper and the cook.

"Oh dear, not again," said Eliza, who stood up and left the room.

"You'll be pleased to hear that we arrested Maisie Hopkins today, Penny," said James. "The young maid hadn't gone far. She was renting rooms near St James's Square and had bought herself some expensive outfits with the proceeds of her crimes."

"What will happen to her now?'

"She'll stand trial, of course, and then I wouldn't be surprised if she were to spend three or four years in Newgate."

"Oh no, really?"

"She's a thief!"

"She stole from Lord Courtauld because she wasn't paid a proper wage!"

"That is no reason to steal."

"No, I suppose not." I sighed. "It's terribly sad that her situation is unlikely to ever improve, especially now."

"Lady Courtauld helped her to leave the workhouse and find paid employment. She was given the opportunity to better herself, yet she decided to steal instead."

"I suppose it just demonstrates how much animosity she bore her employer."

"So much so that she was willing to ruin her own chances of a better life."

"Did she really have many chances of that?"

"She could have worked hard and gained a promotion."

"But would they ever have promoted her? Or would she always have been the girl from the workhouse, forever tainted by her past?"

"That's a good question, Penny, and I don't know the answer."

"People like the Courtaulds are extremely keen to publicly demonstrate their philanthropy, but privately they are equally determined to keep people in their place."

"If it's any consolation to you, a good number of Courtauld's valuables remain unaccounted for."

"I'm not sure whether that is really a consolation. I feel rather sad about the whole affair."

James got up from his chair and walked over to me. "Let's cheer ourselves up a little, shall we? You'll be pleased to hear that I've paid Charlotte the remaining two hundred pounds. I'm sure you'll agree that she doesn't need it – and perhaps she'll waste it all on buying instructional books about writing – but the point I'm making is that the final payment has been made, and I no longer have any obligation toward her whatsoever."

"Meaning?" I felt a grin spread across my face.

Colour rose in James' cheeks and he cleared his throat. He seemed nervous and I gave an involuntary giggle, as if I were a schoolgirl.

"What's funny?" he asked.

"You are."

"I'm funny?" He gave a bemused grin. "You're not supposed to be laughing at me at a moment such as this."

"I'm sorry, you looked rather uncomfortable. Frightened even. I'm not used to seeing you this way!"

We both laughed and James wiped his brow. "Oh dear, and now the moment has arrived I fear that I'm all in a muddle about it."

He reached forward and held my hand. My heart thudded with anticipation.

"I'm wondering, Miss Green —"

"Why Miss Green?" I laughed again.

"Oh Penny, you're not making this easy!"

"I'm sorry."

"I'm wondering, Penny. Actually *Miss Green* sounds more fitting for this occasion." He knelt down in front of my chair. "I'm wondering, Miss Green, if your feelings towards me are such that you would consider marrying me."

"Oh James, you know I will!" I leant forward and flung my arms around his neck.

"Are you really sure?" he said by my ear.

"Yes, completely sure!" My eyes blurred with tears.

"I suppose we must speak to your mother about it."

"I suppose we must."

"Penny, I would have been overjoyed if I had been able to speak to your father about it instead."

"That would have been wonderful."

"But sadly that option is not available to us, so—"

We were interrupted by a loud shriek from somewhere within the confines of the house.

"Goodness! Whatever has happened?" I cried as we separated and leapt to our feet.

Another shriek followed. It sounded like Eliza's voice.

Just as James and I were about to step through the door, Eliza came blustering in. Her face was red and her eyes were wet with tears.

"Good grief, Ellie! Whatever's the matter?" I cried.

She skipped into the centre of the room waving a small piece of paper.

"We've had a telegram!" she shouted. "A telegram from Mr Edwards!"

"Really? And?"

"He's alive?" said James.

"Yes, he's alive all right. And I'll tell you who else is!"

"Not Father?"

"Yes, Penny! He's alive!"

Within seconds Eliza and I were locked in a deep embrace. We half-danced and half-stumbled about the room until we were giddy. I could neither laugh nor cry, but instead I felt an involuntary wail emanating from the very depths of me. The room blurred as tears filled my eyes for a second time.

"Are you sure?" I said eventually. "Are you really sure?"

"Here!"

Eliza pulled away and showed me the telegram. I wiped my face with my sleeve and adjusted my spectacles. The words seemed to swim in front of my eyes:

Happy to report Mr. Frederick Brinsley Green found safe and well. More to follow.

Francis Edwards

THE END

HISTORICAL NOTE

I began my work on this eighth book in the Penny Green series with the idea that I would set the story in the workhouse. I was unprepared for what my research would reveal! The trade between workhouses and medical schools in the latter half of the nineteenth century was something I'd been completely ignorant of. I had assumed the bodysnatchers, such as the notorious Burke and Hare, were confined to the early 1800s. The 1832 Anatomy Act regulated dissection in medical schools and supposedly removed the opportunity for making profits from the dead.

My initial research in the British Newspaper Archive brought up some curious reports from Norfolk in 1901. The *Norfolk News* reported that a body of a workhouse 'pauper' had gone missing. Frank Hyde, 50, had died at Great Yarmouth Workhouse in April 1901 and the workhouse burial register stated that he had been "buried by friends". On investigation it was found that his body was missing from the local cemetery. Allegations followed that his body had been sold to the University of Cambridge for dissection and a visiting committee was appointed to hold an enquiry. The allegation was found to be true and two men at the workhouse were found responsible: the Master's clerk, Mr Adams, and the porter, Mr Hurrell.

Great Yarmouth Workhouse had an arrangement in place with the University of Cambridge to sell the bodies of unclaimed paupers to the school of anatomy. Professor Macalister, chair of anatomy at Cambridge, paid the workhouse six pounds, fourteen shillings and sixpence for each body (approximately £750 / $930 in today's money). Some transactions were properly recorded but others, as in the case of Frank Hyde, were not. It appears that there was deliberate deception about his body being 'unclaimed.'

The porter, Hurrell, was usually paid between six and twelve shillings to find the family of a deceased inmate in the workhouse but in the case of Frank Hyde he purposefully did nothing so that Hyde would remain 'unclaimed'. It transpired that Frank Hyde had been a well-known wire worker in the town and had a wife and three children.

Much of the payment from Macalister for Frank Hyde was used for the transportation of his body by train from Yarmouth to Cambridge. However, it was estimated that Mr Adams had pocketed a profit of between thirteen and seventeen shillings (roughly £78-£100 / $97-£124 today) for "doing very little indeed." (*Norfolk News*, 15th June 1901). The report I read suggested more indignation that Adams had received money for 'doing very little' rather than personally profiting from selling the body of a workhouse inmate and depriving his family of his burial. There are reports that, in some instances, Adams carried out 'mock funerals' with coffins filled with sand, or other materials, but I can't find a full verification for these reports.

According to the *Norfolk News*, the phrase "buried by

friends" was found to have been entered into Great Yarmouth Workhouse's burial registers an astonishing fifty six times. It was a euphemism for sending the body to Cambridge for dissection. In the case of Frank Hyde it couldn't be established whether Adams or Hurrell had falsified the workhouse records. There was no reported evidence that the Master of Yarmouth Workhouse, or any of the board of guardians, knew about the activities of Adams and Hurrell. This doesn't certify for sure that they were ignorant of the practice. The punishment for making a profit from the sale of a body was three months' imprisonment.

I can't find a record of what the men's punishment was and I'm tempted to doubt they received one. Quite shockingly, just a month after the enquiry on 6th July 1901 there was a report in the *Yarmouth Independent* that, "Mr and Mrs Hurrell, porter and portress of Great Yarmouth Workhouse have been appointed Master and Matron of Kenninghall Workhouse."

The profiteering from the bodies of the poor at Great Yarmouth was not an isolated incident. The more I researched, the more cases I found. This one was in Glasgow and reported on 19th September 1891 in *Aberdeen Free Press*:-

"Disposal of the bodies of paupers dying in the City Parish Hospital... One ugly fact after another cropped up, and two or three members of the House Committee quietly continued their investigations, and after six weeks' inquiry made the ghastly discovery that a regular traffic had sprung up in the disposal of the bodies of paupers who were known to have relatives and friends, and therefore supposed to be buried at Sandymount Cemetery, but which were really delivered for dissection at the Anatomical Rooms in College Street. One person only is involved, a man named Daniels, who acted as a coachman at the Hospital, and he is no longer in the employment of the Board, and, it is believed, has left the city."

John Daniel (not Daniels as described above) was later charged with selling thirty-nine bodies for dissection under the pretence that he was authorised to do so.

It appears that scandals and mishaps were commonplace over a period of many years. On 23rd February 1882, the *St James's Gazette* reported that a coffin which was opened at Sheffield Workhouse, "was found to contain the remains of an old man instead of that of a young man whose body had been sent to the medical school for dissection." Presumably the young man was not supposed to have been dissected?

Professor Alexander Macalister, purchaser of Frank Hyde's corpse, receives a chapter of coverage in *Dying for Victorian Medicine, English Anatomy and its Trade in the Dead Poor* by Elizabeth T. Hurren. This sombre and thought-provoking book describes the 'dead train' which carried corpses from London to Macalister at Cambridge:-

"Three times a week an express train left Liverpool Street station in London. It travelled via Cambridge to Doncaster. On its return journey extra funeral wagons were attached discreetly by railways engineers to the rear carriages... This was the 'dead train' that carried corpses to Cambridge. A local undertaker brought the human cargo to the back of the station in a covered carriage."

In her book, Hurren also discusses how 'paupers' arranged to sell their bodies direct to the schools of anatomy. An investigation into workhouse conditions by the *Essex Standard, West Suffolk Gazette and Eastern Counties' Advertiser* in 1885 revealed workhouse inmates had made such arrangements. One report read:-

"'The majority of the old ladies in the House seemed apprehensive lest their mortal remains should be sent to *"Cambridge for dissection"*,... There was one exception however in an elderly inmate who joking remarked that she had already disposed of her body for the modestly low sum of six pence, and when asked where the purchase money had gone she pointed to her nose indicating it had been spent in the much relished delicacy of snuff.'"

Professor Macalister took up his position at Cambridge in 1883 and held it for thirty six years. He was an influential figure in the study of human anatomy and I can find no suggestion anywhere that he acted outside the law when purchasing the bodies of the poor. He was bound by the system which existed at his time:-

"Medical education was a competitive field financed by rising and falling student fees. It was also a business driven by profit margins made from paupers. Macalister for a time lost out to Oxford and Leicester because the former was prepared to pay more for bodies." (*Dying for Victorian Medicine, English Anatomy and its Trade in the Dead Poor* by Elizabeth T. Hurren).

Hurren examined in detail the dissection registers at St Bartholomew's Hospital. Founded in the twelfth century, the hospital soon gained a reputation for medical learning. Hurren has established that between 1832 and 1929, Bart's acquired 6,059 corpses for dissection. Behind the numbers are countless tragic tales of poverty:-

"Body 'number 84', a '22 year old female' called 'Charlotte Burton'... tried to give birth to a concealed pregnancy without medical assistance. Soon after birth her child died and she suffered 'puerperal convulsions'... Charlotte died on the night of '18th February 1834' in abject poverty. Her fellow lodgers sold her body for dissection on '19th February at 8pm'. 'Mr Teale the undertaker' made the body deal and took the cadaver to the Dead House at St. Bartholomew's."

Charles Dickens made outspoken comments about the dissection of the poor in his periodical *Household Words* in 1850. He rejected the common argument at the time that the poor (who were often considered to be responsible for their fate) could atone for their moral failings in life by contributing to the advancement of medical knowledge. Almost forty years later, the debate over dissection still raged as this article from the *Liverpool Echo*, on 22nd November 1889 demonstrates:-

"Yesterday, at the meeting of the Paddington Board of Guardians, held at the workhouse, Harrow-road, the chairman, Mr S. D. Fuller, called attention to the fact that the guardians had now, under the provisions of the Anatomical Act, power to dispose of the bodies of unknown or friendless paupers by allowing them to be used for dissecting purposes at the anatomical schools. Mrs. Charles said she would strongly oppose the guardians so disposing of the bodies of persons dying in the establishment. If the poor cared about anything at all it was to be decently buried... Mr. J. C. Sherrard, J. P., said that when the due interests of science were concerned the opinions of poor people must not be allowed to stand in the way."

The details of dissection were purposefully kept secret by the medical profession because the topic roused strong sentiment. In the 1830s there had been anti-dissection demonstrations in Sheffield and Manchester. By the late nineteenth century, however, it was difficult to stop the emergence of investigative reporting. One such article in the *Pall Mall Gazette* on 19th January 1888 is titled *Horrors of the Dissecting Room* and describes how a body is divided among the students, "One wants a forearm, another a foot, hand..." then "During the cutting up of the body and subsequent dissection of its parts a good many pieces are thrown upon the floor. A porter is employed who goes round at intervals with a brush and pan collecting these morsels, which are removed to a cellar." The article goes on to describe how the parts are then collected into coffins and given a Church of England burial,

"The coffins are flimsy affairs, and one wonders what would happen if one broke at the graveside and the clergyman saw, say, two mutilated heads, half-a-dozen feet and three legs with a gory mass of scraps roll out?"

This article clearly revelled in the grisly details which Victorian readers so apparently enjoyed and characterises the graphic reporting of Jack the Ripper's crimes later the same year. Of course, it has long been speculated that the serial killer known as Jack the Ripper had received anatomical training.

Welfare reform put an end to the anatomy trade. The early twentieth century saw the introduction of National Insurance which provided health insurance for industrial workers. The Old Age Pension was introduced and an act in 1929 closed workhouses and turned them into hospitals. A number of hospitals today in the UK are still housed in former workhouse buildings.

My descriptions of the conditions in the workhouse were informed by contemporary accounts. Included in these is *Tales from the Workhouse – True Tales from the Depths of Poverty*, a compendium of workhouse reports from journalists and former inmates. Notable contributors include James Greenwood and Mary Higgs. Greenwood was one of the first Victorian journalists to disguise himself as a 'tramp' to stay on the casual wards of London's workhouses. His article *A Night in the Workhouse* was serialised in the *Pall Mall Gazette* in 1866. Higgs was a social reformer who investigated poverty by visiting workhouse wards and lodging houses also disguised as a tramp. She published her findings in a series of articles and a book *Glimpses into the Abyss* in 1906.

Sickness and Cruelty in the Workhouse - The True Story of a Victorian Workhouse Doctor by Joseph Rogers was another useful source. Rogers was a physician and a workhouse medical officer who campaigned for poor law reform throughout his forty-year career. His work brought him into contact with Louisa Twining, a member of the famous Twining tea family, who devoted her life's work to improving conditions in workhouses. She visited a friend in the Strand Workhouse in the 1850s and was so appalled by what she experienced that she lobbied the Poor Law Board for over a year to allow her to visit the workhouse and offer comforts to the inmates. Eventually the board relented.

Shoreditch is in London's East End and has an extremely long and vibrant history. The area's traditional working class character has changed over the past thirty years with the gentrification of many streets. These days, Shoreditch is a trendy and expensive place to live but retains some of its traditional, edgier character too. Shoreditch Workhouse was established in the eighteenth century for the poor of the parish and was extensively rebuilt in the 1860s. The interestingly named Land of Promise on Hoxton Street still remains, flanked by The Unicorn pub (now a fast food outlet) and the former poor relief offices. The former administrative building is an impressive facade on Kingsland Road. All the buildings are now part of St Leonard's Hospital.

The Roman Catholic Church of St Monica's Priory in Hoxton Square, Shoreditch, was consecrated in 1875 and is one of over a hundred Catholic churches designed by E.W. Pugin (son of Augustus Pugin, architect of the Houses of Parliament). That E.W. Pugin completed so many churches before his untimely death, at the age of forty one, is impressive to say the least.

Aconitine, a deadly poison, is derived from aconite root which has anaesthetic properties and was once used in the treatment of colds, sore throats, respiratory inflammation, neuralgia, arthritis and a number of other aches and pains. Aconite is more commonly known as monkshood or wolfsbane among other names. Several varieties are attractive garden plants. A famous case of aconitine poisoning was carried out by a doctor, George Henry Lamson, in 1881. He acquired a morphine habit, fell into financial difficulties and decided to poison his young brother-in-law, Percy John, to secure more of his wife's inheritance. His position as a doctor enabled him to acquire aconitine from a pharmacist and he persuaded Percy to take capsules of the poison during a visit to his boarding school in Wimbledon. Lamson had chosen aconitine because he believed it would be untraceable in the body after death. While this had once been true, Lamson hadn't reckoned on the expertise of Dr Thomas Stevenson, a renowned toxicologist and forensic chemist, who was able to find traces of the poison in Percy's body. Lamson was hanged for his crime in 1882.

Madame Tussaud's, in Baker Street, was a popular attraction in the nineteenth century and remains so today. In Victorian times, Tussaud's knew how to draw the crowds by being quick to model the famous and notorious people of the day. Infamous criminals were displayed in the Chamber of Horrors. Marie Tussaud was a French artist who became famous for her wax models of celebrities in the late 18th century. During the French Revolution she was employed to make the death masks of famous guillotine victims Louis XVI, Marie Antoinette among many others. In the early 19th century Tussaud travelled to Britain to exhibit her wax models, she remained in Britain for the rest of her life. She toured the country for a number of years before establishing her permanent exhibition in Baker Street in 1835. After her death aged

88 in 1850, Tussaud's work was continued by her sons then grandson.

The quirky shop Marshall & Hawes is based on Millikin & Lawley which was one of the largest suppliers of human skulls and skeletons in the world. The shop was located on The Strand, close to the medical school at nearby King's College. Rather oddly, the shop also stocked watches, conjuring tricks, model boats and magic lanterns. It must have been an interesting place to visit. Millikin & Lawley's osteology sets still come up for purchase now at various auction houses. But the question Penny asked still endures - who did those bones once belong to?

If *Death at the Workhouse* is the first Penny Green book you've read, then you may find the following historical background interesting. It's compiled from the historical notes published in the previous books in the series:

Women journalists in the nineteenth century were not as scarce as people may think. In fact they were numerous enough by 1898 for Arnold Bennett to write *Journalism for Women: A Practical Guide* in which he was keen to raise the standard of women's journalism:-

"The women-journalists as a body have faults... They seem to me to be traceable either to an imperfect development of the sense of order, or to a certain lack of self-control."

Eliza Linton became the first salaried female journalist in Britain when she began writing for *the Morning Chronicle* in 1851. She was a prolific writer and contributor to periodicals for many years including Charles Dickens' magazine *House-hold Words*. George Eliot – her real name was Mary Anne Evans - is most famous for novels such as *Middlemarch*, however she also became assistant editor of *The Westminster Review* in 1852.

In the United States Margaret Fuller became the *New York Tribune*'s first female editor in 1846. Intrepid journalist Nellie Bly worked in Mexico as a foreign correspondent for the *Pittsburgh Despatch* in the 1880s before writing for *New York World* and feigning insanity to go undercover and investigate reports of brutality at a New York asylum. Later, in 1889-90, she became a household name by setting a world record for travelling around the globe in seventy two days.

The iconic circular Reading Room at the British Museum was in use from 1857 until 1997. During that time it was also used as a filming location and has been referenced in many works of fiction. The Reading Room has been closed since 2014 but it's recently been announced that it will reopen and display some of the museum's permanent collections. It could be a while yet until we're able to step inside it but I'm looking forward to it!

The Museum Tavern, where Penny and James enjoy a drink, is a well-preserved Victorian pub opposite the British Museum. Although a pub was first built here in the eighteenth century much of the current pub (including its name) dates back to 1855. Celebrity drinkers here are said to have included Arthur Conan Doyle and Karl Marx.

Publishing began in Fleet Street in the 1500s and by the twentieth century the street was the hub of the British press. However newspapers began moving away in the 1980s to bigger premises. Nowadays just a few publishers remain in Fleet Street but the many pubs and bars once frequented by journalists – including the pub Ye Olde Cheshire Cheese - are still popular with city workers.

Penny Green lives in Milton Street in Cripplegate which was one of the areas worst hit by bombing during the Blitz in the Second World War and few original streets remain. Milton Street was known as Grub Street in the eighteenth century and was famous as a home to impoverished writers at the time. The street had a long association with writers and was home to Anthony Trollope among many others. A small stretch of Milton Street remains but the 1960s Barbican development has been built over the bombed remains.

Plant hunting became an increasingly commercial enterprise as the nineteenth century progressed. Victorians were fascinated by exotic plants and, if they were wealthy enough, they had their own glasshouses built to show them off. Plant hunters were employed by Kew Gardens, companies such as Veitch Nurseries or wealthy individuals to seek out exotic specimens in places such as South America and the Himalayas. These plant hunters took great personal risks to collect their plants and some perished on their travels. The *Travels and Adventures of an Orchid Hunter* by Albert Millican is worth a read. Written in 1891 it documents his journeys in Colombia and demonstrates how plant hunting became little short of pillaging. Some areas he travelled to had already lost their orchids to plant hunters and Millican himself spent several months felling 4,000 trees to collect 10,000 plants. Even after all this plundering many of the orchids didn't survive the trip across the Atlantic to Britain. Plant hunters were not always welcome: Millican had arrows fired at him as he navigated rivers, had his camp attacked one night and was eventually killed during a fight in a Colombian tavern.

My research for The Penny Green series has come from sources too numerous to list in detail, but the following books have been very useful: *A Brief History of Life in Victorian Britain* by Michael Patterson, *London in the Nineteenth Century* by Jerry White, *London in 1880* by Herbert Fry, *London a Travel Guide through Time* by Dr Matthew Green, *Women of the Press in Nineteenth-Century Britain* by Barbara Onslow, *A Very British Murder* by Lucy Worsley, *The Suspicions of Mr Whicher* by Kate Summerscale, *Journalism for Women: A Practical Guide* by Arnold Bennett, *Seventy Years a Showman* by Lord George Sanger, *Dottings of a Dosser* by Howard Goldsmid, *Travels and Adventures of an Orchid Hunter* by Albert Millican, *The Bitter Cry of Outcast London* by Andrew Mearns, *The Complete History of Jack the Ripper* by Philip Sugden, *The Necropolis Railway* by Andrew Martin, *The Diaries of Hannah Cullwick, Victorian Maidservant* edited by Liz Stanley, *Mrs Woolf & the Servants* by Alison Light, *Revelations of a Lady Detective* by William Stephens Hayward, *A is for Arsenic* by Kathryn Harkup, *In an Opium Factory* by Rudyard Kipling, *Drugging a Nation: The Story of China and the Opium Curse* by Samuel Merwin, *Confessions of an Opium Eater* by Thomas de Quincy, *The Pinkertons: The Detective Dynasty That Made History* by James D Horan, *The Napoleon of Crime* by Ben Macintyre and *The Code Book: The Secret History of Codes and Code-breaking* by Simon Singh, *Dying for Victorian Medicine, English Anatomy and its Trade in the Dead Poor* by Elizabeth T. Hurren, *Tales from the Workhouse – True Tales from the Depths of Poverty* by James Greenwood, Mary Higgs and others, *Sickness and Cruelty in the Workhouse - The True Story of a Victorian Workhouse Doctor* by Joseph Rogers. The *British Newspaper Archive* is also an invaluable resource.

THE GANG OF ST BRIDE'S

A Penny Green Mystery Book 9

A gang of lady thieves is targeting Piccadilly's wealthy shoppers and no one seems able to stop them. As frustrations build, the body of a young woman is pulled from the River Thames. Reporter Penny Green has a lot to write about, and she faces a new challenge when a stranger approaches her with a riddle. Could it lead to a killer?

Time is running out for Penny – her impending marriage to Inspector Blakely signals the end of her Fleet Street career. The riddle could be the last case she works on and it's not without its dangers. Someone seems keen to ensure that Penny doesn't make it to her wedding day at all.

Find out more at: emilyorgan.com

THANK YOU

Thank you for reading *Death at the Workhouse*, I really hope you enjoyed it!

Would you like to know when I release new books? Here are some ways to stay updated:

- Join my mailing list and receive a free short mystery: *Westminster Bridge* emilyorgan.com/westminster-bridge
- Like my Facebook page: facebook.com/emilyorganwriter
- View my other books here: emilyorgan.com

And if you have a moment, I would be very grateful if you would leave a quick review of *Death at the Workhouse* online. Honest reviews of my books help other readers discover them too!

GET A FREE SHORT MYSTERY

꧁꧂

Want more of Penny Green? Get a copy of my free short mystery *Westminster Bridge* and sit down to enjoy a thirty minute read.

News reporter Penny Green is committed to her job. But should she impose on a grieving widow?

The brutal murder of a doctor has shocked 1880s London and Fleet Street is clamouring for news. Penny has orders from her editor to get the story all the papers want.

She must decide what comes first. Compassion or duty?

The murder case is not as simple as it seems. And whichever decision Penny makes, it's unlikely to be the right one.

Visit my website to claim your FREE copy:
emilyorgan.com/westminster-bridge

THE CHURCHILL & PEMBERLEY SERIES

Also by Emily Organ. A cozy mystery series set in an English village.

☙❧

1932. Armed with a handbag and fuelled by cake, Annabel Churchill is a mature yet tenacious private detective. Together with her quirky sidekick, Doris Pemberley, she's determined to solve mysteries and chase down criminals in the sleepy Dorset village of Compton Poppleford.

Find out more here: emilyorgan.com

Made in the USA
Columbia, SC
24 May 2020